TARA SUE ME

SEDUCED
BY FIRE

headline
ETERNAL

Published by arrangement with New American Library
a member of Penguin Group (USA) LLC.
A Penguin Random House Company.

First published in Great Britain in 2014
by HEADLINE ETERNAL
An imprint of HEADLINE PUBLISHING GROUP

5

Cataloguing in Publication Data is available from the British Library

ISBN 978 1 4722 0816 3

Offset in Bembo by Avon DataSet Ltd, Bidford-on-Avon, Warwickshire

Printed and bound by CPI Group (UK) Ltd, Croydon, CR0 4YY

Headline's policy is to use papers that are natural, renewable and
recyclable products and made from wood grown in sustainable forests.
The logging and manufacturing processes are expected to conform
to the environmental regulations of the country of origin.

HEADLINE PUBLISHING GROUP
An Hachette UK Company
338 Euston Road
London NW1 3BH

www.headlineeternal.com
www.headline.co.uk
www.hachette.co.uk

To Ginger, who unknowingly
started everything.

ACKNOWLEDGMENTS

This novel holds a special place in my heart as it was written following a very difficult time in my personal life. They say when a door closes, a window opens. If that's the case, *Seduced by Fire* is my window.

There were many people who helped make this book what it is and I am forever grateful to them.

To Rebecca Grace Allen, who has been the world's best crit partner, brain stormer, chat buddy, and friend a person could ask for. You stuck with me in the early days and wouldn't let me give up. Thank you.

To Cyndy Aleo, who forces me to be better and never lets me settle. You'll never know how much your support has meant. Thank you.

To Danielle, who makes me laugh, makes me think, and helps in innumerable ways. You have been indispensable and I can't imagine doing this without you. Thank you.

To Lauren and Christina, who encouraged me to continue. You guys . . . there aren't enough words. Thank you.

To Lauren and Tonya, who gave feedback that helped tremendously. I hope you know how much I value your comments. Thank you.

To Claire Zion, who took my words and made them so much better. I am blessed to have you as an editor. Thank you.

To Kathy, who is always there to offer just what I need. You're good people, Kathy. I hope you know that and I hope you know how much you mean to me. Thank you.

To my husband, who is my support, my encourager, my idea bouncer offer, and my champion. I don't know how you manage to do it all and stay sane. Thank you.

And to my readers, who allow me the privilege of telling them a story. I am honored. Truly. Thank you.

SEDUCED

BY FIRE

ONE

*A*ccording to Julie's best friend and business partner, Sasha, men only bought flowers for two reasons: to get in your pants, or to get back in your pants. While Julie didn't think that to be an absolute truth, once Sasha made up her mind, she didn't often change it.

The front door of Petal Pushers, the floral shop they owned together, opened with a melodic ring. After seeing the two customers walk in, Julie decided to make her case once again.

"Look at those two," she said with a whisper, making sure the customers couldn't hear. "I highly doubt he's trying to get into *her* pants."

Sasha looked up from the computer where she was placing an order for next week's stock. The "he" in question was tall, with sculpted angular features, and dirty blond hair, but the woman by his side wasn't the usual trophy girlfriend. She was an older woman, dressed for the chilly weather in Wilmington, Delaware, in a winter white coat that probably cost more than Julie made in a year.

"Never know these days." Sasha punched a few keys on the computer. "I need to make a few calls. Can you handle these two?"

Julie waved her to the back office and turned her attention to the couple still standing by the door. This time she noticed how expensive the guy's coat was while he talked on his cell phone. The woman with him admired a floral arrangement displayed for an upcoming wedding.

"Good afternoon," Julie said. "Welcome. Can I help you with something?"

The older lady smiled. "My great-granddaughter has a ballet recital tonight. I wanted to pick up some flowers." She turned to the guy, still on his phone. "Daniel, do put that away and come here."

The man at the door spoke a few more words before disconnecting. "Sorry, Grandma. It couldn't wait."

She rolled her eyes. "It never can."

"I heard that." His voice was low and deep and as he approached, his gaze met Julie's. Blue steel was her first thought when she saw his eyes. Hard and immovable. She actually squirmed under their scrutiny.

For a second, she thought he realized the effect he had on her, because something in his expression flickered with understanding. Just as quickly, though, his mouth upturned into a soft smile. "We're looking for something to thrill the heart of a five-year-old ballerina."

Julie stood and told herself to focus on the sale, not the customer's eyes. "Your daughter?"

The older lady laughed. "Heavens no, dear. Not Daniel," she said as if the idea of Daniel having a daughter was the most humorous thing in the world. "It's for his niece."

Daniel appeared unaffected by his grandmother's words. He only raised an eyebrow to Julie and proceeded to take off his leather gloves.

He pulled one finger at a time free, and for whatever reason, Julie found herself unable to stop watching the mundane task. His fingers were long, and as he took the last glove off and kept it in his fist, she admired the elegant but subtle strength in the way he moved. Her mind drifted, imagining those fingers brushing her skin. Those hands on her . . .

How would his touch feel cupping her chin, trailing downward, across her breasts? Lower, brushing her hips, inching closer—

He smacked the gloves against his palm.

"The five-year-old in question," he said, eyes lighting at her startled expression, "loves ruffles, ponies, and all things princess."

Focus, she scolded herself. Flowers.

"Sounds like she would love pink roses."

"Pink roses. Excellent suggestion, Ms. Masterson," he

answered with a whisper and a glance at her name tag. "That's exactly what I thought, but Grandma thought wildflowers."

"Based on what you said, the roses. Definitely pink roses."

"We'll take a dozen." His blue eyes were steady on hers and she leaned closer as his voice dropped further. "How about you, Ms. Masterson, what type flowers do you like?"

"I'm not really a flower-type girl."

"Really?"

She shrugged. "I guess it comes from working with them all day."

It wasn't that she didn't like flowers; she just didn't like getting them from men. In her opinion, there were plenty of other more romantic gifts.

"Daniel," his grandmother said. "Have you decided on something?"

He winked at Julie. "We're going with pink roses. She's guaranteed to love them."

After they left with the roses, Julie tried to decide what it was about him that made her react the way she did. He had a breezy confidence about him, but a lot of her male customers did. There was something, though, about the way he moved that seemed somehow *more*.

"They leave?" Sasha asked, returning from the back office and running her fingers through her dark spiky hair.

"Yeah. And you were wrong—he wasn't trying to get into anyone's pants. He was buying flowers for his niece."

Sasha flipped through the day's receipts. "Daniel Covington doesn't have to try to get into anyone's pants. Women just drop them at the mere sight of him."

Julie looked up from the new arrangement she had been working on. "You know him?"

It really shouldn't have surprised her. Sasha knew everyone. It was one of the reasons the shop had been so successful. Julie was the business-minded one, Sasha the people person.

Or maybe she had dated him. Sasha was known for her ability to run through men like tissue paper. Every other month, it seemed she was on the arm of a new guy. *New and improved. Highly disposable.* But certainly Julie would have remembered Daniel.

"I don't *know* him, know him," she said. "But I know of him. He's the senior vice president of Weston Bank."

Second-largest bank in Delaware.

That certainly explains why he didn't blink at the cost of a dozen pink roses in January.

"Wealthy and good-looking," Julie said with a sigh. "The universe is so unfair."

Sasha's head snapped up. "Not you, too."

"Not me, too, what?"

"Wanting to drop your pants for Daniel."

Julie picked up the flower she'd been trimming and twirled it between her fingers, trying not to remember how she had imagined Daniel's hands and what they'd feel like on her body. "I don't want to do any such thing. What's it to you, anyway? You're always telling me to get out more."

"I didn't mean with *him*."

"Are you telling me I'm not good enough for the senior vice president of Weston Bank?" She pointed the flower at her friend. "Don't make me come over there."

She added the last as a joke, but in reality she was just covering the hurt at the suggestion she wasn't good enough for someone like Daniel. Hurt, yes, but there was also anger at her friend. How dare she insinuate she couldn't date an executive? Besides, who was Sasha to judge? It wasn't like she had a stellar record with the opposite sex.

"I'm just telling you, you're not compatible."

"And I thought you didn't know him."

"I don't," Sasha said in the tone of voice that told Julie the topic wasn't up for further discussion.

Julie tried to decide if she wanted to push it. What did Sasha know about Daniel that made her so certain they weren't compatible? She wondered again for just a second if they had dated.

"Doesn't matter anyway," Julie finally said. "He just came in to buy roses. It's not like I'll ever see him again." Because the universe really wasn't fair.

Sasha looked at her apologetically and nodded toward the trimmed flowers Julie was working with. "On the other hand, people we would be okay never seeing again always seem to pop up. I took a phone call in the back."

Julie dropped the flower. "Mrs. Grant? Again? She's already changed her order twice."

"She read an article."

"Of course she did."

Sasha dug in her pocket and pulled out a ten-dollar bill. "Why don't you go grab us some mochas? I'll handle her this time."

Julie took the cash. "You're the best."

"Don't you forget it!" her friend teased as she left.

The sound of flesh slapping flesh rang out in the otherwise silent room as Daniel watched the couple in his playroom. Ron was his new mentee, a highly coveted position in their local BDSM group. Daniel had held several conversations with the young man, but this was the first time he had watched him with a submissive.

The submissive, Dena, was an experienced sub in their group. A good choice for a Dom in training, which was why Daniel had asked her to join them for the afternoon.

Daniel walked to where Ron had her positioned over a padded table. "Nice location," he said, in response to the spanking the young man had just administered. "But do it again. Harder this time." He ran his hand over Dena's ass. Barely warm. "She's no masochist, but she needs to feel it."

Ron nodded and went back to spanking.

"Watch for signs," Daniel instructed. Dena hadn't been commanded to be still and she wasn't bound. "When she starts to get aroused, she'll lift up to you. Listen to her. If she's not required to be silent, you can judge her response by her moans." He lifted his voice for her benefit. "But I did command silence today, so if she gives so much as a whimper, you can watch me punish her."

He didn't miss the hitch in her breathing. He smiled in response and walked to stand by her head. "Don't get too excited, girl, I call it punishment for a reason. You won't like it."

Dena steeled her body and if Daniel were a betting man, he'd guess there would be no disobedience today. He took a step back so he could keep both participants in his sight. Ron was putting more power into his strike and she loved it.

"Run your hand between her legs," Daniel instructed. "It'll allow you to see how wet she is and heighten her arousal."

Ron gave her one more slap on the backside and then slipped his hand between her legs. "She's soaked."

"Smack her pussy quick and hard a few times. Tell her she's been a good girl."

Ron continued with the lesson, following Daniel's advice, correcting himself when needed, and bringing Dena closer and closer to climax. While watching his mentee pleasure the submissive orally, he recognized his own need. It had been weeks since he'd played with anyone. Far too long since he'd held a woman's submission in his hands and showed her the pleasure he could bring her.

Without even thinking about why, his mind wandered back to the petite florist with the long dark hair he'd talked with days earlier. There had been an air about her. Something beyond her physical beauty drew him to her. Maybe the intelligent and self-confident look in her eyes or the unveiled way she'd sized him up. Certainly, there'd been some kind of sexual awareness between them. What would it be like to have her submission? To control her pleasure? It was far easier to picture her on her knees before him than it should be.

Forget it, he told himself. *She's strictly vanilla.*

Not that he knew it with any certainty, but he'd learned a long time ago it was best to assume a woman was vanilla until proven otherwise.

He forced his attention back to the couple before him. Ron needed a lesson in how to care for a submissive after play ended. Any thoughts having to do with the beguiling florist would have to wait.

Because as much as he tried to think otherwise, he knew it to be only a matter of time before she joined him in his fantasies.

"*D*ena," he said, as Ron left the house. "Would you mind staying around for a bit?"

Dena glanced back at him and nodded, a look of anticipation on her face.

Damn. She probably thinks I want to play.

Not that it would be unheard of. They had played together before. She was an attractive woman and had fully embraced her submissive spirit. He had asked himself before why the two of them had never been a couple, but never came up with an acceptable answer. Finally, he chalked it up to not being ready for a serious relationship.

Once in the kitchen, he poured her a glass of water and pulled a chair out for her.

"Thanks," she said, sitting down. She cocked her head. "Everything okay?"

"Yes, of course." He poured himself a glass and sat across from her. "What did you think of Ron?"

"He has potential. I've served worse." The corner of her lip upturned a bit. "Of course, I've served better."

Her sly comment drew his thoughts to the last time they'd played. Surprisingly, though, the memories dimmed in comparison with the fantasies he'd had of the florist. Unbidden, the image of her on her knees before him beckoned.

Stop! He clenched his fist. He would master his thoughts. They would not get the better of him. He forced his attention on the conversation at hand. "I think he shows potential as well. An eager learner."

Daniel had lived the lifestyle of a Dom for over ten years, been a mentor for five. In that time, he'd seen plenty of men, and women, who wanted to become Doms or Dommes. Often, it never worked because they saw BDSM as a way to meet their own needs, to control, to exert power over a submissive. And while there was a place for that in his view of a power exchange, so much more important, he thought, was the protective care a Dom took of his submissive. How he graciously took her trust and used it to bring them both pleasure.

His thoughts once more drifted back to the florist. What would it be like to be entrusted with her submission? He pictured her bent over his table in the playroom downstairs: ass facing him, legs spread, her body willing and eager for whatever he chose to do to it.

His cock hardened just thinking about it.

"You seem a bit distracted today, sir."

"Sir" was how submissives in their group were to address Doms when not out in public. Daniel had given Dena permission to use his name when they weren't in a scene, so it wasn't difficult to see she'd addressed him more formally as a subtle hint of her interest in playing.

He needed to get her focus on something else. "I've just got a lot on my mind lately." Before she could offer to distract him, he continued. "I told Ron to call you in the next day or two, so let me know if he doesn't. I'd also like your thoughts on areas he needs help in."

She nodded, unsurprised. She had worked with Doms in training before and knew what was expected. "I'll e-mail you by the end of the week."

"Anything that happened today you'd like to talk about?"

She shook her head. "Nothing stood out as out of the ordinary or unexpected."

"Good."

TARA SUE ME

"Are you still planning to speak at the next meeting?"

Their local group held meetings once a month, generally before a party, and he was scheduled to speak at the next one. "Yes."

"Let me know if you need help with a demonstration or anything."

He felt the need for a long, hard jog. It was time for her to leave. He drained the last bit of his water and pushed his chair back. "I think I'll be fine, but thank you for the offer. Come on. I'll walk you out."

She didn't so much as move and her lips curled up into a sly smile. "I was rather hoping we could spend some more time in your playroom, sir."

It would be so easy. A simple word, a slight nod of his head, and she would be his for the next hour or so. She offered her body for his pleasure and a part of him wanted to take it. To use it. To use her. But the larger part of him knew he wasn't in the right frame of mind for the playroom. To take her there would be greedy and unwise. So he held his need in check and simply shook his head.

"Not today, Dena." He stroked her cheek hoping to ease any embarrassment on her part. "I need to run and make a few phone calls."

As soon as she left, he changed and went for his run. Afterward, he showered and then flipped his laptop open and scrolled through the e-mails his administrative assistant had sent him over the last few weeks. Something had sprung to his mind during his run and he knew from past experience his mind wouldn't rest until he checked it out. He looked through all the e-mails searching for one in particular.

And there it was.

He skimmed the e-mail and drummed his fingers on the tabletop for just a second or two before sending a reply.

"I can't believe you didn't tell me we had a gig with Weston Bank." Julie slammed and locked her car door as she shot Sasha a nasty look. "Daniel Covington probably thinks I'm an idiot for not mentioning it last week."

Sasha had oh so slyly mentioned yesterday that they had a meeting at the bank at two o'clock today to discuss floral arrangements for the black-tie melanoma fund-raiser in two weeks.

Sasha walked beside her. "Seriously, Jules, I'm sure Daniel Covington has no idea who's providing flowers."

Tap. Tap. Tap. Julie concentrated on the sound her heels made on the sidewalk. She couldn't afford to be flustered at this meeting. The benefit was a big event and if everything went well, it could lead to larger jobs in the future. Besides, Sasha had done the right thing. Had Julie known about the meeting, she'd only have worried about it. Odds were, Daniel probably thought flowers appeared out of thin air.

"You're right. Besides, it's not like you knew he'd be

stopping by with his grandmother," Julie said, pushing open the door. "This meeting goes well, I'm taking you to dinner."

"Thank goodness, all I have at my place is an overripe banana."

The front desk receptionist took their names and then showed them to a small conference room. "Mr. Covington will be right with you."

Julie's head spun to Sasha. "What did she say?"

Sasha looked just as surprised. "Apparently he has an idea about the flowers after all."

Fortunately or unfortunately, depending on how she looked at it, Julie didn't have time to dwell on anything. Within mere seconds, the door opened and Daniel breezed into the room. He wore a light gray suit and a bright blue tie that complemented his eyes. There was a look of momentary surprise as he noticed Sasha, but he was all smiles when he turned to Julie and held out his hand.

"Ms. Masterson, good to see you again. My niece loved the roses."

Then he looked to Sasha and shook her hand. "Ms. Blake."

There was a hint of recognition between the two. Julie picked up on it immediately. Neither Sasha nor Daniel seemed to acknowledge it, almost as if they had silently agreed to act as if they didn't know each other.

Daniel waved toward the chairs. "Let's have a seat and finalize these plans, shall we?"

Surely a vice president had better things to do than to discuss flowers for a benefit? But it wouldn't be proper to ask, so Julie did as suggested and sat.

"This benefit is near and dear to my heart," Daniel said. "My grandfather died of melanoma."

"I'm sorry to hear that," Julie said.

"Thank you, but it was years ago. The flowers we had at last year's event were subpar and I wanted to ensure the same didn't happen again. That would be why we hired you this time."

"I assure you, the Petal Pushers don't do subpar," Julie said.

"That's what I like to hear." His smile was easy and gentle, but his eyes held a tinge of desire.

Twenty-five minutes later, they'd negotiated all the floral arrangements and pricing. With a deft sweep of his pen, Daniel signed the contract and smiled.

"Pleasure doing business with you. I can already tell I'm in expert hands."

As they all stood to leave, he addressed Sasha. "Can you give me a moment with Ms. Masterson?"

A wary expression crossed her friend's face, but Sasha pursed her lips together and nodded. "I'll be in the car, Julie."

Julie's heart raced and she felt certain the temperature had risen in the small room by at least fifteen degrees.

"Julie," Daniel said when the door closed. "It fits you. May I call you Julie?"

Determined not to appear as flustered as she felt, she smiled. "If I can call you Daniel."

"Of course." Was it her imagination or did his eyes darken as he spoke? "I was wondering, *Julie*, if you would be at the benefit outside of your professional capacity?"

The tickets were a hundred dollars a plate, nothing she could afford. "No, I'll be there before it starts, but I'll leave after everything's set up."

He took a step closer to her and her heart raced faster. "Would you come, then? As my date?"

Sasha's words of warning repeated themselves in her head, but she refused to listen to them. There was obviously something, some chemistry, between her and Daniel. She'd felt it the first time she met him and obviously he felt it, too; she'd be a fool not to explore it.

Yet, how could she both set up for the benefit and get ready to attend as a guest?

The simple answer would be to book a room at the hotel it was being held at. The problem with that was the five-star price associated with the five-star accommodations. An image of her on a date with Daniel flickered in her brain and she knew she'd pay it.

"You can say no. I promise I can take it."

Her head jerked. "What? Oh, no. I was actually just trying to work out the logistics in my head. I mean, I'd love to accept."

"Did you?"

No. She had no idea how it would all work, how she'd

manage to do everything. She didn't even want to think about what Sasha would say. But one look into his captivating eyes, a glance at his easy smile, was all she needed.

"Not yet, but I will."

"Would it be pushing my luck to ask you out to coffee sometime next week? Before the benefit?"

Two dates in one week? "Thursday afternoon?"

He took a business card from the papers on the table and wrote something down. "Here's my cell. Call me."

She would. She definitely would.

A week later, she was putting the final touches on a funeral arrangement when Sasha came through the door. It was Wednesday. Recently, Sasha had been taking a long lunch on Wednesdays to spend time with her latest boyfriend, Peter.

"How was lunch?" Julie asked. She really didn't have to. Sasha nearly screamed "satisfied woman" the way she strolled into the shop, stopping here and there to touch a petal.

"Now, you know I didn't eat anything." Her eyes grew dreamy and she smirked. "But, since you mentioned it. While I was—"

"Stop it right there. No kinky sex talk in the shop. Someone could walk in."

Julie knew her friend Sasha was a sexual submissive, and she understood a few details of what that entailed. Whenever Sasha played with a new Dom privately, Julie acted as her safety call, waiting a specified time for Sasha to text or call with a secret code so Julie would know all was well. Truth be told, even though some part of her thought there should be something scary about needing a safety call, a bigger part of her had always wondered what it'd be like to submit sexually.

"Just saying," Sasha said. "You can always tell a good one. It's like they can read your mind. Kinda freaky."

"Good what?"

"Good Dominant."

"The guy in charge?"

"It's so much more than that. It's like an itch, an ache. And when you're with the right Dom, and he scratches it just so?" Sasha sighed with deep satisfaction and simultaneous excitement.

Hearing Sasha talk about it made Julie want to try it all the more. After all, it seemed to suit Sasha. And just because she tried it didn't mean she had to do it forever. She could just see if she liked it.

But no sooner had that thought passed through her mind than she wondered what it would be like to submit to Daniel. Would he be gentle in bed or was he into taking what he wanted hard and fast?

"You're sighing," Sasha said. "What's on your mind?"

Had she sighed out loud? She didn't even realize it. "Just thinking about something."

"Would that something happen to be a certain vice president?"

"Here lately, it's always about him."

"Just be careful, okay?"

But that was the problem. She was always careful. For once she wanted to take a risk.

---

*D*aniel was standing inside the coffee shop, waiting, when Julie arrived on Thursday. She took a second to watch him from the window. Having arrived after work, he was wearing a beautiful dark suit that emphasized his blond good looks. He was drawing admiring glances from several women.

Locally owned, the coffee shop was her and Sasha's favorite hangout. Furnished with plush leather couches and handmade bookshelves, it was the perfect place to spend a winter afternoon. She wondered if Daniel had ever been inside before. Right now he was looking at the far wall, frowning at something she couldn't see.

Must have been a bad day.

She looked down at the polo shirt she always wore to work and wished she'd had time to run home and change into something nicer. It wouldn't look like she belonged with Daniel when she joined him. Shaking her head, she pushed open the door. Let people think what they would. For the moment, she was with Daniel and that was all that mattered.

His expression lightened when he saw her and he walked over. "Hey, come on in. Let me take your coat."

She shrugged out of her winter coat, trying hard not to react when their hands brushed. "Thanks."

He seemed completely unaffected, hanging the coat on the rack beside the door. "You want to get a table while I order?"

She told him what she wanted, medium latte and a blueberry scone, then found a secluded corner table and waited. He hadn't been in line long when a young woman approached him. He shook his head at whatever it was she said. The lady reached out to touch him, but he shot her a look that froze her in her tracks.

The look troubled Julie a bit. It had been so cold and stern, and seemed totally out of character for Daniel. At least, it seemed out of character for what she knew of Daniel so far. Maybe she hadn't read him as well as she thought.

She asked him about it when he found her minutes later. "Did that chick hit on you?"

He placed her latte and scone in front of her. "Yes, some people can't take no for an answer."

"Some people are really bold. I can't imagine approaching a stranger in a coffee shop."

He took a sip from his cup. "She wasn't a stranger."

Did that make her an ex, a friend who wanted more, maybe a business associate? She wanted to ask, but didn't. It was their first date; she had no claims on him and he owed her no explanations.

"I'm very selective about who I go out with," he said.

She raised an eyebrow and he laughed.

"That sounds a bit snobbish, doesn't it?" he asked.

"Slightly. You make it sound like you think the rest of us will date anyone with a basic grasp of the English language and most of their teeth."

"Let me rephrase, then." He sat thinking for several seconds before finally giving up. "Nah. I've got nothing."

"That's okay, I understand. You have certain criteria you'd like in a woman and some people don't make the cut. I'm selective about who I go out with, too."

"I'm glad I fit the bill."

She shrugged. "What can I say, I'm putty in the hands of a man who talks in complete sentences."

He didn't take it like the joke she'd intended; instead, his eyes flashed with desire. "I doubt you'd be putty for just any man no matter how well he spoke."

Damn near every conversation she'd ever had with Sasha about submission ran through her mind, but she pushed them out of her head. She focused her attention on Daniel, trying hard not to imagine being putty in his hands.

"It's a figure of speech. I'm a self-made businesswoman. I'm putty in no one's hands and I don't intend to be."

"Is that so?" His eyes looked so deeply into hers that she wondered if he saw through her words.

"Yes," she said, but even she didn't believe her response. From the look he gave her, she could tell Daniel didn't either.

"That's too bad."

He spoke the words so softly, she wasn't sure she was meant to have heard them.

He changed subjects, bringing up the benefit on Saturday. Julie asked about his grandfather and he was happy to talk about him. He shared some stories about fishing as a young boy with his grandpa that made her laugh, but also realize the warmth and love that had been between them. Her own grandparents had died before she was born, so she didn't have a connection like Daniel did. She admired the love he obviously felt toward his grandfather, and was moved that he expressed it by organizing the melanoma fund-raiser every year.

She found Daniel easygoing and fun to talk with. He had an air about him that set her at ease. Except for the times—and it happened more than once, so she knew it wasn't her imagination—that he looked at her with those blue eyes and the intensity took her breath.

There was something unusually captivating about Daniel. She just couldn't quite put her finger on it.

TWO

*T*he day of the melanoma benefit brought the exact
amount of chaos and problems Daniel had come to
expect of large fund-raisers. Which was why he was glad
he'd paid knowledgeable contractors good money to handle the issues as they cropped up.

He'd arrived at the hotel three hours before the first
guest was due to arrive. The time allowed him to oversee
everything and still leave to change into his tux before he
was scheduled to appear.

That's not the real reason you came early.

No, the real reason was so that he could see her. Julie.

Who at that very moment was giving some poor deliv-
ery boy a firm talking-to about something. Her hands were
on her hips and every once in a while, she would point to a

nearby vase of flowers. The sight of her taking charge and setting whatever wrong to right made him grow uncomfortably hard.

Her brown hair was pulled haphazardly into a knot on top of her head. All too easily he imagined taking it down, running his fingers through it, giving it a sharp tug as he thrust into her needy body.

She turned and saw him. "Mr. Covington."

Thoughts of Julie's hair and what he wanted to do with it faded as the woman in question walked toward him. He hoped she didn't see the erection those thoughts left in their wake.

When she stood before him, he noticed several strands of hair had fallen from the knot. He reached out and tucked one wayward piece behind her ear.

"I thought I gave you permission to call me Daniel?"

"It seemed more professional the other way."

"Sir," I want you to call me "sir." But he knew he couldn't speak those words out loud to her. "As long as you call me Daniel tonight."

She nodded in response, a flush creeping up her neck. She cleared her throat. "Everything's set up. Except for the centerpiece for the head table and that will be corrected in a few minutes."

"Everything looks great. Your team's done an outstanding job."

"Thank you."

He would look over everything in a few minutes.

Though he really doubted he needed to. Julie and Sasha's team really had done an amazing job. But for the moment, he had more pressing things to address. When he had asked her to accompany him, he'd forgotten something.

"Where should I pick you up tonight?" he asked.

She hesitated for a second. "We could meet in the lobby."

"The lobby? No. Tell me where you live and I'll pick you up."

"I actually booked a room here tonight. My stuff's upstairs, so I have time to change."

"You booked a room? Why? Oh. *Oh,*" he said as understanding dawned.

She tapped her pen against the clipboard in her hand. The pink polo shirt she wore had not only her shop's logo on it but several smears of dirt and green stains of some sort.

"Julie, I'm sorry. I gave little thought to how hectic the day would be for you."

I only thought of myself. I wanted you on my arm for the night.

She waved her hand as if shooing away his comment. "You men. You put on a tuxedo and all is well. We women have to do our hair, makeup, and try to pull up sheer hose without messing up our manicures."

Sheer hose. Her legs.

His hands spreading her knees.

"Don't wear the hose," he said through clenched teeth.

"What?"

Idiot.

"I mean, if it's that much trouble." His voice sounded coarse to his ears.

"Lucky for me, I didn't actually bring hose. And"—she wiggled the fingers of one hand at him—"in any case, I have florist fingers."

"You see, I look at those fingers and I see the hands of a woman who's worked hard to get what she wants."

"I suppose. But sometimes I think it'd be nice to have girlie nails."

"It's all about sacrifice."

Her expression was thoughtful. Suddenly, he wished their date wouldn't be shared by a hundred people. He wanted to get her alone and learn everything about her. Talk to her. Find out where she went to school, if she had any siblings, what her favorite food was.

Right. Because if you got her alone, that's what you'd do. Talk.

Talk would be all they'd do, he reassured himself. The assumption had to be she didn't live his lifestyle. Wouldn't be interested in it. Even with that assumption, he was still drawn to her and wanted to spend time with her. What little he knew about her made him curious to know more. Plus, there was a certain look she'd had in her eyes that day at the coffee shop when she'd said she didn't intend to be putty in anyone's hands that indicated the exact opposite.

She was also Sasha Blake's friend and business partner. Would she know about Sasha's lifestyle? Had they talked about dominance and submission? Did that explain the sensuality she exuded? Questions for another place and time.

"Will you have time to get ready?" he asked.

She glanced at her watch. "The way I see it, I'll need an hour and a half to finish up here. That leaves me plenty of time to get ready."

"Ms. Masterson!" A hotel employee ran up to them.

Daniel moved out of the way. "I'll let you get back to work. Meet you in the lobby in three hours?"

"Sounds good," she replied before turning her attention to the young man at her side.

He arrived back at the hotel, dressed, two hours and forty-five minutes later. Though he always tried to be punctual, he had another reason for not being late that night: he wanted to watch Julie make her entrance.

When he reached the hotel, he saw a few early guests had arrived. They lingered in the lobby, making small talk before wandering to the ballroom. Daniel waved at a few people, but his gaze kept returning to the elevator doors.

They finally opened and she stepped out.

His breath caught.

Ninety-nine percent of the women attending the fundraiser would dress in black. Julie Masterson was not ninety-nine percent of women.

Gone was the harried and stained florist from earlier in the day. In her place was a siren. Her gown was white and fit close to her skin, showing off the curves he imagined buried beneath her standard pink polo. Sheer beading draped itself over one shoulder, allowing just a peek of skin. Her hair was twisted up, leaving her neck long and bare. She looked even better than his fantasy.

She looked around the lobby for him and once her gaze settled on his, her mouth formed an O of recognition. She walked toward him, her hips swaying ever so slightly. Every step she took gained her more and more attention from the lobby crowd.

"Let me assure you," he said when she finally stood before him, "that no one is looking at your fingers. You are stunning."

"Thank you. My sister's a buyer up in New York. She got this for me and tonight's the first chance I've had to wear it."

"You'll have to give me her address."

"You're into clothes?"

"No. I want to send her a thank-you note."

Her laugh was low, throaty, and the most seductive sound he'd heard in years. Once again, he was sure the intense sexuality he sensed in her was there.

He held out his arm. "Shall we?"

People surrounded them as soon as they entered the ballroom. Daniel was well-known for his work raising money for cancer awareness and research. While most of the time he was content to talk with anyone about his involvement, at that moment, he simply wanted to be left alone with Julie.

But that wasn't an option. So he greeted everyone warmly, and thanked them all for coming. She stayed by his side while he talked, looking at him every once in a while with a curious grin on her face. She looked so lovely, he wondered idly if he'd have so many people swarming around if it wasn't for his date.

They eventually made their way to the head table, where, finally, he could hear himself think. They sat next to each other, and he let out a deep breath.

"That was certainly interesting. Do you always inspire such an entourage?" Julie asked.

"Only when the woman by my side is wearing a gown like the one you have on."

He was pleased to see she could handle a compliment. It bugged him when a woman got all flustered just because someone said she looked nice. But Julie just smiled in recognition of his kind words. "There were a good number of women in that crowd. They definitely liked the way the man by my side looked in his tux." Her eyes were dark.

He leaned close so he could smell her. She smelled of oranges. "What about you? How do you think he looks?"

"You look perfectly adequate." She said it with a straight face, but her eyes were laughing at him.

"You're a dangerous woman, Julie Masterson."

She placed her napkin in her lap with the utmost care

and attention. "If that's not the pot calling the kettle black, I don't know what is."

"I'm just dangerous to my competitors."

"Remind me to never get on your bad side."

He had a feeling he didn't have a bad side where she was concerned. He felt comfortable and easy around her. She was an intelligent self-made businesswoman. She made him laugh and she looked fantastic. And she was the sexiest woman he'd met in years.

"Tell me," he said to her. "Why flowers?"

She shrugged. "My mom loved flowers. She had them all over the house and always said it was a travesty to save them for special occasions. I wanted to share her love and beliefs with everyone. Sasha and I found the shop a few years ago while walking through the historic district. We bought it and the Petal Pushers was born. Now it's like I spend part of each day with my mom."

"And yet you said you weren't the flower type of girl."

Her body stilled. "You remember?"

He ran a finger across her hand, swirled a figure eight on the top. "I remember everything about you."

For the briefest moment, when he looked into her eyes, it was as if the rest of the room disappeared and there was nothing in the world except the two of them. Her hand turned over on the table, so the palm faced up. He dragged his finger along the lines there before settling his hand over hers.

How simple it was to engulf her hand in his. He had an

overwhelming desire to engulf her entirely. Surround her. Protect her.

Tease and tempt her.

They jumped apart when a waiter placed their salads in front of them. Daniel looked up to find their dinner companions watching them intently. He was almost embarrassed to realize they hadn't even noticed when the other diners sat down. But the truth was, he didn't care. He couldn't when she was overwhelming him like this. Now their dinner companions all averted their eyes, obviously embarrassed on their own parts to be caught staring.

"It must be you," Julie said all calm and cool. "People never stare at me like that."

"Maybe it's the combination of us together."

The air between them pulsed. Surely she felt it, too. They would probably be a dangerous combination together. Even more so alone. He wanted to test that theory.

Badly.

But the benefit wouldn't be over for hours.

He pressed the palms of his hands against his thighs. Refocused his attention on the three other couples sitting at the table. Before he'd asked Julie to be his date, he'd been looking forward to discussing several new oncology breakthroughs with those in attendance. At the moment, though, all he could muster was small talk. After a few minutes, the other couples were talking among themselves and he could finally turn back to Julie.

"What does your mom think of your business?" he asked.

"She passed before it opened."

"I'm sorry to hear that."

She took her time cutting her salad. She was very meticulous about it, cutting each piece into nearly identical sizes. "How about you? Why banking?"

Obviously, the conversation about her mother was over. He took a moment to follow her lead and cut his salad.

"It's a family business. Something it was always assumed I'd do."

"Is it what you really want to do?" Questioning eyes met his. "If you could do anything, what would it be?"

He chuckled. "What do I want to be when I grow up?"

"Something like that."

"Outside of the fact that I'm thirty-five, I suppose when I grow up, I just want to know I've changed the world for the better."

She muttered something under her breath, but all he could make out was "no wonder" and "pants."

"What?"

"Nothing, just something Sasha said."

Their conversation flowed smoothly throughout dinner. Julie proved to be witty and warm, a delightful combination. But as she talked about what she'd done to reach her goals, and the obstacles she'd overcome, she also showed him a will of iron. Her father had left when her sister was born. After her mother died, she'd worked two jobs while going to school. Somehow, she and Sasha had secured a loan for the shop and turned it into a successful business. He had a strong desire to bend that will of hers to his own, to show her what it was like to have someone protect her and take care of what she needed.

Careful, he told himself.

He had succeeded in arranging for one of the leading oncologists in melanoma to speak at the benefit, and for months he had been looking forward to the event. But sitting next to Julie close enough to hear her breathing and smell her orange scent made listening as the speaker went on and on about biomarkers almost more than his patience could bear.

When the gentleman wrapped up his speech, Daniel joined the audience in a standing ovation, but the truth was he already couldn't remember what had been said and he clapped only because the talk was over. Julie was up on her feet beside him. She leaned her head near his.

"What a fascinating speech," she whispered.

"I only heard every third word."

She laughed, but he lifted an eyebrow to let her know he wasn't joking.

They sat back down and chatted with their table companions while the orchestra set up. The local hospital's chief of staff was seated across from Julie and she quickly became deeply engaged in conversation with him about ongoing research at the hospital. He was so impressed by how relaxed she seemed, despite the heady dignitaries she spoke with. All her questions were intelligent, and her tone was confident and friendly. Apparently, making her own way in the world as she had was its own reward.

When the first notes sounded from the nearby violin, the executive excused himself and took his wife's hand.

"She always insists on dancing the first dance," he explained.

Daniel waited until the older couple made it to the dance floor. Then he stood and held out his hand to Julie. "Dance with me?"

She didn't hesitate, but silently took his hand and came to her feet.

For the most part, Daniel could take dancing or leave it. He would join in when the situation called for it. Other times, he would sit out and people-watch. But tonight, outside of wanting to hold Julie, he had another purpose in asking her to dance.

You could tell a lot of information about a person by the way she danced. There were the obvious things: grace and agility. But Daniel was looking for more from Julie.

They settled themselves onto the dance floor, one of her arms around his shoulder, her other hand held gently in his. He slipped his free arm around her waist and pulled her close. As he began to move, she followed.

"Thank you for coming with me tonight," he said.

She settled farther into his arms. "Thanks for the invite."

"Can you do dinner next week?" He had the group meeting Thursday night and the play party Friday night, but he was free on Saturday.

"Yes." She smiled up at him as she answered.

They could work out the details later. For the moment, he only wanted to hold her. She was an astute dancer, following his lead, her body answering his movements. It told him what he had been looking for, and now it was far too easy to picture her body answering his in a much more intimate manner. Would she be as pliable in bed? Dare he hope?

He wanted to ask if she was staying the night at the hotel, but he didn't want to come across as a jerk who only wanted her for one thing. The truth was, he didn't just want to go to bed with her; he wanted to get to know her. For now, he would ignore the side of himself that whispered it would do him no good to get to know her if she didn't share his sexual desires.

He had dated so-called vanilla women before. It was adequate. Filled some of his needs. But he knew that it could never be truly satisfying to him unless his sexual partner genuinely submitted to him. At least in the bedroom.

The woman in his arms might test that need. If they continued on their current path and he found himself even more attracted to her . . .

Well, that was something they would have to explore later.

"You seem far away all of a sudden."

Yes, he had been and that was a travesty with such a remarkable woman so close. "Forgive me?"

She pulled back slightly and gave a sly smile. "Maybe. If you make it up to me."

Forget about getting to know her better. When she teased him like that, all he could think about was dragging her off the dance floor and taking her upstairs.

He risked sliding his hand a bit lower down her body so his fingers brushed the top of her ass, and pulled her toward his groin. "Don't start something you're not ready to finish."

"I'm not a tease."

"Didn't think you were, just wanted you to know you're playing with fire."

She pulled his head down and whispered in his ear, "Would you like to join me in my room for a drink?"

Julie didn't know what had gotten into her. Probably it was the combination of being dressed up in the gorgeous gown her sister had given her, Daniel, and the dancing. Not to mention, Sasha's words from over a week ago replayed in her mind all night. She still felt like her friend's insinuation that Julie wasn't suitable for Daniel was a challenge of some kind.

All night she'd been basking in the heat between them, acutely aware of the overwhelming powerful maleness of him. He brought out a part of herself she'd rarely experienced. He made her bold. And the way he looked at her? As if she were a rare treat he wanted to savor. Or possibly devour in one bite.

He walked behind her as they left the elevators and moved down the hall toward her room. His hand never left the small of her back, a subtle reminder of his warning downstairs. He was fire and she could either accept his power or not, but he would make no excuses for what he was.

"This is it," she said, stopping in front of her door.

"Allow me." He took the key from her and unlocked the room, holding the door open and letting her pass.

Nervous excitement bubbled in her stomach. He looked so *male* in the middle of the room. So *there*.

"I actually don't have anything to drink," she admitted. "We can order room service or raid the wet bar."

He started untying his tie. "No problem. I'm not really thirsty."

He slipped the tie from his neck, placed it on an end table, and started removing his cuff links.

Dear heavens, was he going to strip down just like that?

He nodded to the couch and smiled as if aware of a joke she wasn't in on. "Have a seat, Julie. I won't bite. I'm just getting comfortable."

There were moments that defined your life. Julie knew that. The day she decided to get her MBA. The afternoon she and Sasha found the building they eventually remodeled into the shop. Somehow, she knew, this moment with Daniel was another one.

She was a woman who took what she wanted and in that moment, she wanted Daniel.

"Good idea." She walked to where he stood and turned so her back faced him. "Help me get this off, will you?"

"Julie." His voice was a warning. And a promise.

"I just want to get comfortable."

His hands brushed her shoulders, teased the nape of her neck. She barely had time to take a ragged breath before his lips replaced his fingers and he pressed a soft kiss on the top of her spine.

"If I help you get the gown off, I'll have you naked and beneath me on that bed in less than ten seconds."

"I certainly hope so."

The hands on her shoulders tightened. "There are . . . things you don't know about me."

She turned back to face him, met his eyes. "Are you a deranged serial killer?"

There was a smile in his response. "No."

"Do you kidnap small children?"

"No."

"Are there any outstanding warrants for your arrest? Does anyone have a restraining order out against you? Have you jumped bail?"

"No. No. And no."

"Do you have a condom with you?"

"Damn straight I do."

"Then that paired with what I already know about you is enough." She turned around again and lowered her neck to give him better access. "Will you help me with the gown?"

He didn't unzip it immediately. Instead, he placed several kisses along the bare skin of her back. "I've wanted to taste you all night. All week."

She trembled at the feel of his mouth on her, at the sound of his words. He'd been thinking of her just like she'd been thinking of him.

"You taste even better than you did in my fantasy."

Instead of unzipping her, his hands went to her hair and gently removed each pin. Her hair fell in waves around her face and she moaned in pleasure when he rubbed her scalp, his fingers easing away the soreness of having it up for so long.

"That feels good," she said, thrilled to have her hair down and even more thrilled at his touch.

"That's my plan."

Ever so slowly, the zipper slid down, gradually exposing her to him. His lips followed the path until finally coming to a stop at the small of her back. Two large hands gently pushed the gown from her shoulders.

She turned around as the silken material slipped off her body. The gown didn't allow for a bra, so she was topless when she faced him. One by one, she undid the buttons on his shirt. "I believe your ten seconds are up."

He took her hand in his and placed a kiss on her palm. "There's been a change of plans. Rest assured, though, I'll still have you under me at some point."

She couldn't wait to feel him above her, pressing into her. "Then you better let go of my hand so I can finish unbuttoning your shirt."

He hesitated for the briefest of moments, but then his easy smile came back. "I suppose it's only fair since I undressed you."

Quicker than before, she undid his buttons. The shirt fell away, revealing his hard chest. She ran her hand down the sculpted muscles. "My, my, my. Looks like someone works out."

"The better to fuck you, my dear."

Her knees quaked at his dirty talk. She loved a vocal man. "Really? I would have thought that depended on another part of your anatomy." Her fingers drifted to his waistband.

"When done correctly, it's a whole body activity."

How long had it been since she'd been with someone who really knew what he was doing in bed? She couldn't count in months; years would be closer to the truth.

She started to drop to her knees, but he stopped her.

"Not tonight, Julie."

She looked up, puzzled.

"My plan is for this to actually last longer than ten seconds," he said, but something else lurked behind his expression.

Without explaining further, he pulled her into his arms and kissed her. Softly. As if she were fragile. Little by little, he backed her toward the bed, so she sat on the edge of the mattress wearing only a tiny pair of panties.

He stood above her, his fingers swirling over her chest, lightly brushing her nipples. He dropped his mouth to one and gave it a gentle suck. Her back arched, silently begging for more. Asking to be taken deeper. To be engulfed.

"Lie back," he said, his voice low and commanding.

She obeyed, situating herself on the bed with her legs hanging over the side. He was still standing, his hands lightly brushing over her body. Rougher than a tickle, his touch teased her mercilessly. Desire pooled between her legs, but that was the one area he avoided.

"Please," she begged, lifting her hips in silent invitation.

"Some part of you feeling neglected?"

"You did say it was a whole body activity." She playfully pouted.

He chuckled. "I did, didn't I? How rude of me not to involve all your parts."

His finger teased the leg of her thong. Her legs shook. She felt desperate for him to touch her. One glance revealed him kneeling between her legs. She watched as he hooked a finger inside her underwear and slowly pulled it off.

Naked under his gaze, she didn't feel exposed. She felt powerful and needy and wanting. Oh so wanting.

"Please," she said again.

"Is your pussy feeling deprived?" He trailed a finger up her thigh, inching closer. Drifting away.

"Yes," she said, not caring that her voice sounded like a whine.

"Keep your legs spread nice and wide for me." He pushed them farther apart. "Just like that."

Bending down, he placed a single kiss on her upper thigh. Then he wrapped his arms around her waist and licked her slit, the scruff of his upper lip brushing her clit.

Her hips jerked off the bed and she fisted her hands frantically in his hair. "Yes."

He was warm and big and the craziest combination of rough and tender. He would nibble her almost playfully while his hands roamed her body. He blew a stream of air across her clit while at the same time pinching a nipple slightly.

She muttered curses under her breath.

But just when she was coming close, right as she teetered on the edge of orgasm, he pulled away completely, leaving her achy and alone. She peeked out of one eye. He stood by the bed, panting, rummaging in his pocket.

He found the condom, shoved his pants down, and then ripped the package open. She didn't see much before he covered himself, but what she saw looked downright delectable.

The ache between her legs pulsed impatiently. She wanted him. Wanted him badly. And from the looks of it, he wanted her just as much.

He crawled onto the bed with her, his toned body taunting her. She wanted to take her time exploring it, but at the moment what she wanted more was for him to fulfill his promise.

He didn't disappoint her. Without saying a word, he came up over her, spread her legs even wider, and positioned himself at her entrance.

"Does your pussy need even more attention?"

She tried to wiggle in an effort to draw him in, but he held her waist still and when he spoke, his voice was low and unyielding. "I asked a question."

"Damn it, Daniel, yes." Her eyes closed in anticipation.

"Look at me," he said, and when she did, she saw her need echoed in his eyes.

His gaze stayed locked with hers as he oh-so-slowly pushed inside. It had been a long time since her last boyfriend and she felt every delicious inch Daniel gave her. The stretching felt so good, she whimpered.

He stilled. "Are you okay?"

She could have howled at the loss of his pressing forward. "Don't stop, feels too good to stop."

As if that was the signal he had been waiting for, he held her waist and thrust to the hilt with one push. He held still for a moment and she took a few breaths to accustom herself to the size of him. He didn't move his lower body, but leaned over and kissed her.

"Damn, you feel good," he whispered against her lips.

"Let me make you feel better," she said with a shift of her hips.

He answered with a shift of his own. "Like this?"

The sweet ache of him moving inside her, the hypnotic push and pull, was too much. She closed her eyes in an attempt to contain the sensations he created. His arms held her tightly while he settled into a pounding rhythm. Her own hands found purchase on his backside and she scratched the clenched muscles of his ass.

"Wrap your legs around me," he ground out.

She obeyed, and when he slid even deeper, she hissed in response. There were no words then, just their breathing, his grunts, and her cries of pleasure. He dropped a hand between them, and began to circle her clit with a fingertip.

Her hips bucked; it was too much. "Oh, fuck, yes, Daniel, yes."

"I want to feel you come. Come hard and fast all around my dick."

She already was, it started low in her belly, concentrated itself between her legs, and then shot outward, encompassing her entire body. She was only slightly aware of Daniel's last few thrusts, of his body stilling within her as he came, and his sigh of satisfaction as he rolled them to their sides.

His lips were on her cheeks, her nose, and her ear. "I was a bit rough. I didn't hurt you, did I?"

She ran a hand across his back, down his arm, and back again. There was a pleasant ache between her legs, and she knew she'd feel him for days. "Only in a good way."

They stayed in silence for a few minutes, allowing their breathing to return to normal, simply enjoying being in each other's arms. She stretched out beside him, trying to remember the last time she felt so good. Probably never.

Suddenly shy, she traced a finger along the muscles of his chest. She hoped he knew she wasn't wanton as a general rule. She wasn't sure she recognized the woman she became in his presence, but she rather thought she liked her. Julie Masterson, the seductress. A giggle escaped before she could stop it.

Daniel cracked one eye open. "That's a sound no man wants to hear in bed."

Feeling bolder, she pressed a kiss to his shoulder. "I was actually thinking about the way being around you makes me feel all wanton and wicked."

"And that's worthy of a giggle?"

"It's just not like me."

"Maybe it's more like you than you realize."

His words struck a chord within her. Maybe he was right and she had just needed the right man to show her the woman buried inside and longing to be free.

"Julie, I—," he started, but stopped when a cell phone rang.

"Must be yours. That's not my ringtone."

"It is. I'm sorry. It's my private line. Do you mind?"

She sat up, dragging the sheet with her and wrapping it around her chest. "No, go ahead."

He rummaged through the pile of clothes, finally pulling the phone from his discarded pants. A frown crossed his face when he saw the display. "Tess?" he asked, answering the call. The frown changed into an expression of worry. "How long ago? Where's she at now?" Silence followed as whoever he was talking with replied. He looked down at his watch. "I'll be there in thirty minutes. No, I can't get there any faster."

He ended the call with a sigh and turned to her. "I'm sorry. My grandma's had an episode. . . . She's not in the best frame of mind sometimes. That was my sister."

Julie swallowed her disappointment; she'd hoped he could stay longer. Selfish of her to feel that way with his grandmother ill, but there you go. She wasn't just a seductress; she was a selfish seductress.

But she waved at him. "Don't think twice about it—you need to be with your family."

He shrugged his shirt on. "I feel like a jerk, leaving like this."

"Don't. You'd be a jerk if you didn't go."

His tuxedo pants were quickly donned and he haphazardly stuffed his shirt in. When he was dressed, he walked to the bed and cupped her face.

"You are an amazing woman and I promise I will make this up to you." He leaned down for a soft kiss, promised to call, and then left.

With a sigh, Julie collapsed back onto the bed and snuggled into the downy comforter. She eventually fell asleep to one thought: she was willing to bet she would thoroughly enjoy Daniel making it up to her.

THREE

*T*he week passed slowly. Daniel called twice and they sent a few texts back and forth, and even planned a date for Saturday, but he seemed distant. Julie remembered his words from the benefit, that there were things she didn't know about him. Did that explain the distance? Or did he think her cheap and easy after the night in her hotel room?

On Thursday night, she sat in the shop, counting down the minutes until she could lock up. Then it would be back to her place for takeout and a good book. At least she had Saturday night to look forward to. Saturday night she'd keep her clothes on for the entire date. Or at least until they could talk about why he was so distant.

If there was a following week. Sasha had said she

wouldn't be compatible with Daniel. Maybe she was right. Earth-shattering sex aside, because they'd certainly seemed compatible in bed.

She drummed her fingers against the countertop. She'd had the dream again. The one that had started during college. Though it'd always been the same, last night it'd ended differently.

The room is dark. A single candle provides the only light. He'd told her to keep her eyes closed, but she risks a small peek to try and see him. Always he was cloaked in darkness. Always. Tonight is no different.

"Did you open your eyes?" His voice is thick with displeasure.

She whispers her apology, but it's too late. One hand covers her mouth, while the other slips her panties down her hips.

"I'll teach you to disobey a direct order."

Somehow, she is on her stomach and he is spanking her. It doesn't hurt, it simply turns her on more, and she wiggles in a desperate attempt to alleviate the needy ache between her legs.

"Look at you getting horny by being spanked." He rains more slaps against her flesh. Harder. Harder. "The harder I spank you, the more desperate you are to come."

He's right. There's no sense in even trying to deny it. He circles her clit and she comes with a yelp when he sweeps a finger across her hungry flesh.

"I didn't give you permission."

He flips her over, onto her back, and for the first time ever, she sees him clearly.

"Daniel!"

"Thinking about a certain banker again?" Sasha flipped the sign over the door to CLOSED.

Julie couldn't believe she'd spoken aloud, but just remembering the dream had surprised her again. Now she blushed and tried to explain. "No, I just thought I saw someone who looked like him walking by out the front window."

Sasha looked at her funny, but didn't point out it was too dark outside to see anyone walking by. Julie decided to change the subject. "Time for me to curl up with a good book. What are you doing tonight?"

"It's my monthly group meeting." Sasha tilted her head and gave a sly smile. "Come with me?"

"What? No. I'm not like that." She didn't know why it was so difficult to admit her interest.

"I've seen the look in your eyes when I talk about it. I know you're curious. Come check it out. Trust me. You won't regret it."

Julie was so tempted.

Sasha held out her hands as if weighing something. "Lonely Thursday night or meeting cool people? Romance novel or acting out your fantasy?"

She would never stop wondering what BDSM was all about until she learned more. Though she'd never admitted it to Sasha, she was extremely curious and the reoccurring dream had been at the forefront of her mind all day. She knew the meeting would be safe. And Sasha would know everyone. "Oh, okay. I'll go."

Her friend applauded. "Good for you. Take charge. Come on, I'll brief you in the car."

During the drive to the community center that housed the meeting, Sasha chatted about what to expect. Namely, that everyone would have a bracelet on. As a first-time guest, Julie's would be white. Sasha, a submissive, wore red. Switches wore green. Doms wore black.

When she entered, she'd be given paperwork to look over and complete if she would like to come back or attend the party the next day. After a brief meet and greet time, a senior member would lead the group in either a teaching session or a roundtable discussion.

"What's the topic tonight?" she asked Sasha.

Sasha stared intently at the red light they were stopped at. "I'm not exactly sure."

"I don't know if I'm ready to talk sex with a roomful of strangers."

"Only roundtables involve group discussion and even then, they won't make you talk."

Julie squirmed in her seat. She wasn't a prude. Heaven knew, she had only to look back to last weekend to figure that out. She just wasn't sure she was open-minded enough for the next few hours.

"You going to the play party tomorrow?" she asked Sasha.

"Yeah, Peter and I are doing a demo." She turned and gave Julie a wicked smile. "Wanna come?"

"I'll probably pass."

"Invitation's open."

She loved Sasha as much as she loved her sister; she just didn't know if she wanted to see her participating in whatever it was she was demoing with her latest fling.

They pulled into the parking lot and there were a lot more people present than she'd anticipated. Even though Sasha told her not to worry and that the group held confidentiality in the highest regard, she still feared running into someone she knew. Or running into someone next week that she'd met at the meeting.

A friendly-looking young guy wearing a green bracelet greeted Sasha warmly and handed Julie a stack of papers and a white bracelet.

After slipping the plastic band on her wrist, she flipped through the papers.

"Don't let the checklist freak you out," Sasha whispered.

Julie glanced at a few items on the list and decided it would be best to read through it later. In private. And with the Internet handy.

The forms she didn't pay much attention to, since she wouldn't be going to the party the next day. She'd take them home, too. If she ever decided to come back, she'd fill them out then.

Sasha introduced her to a few people and Julie began to relax. Everyone was open and friendly. There seemed to be an equal number of men and women present, representing a wide age range. Sasha addressed the people wearing black bracelets as either "sir" or "ma'am," but since Julie was new, they insisted she use their first names.

Julie was standing with Sasha, talking to a group of women wearing red bands, when a familiar voice rang through the room.

"Sorry I'm late. Everyone go ahead and take a seat. We'll get started right away."

She spun around to find Daniel striding through the crowd. On his wrist was a thick black band.

"What the hell, Sasha?" Julie asked when her mind cleared somewhat and she found her voice.

Sasha sighed. "You needed to know."

Holy fuck. Daniel was a Dom.

She couldn't be more shocked. Clearly this was what her dream was trying to tell her, and she hadn't been listening. She was certain if she thought about it, it would make sense. Maybe. But at the moment she was still dealing with the shock of seeing Daniel. At Sasha's BDSM group meeting. Where he was a Dom.

"What?" Julie questioned. "So you thought dragging me here was the best way for me to find out?"

"You're getting more and more involved with him and he obviously isn't telling you. I know something happened last weekend—it was written all over your face on Monday. Don't look at me like that. I'm not an idiot."

Last weekend. Daniel's insistence she needed to know more about him. Her lighthearted brush-off of that insistence.

The two of them were starting to draw attention. The group of submissives moved away to find seats. A black-bracelet-wearing man she'd been introduced to moments earlier came up to them.

"Is there a problem here, ladies?" He looked cold and hard. Julie guessed he didn't smile often.

"No, sir," Sasha replied. "No problem here."

Julie wondered if she could slip out of the room without Daniel seeing her. But their little commotion had grabbed his attention. He caught her gaze and his eyes widened in shock.

"Julie?" Then he looked to the woman at her side and understanding crossed his face. "Sasha," he said, his voice low and commanding, allowing no possibility of disobedience. "Side room. Now. Dena, run a roundtable discussion."

Sasha straightened her shoulders and, looking like a condemned prisoner walking to meet her fate, followed Daniel out a side door. The man who had approached her and Sasha went with her.

A leggy blonde jumped up. "Um, since Master Covington has been detained, let's have whoever wants to share tell one thing that can improve communication between Dominant and submissive."

Not jumping their bones when they tell you there's something you need to know.

Several heads turned in her direction.

Damn it all, did I say that out loud?

Luckily she hadn't, and the conversation began to flow around her. She found she couldn't concentrate on the words. Instead, she unsuccessfully tried to hear what was happening in the side room. There wasn't any yelling or shouting that she could hear. Then again, Daniel didn't seem like the yelling sort.

And why had the blonde called him "Master"? Didn't that speak to a deeper intimacy?

The side door eventually opened. Sasha slipped out and sat down beside her. "They want to speak to you," she whispered.

"They do? Why?"

"It'll be fine. Just go on."

Julie stood up on trembling legs, stopping only when Sasha grabbed her hand and whispered, "I only did what I thought best. I hope you know that."

Julie squeezed her hand and walked to the door. Deep inside, she knew Sasha had acted out of a good heart. That didn't mean she wasn't still upset at the way she handled the situation.

Her heart raced as she entered the side room, but she didn't want to look anything less than calm, cool, and collected to Daniel. Even if she was the exact opposite.

A row of chairs was placed in a semicircle in the middle of the room. Daniel sat in one, but stood at her entrance. He gave her a tentative smile. She took a deep breath.

"Daniel, I—"

He held a hand up. "Jeff. Leave us."

She'd forgotten about the other guy.

Jeff stood up from his chair. "That goes against protocol."

"I know."

"You helped write the protocol."

"I know."

"So then, you understand why I strongly suggest someone else be present."

"Jeff, I heard you, but with all due respect, I'm going to politely tell you to leave one more time." It was a no-argument-allowed, don't-even-think-of-disagreeing voice.

It appeared as if Jeff gave serious thought to disagreeing, but he eventually nodded. "Right. I'll go help Dena with the roundtable. You take as much time as you need."

Daniel only turned his attention back to her when the door closed. His eyes looked tired and there were crease lines in his forehead. "I'm sorry. I never imagined you finding out like this."

She thought about going and sitting down next to him, but decided to stay where she was for the moment. "How did you imagine me finding out?"

The corner of his mouth lifted. "I do like your spirit."

"Are you avoiding the question?"

The smile left. "Come, sit down."

"First tell me what's going to happen to Sasha."

Though she was still irritated with Sasha, she knew

how much her friend enjoyed the group. It would be upsetting if they kicked her out. Surely, she hadn't done anything to warrant that.

Daniel seemed to sense her concern. "Very well. Nothing's going to happen to Sasha. Assuming, that is, your story matches hers."

Her mouth dropped. "You brought me in here for an interrogation?"

"I think 'interrogation' is pushing it a bit, but yes, I have to question you. And it was either in here or out there. Personally, I thought you'd prefer it be just the two of us talking instead of doing so in front of the entire group."

In front of the entire group? He would do that? Her heart rate had slowed a bit. At his suggestion he could question her in front of the group, it started pounding again.

It was as if Daniel sensed her unease. "You have to understand how important we hold each other's confidentiality. Our lifestyle isn't commonly accepted. If I . . . *we* found out that she had told you about me, about anyone . . ."

"She didn't. She's actually invited me several times to come in the past. We were closing the shop tonight, she mentioned she was coming." She shrugged. "I didn't have anything to do. And I've always . . ."

"Yes?"

"Wondered." There. She'd said it out loud. To Daniel even.

But he showed no reaction to her confession. "That's

pretty much what Sasha said. Except you know, of course, that she was aware I'd be here and she knows you and I are . . . involved."

"Yes, I know. I'm still pissed at her about that."

"As your friend, I can see how you'd be upset, but as a senior member of Sasha's BDSM group, I understand why she went about it the way she did."

"Which brings us back to my original question. How did you imagine me finding out?"

He sat back down in his chair. "Come sit with me, please?"

Warily, she crossed the floor to him. When she took the chair beside him, he held out a hand. She placed hers on it and their fingers intertwined.

"I was going to tell you Saturday night."

She believed him. Though he hadn't told her everything about himself, she knew enough about him to know he wouldn't lie.

"Why did that woman call you 'Master Covington'?"

"Dena? The blond submissive?" At her nod, he continued. "It's a title used by the group's submissives when addressing the senior Dominants."

She gave a sigh of relief. "I thought you and her, maybe, you know."

The hand holding hers tightened a bit. "No, we're not. I'm not with anyone right now except you."

Her heart gave a little flutter and she squeezed his hand back. His thumb stroked her palm.

"Now," he said. "About that wondering part you mentioned."

"I'm not sure I'm ready to talk about it right now. Just seeing you here. Finding out you're a Dominant. It's just . . . I need to let it sink in."

"Fair enough, but will you answer one question?"

"Maybe?"

His thumb continued stroking hers. "When you were wondering, what role were you in? Were you a Domme, with a submissive worshipping you? Or was it you who kneeled? Did you find your strength in control or yielding?"

She closed her eyes against the sensation his touch created. Behind her closed eyes she saw it so clearly: her body, given to him, for his use.

"I yielded," she whispered.

"Oh, Julie." He untwined their fingers and stroked her cheek. "Open your eyes. Look at me." When she opened them, he continued. "Never doubt the strength to be found in yielding. A good Dominant understands that strength. Protects it. Makes it flourish."

Her mouth was dry. "And you? Are you a good Dominant?"

The look in his eyes spoke of one at complete ease with who he was. "I'm the best."

Daniel watched as her expression changed from shock to desire. She might not be ready to discuss her interest in submission, but her body knew what it wanted. He could wait for her to be ready. He'd seen the same look in the eyes of numerous submissives. It was only a matter of time. What she needed was the space to think.

"Do you still want to have dinner Saturday?" he asked. If not, if the shock of seeing him at the meeting had been too much, they could reschedule.

"Yes."

He dropped his hands, afraid of appearing too forward and eager. "If it's okay with you, why don't you come over to my place and let me cook?"

"Your place?" She had an I-know-what-you're-doing look in her eye.

"Trust me when I say it's not like that. It's just that if you want to discuss anything, I thought you'd prefer to do so in private."

She nodded. "Your place."

"Until then, if you have any questions, I'm sure Sasha would be more than willing to answer."

Finally. She laughed. Progress.

He saw the question in her eyes before she asked it. "Have you and Sasha ever . . . played?"

"No."

"Will you be at the party tomorrow?"

"Yes, though I'm not sure you're ready to attend one yet."

"That's not why I was asking." She looked down at her hands. "I was wondering if you would be with anyone there."

He waited until she lifted her head again before answering. "I'm a senior member of the group. I need to be there and I'll be serving as Dungeon Monitor, making sure group rules are followed, being an overseer. But for right now, I'm only with you and I won't be playing with, or seeing, anyone else."

He stood up and reached for her hand. "We should get back into the other room. The meeting's probably almost over."

"You didn't get to give your presentation."

"But you and I talked, and in my mind, that's more important."

"What was it going to be about?"

Oh, yes, there was interest behind that inquisitive glance. Just thinking about being the one to reach inside and bring out her submissive side made him hard.

"The Importance of Being Teachable."

"Huh," she said, sounding slightly disappointed. "Not exactly what I was thinking it'd be."

"There are breakout groups that meet every other week. One for Tops, one for bottoms. If you get to the point you'd be interested, Sasha can give you more information."

"Sasha? Not you?"

He led her to the door, his hand on the small of her back. Chatter was coming from the other room. The meeting had ended.

"Sasha's a submissive. I could give you my opinion, but

it would mean more coming from someone living the role. More importantly, though, Sasha is a friend of yours and has your best interest in mind. I don't want you to think I'm being self-serving."

She turned to him, her eyes soft. "I could never think of you as self-serving. You've been nothing but selfless."

He brushed her cheek. "Ah, but you're wrong. When it comes to you, I'm totally selfish. I want to keep you all to myself."

She grinned and reached for the doorknob, but he stopped her. There was something she had to understand.

"Julie, I want you to know that what happened last weekend was amazing."

She turned back to face him, her hazel eyes darkened. "For me, too."

"It's just, I know I've been distant this week and I didn't want you to think it was because I found anything lacking between us. I felt guilty at keeping this part of me from you."

She was being far too quiet. It tested his resolve to give her space. But first, he needed some reassurance himself. "And, if it's okay with you, I'd really like a kiss."

"I'd really like that, too."

He took her face in his hands. "Then why deny ourselves what we both want?"

He meant for the kiss to be tender and gentle, but when his lips touched hers, she moaned and rocked her body into

his. He ran a hand behind her head and held her close, parting her lips and tasting. Her hands fisted in his shirt, her
need as desperate as his.

A knock on the door brought them both back to
reality.

"Daniel?" It was Jeff. "There are some people who need
to speak with you."

"Saturday," Daniel whispered to Julie before pulling
away and opening the door.

FOUR

The next night, Daniel arrived a bit early to the host's home. The party would be held inside the house and grounds, so he started by peeking into the garage where the playroom had been set up. Several pieces of equipment had been placed around the unfinished room. With the concrete floor and hooks and chains attached to unpainted drywalls, the space certainly had the feel of a dungeon.

Before too long, people started arriving and filling the room. His gaze wandered from couple to couple, making certain everyone was okay and following the agreed-upon party rules. Ron and Dena stood talking in a corner. From the looks of it, Ron was trying to talk her into playing. She appeared uninterested.

Dena truly was a beautiful woman. Tonight she was

dressed in her usual party outfit: spiked heels, black lace corset, and dramatic makeup that made her blue eyes stand out more than usual. As he watched, she called to another submissive and introduced her to Ron. The three of them walked to a nearby couch and sat down.

"Master Covington."

He turned to find a petite redhead. "Hello, Rachel."

She was a relatively new submissive to the group, and he thought this was probably her second party. As far as he knew, she didn't play with anyone at the moment.

"I thought maybe we could . . . but I didn't see . . ." She waved at his armband.

He wore a yellow armband in order to be identified as the Dungeon Monitor. Everyone in the group knew he'd be overseeing the party, ensuring everyone's safety, and that his rule was law.

"Outside of the fact that I'm not currently available," he said, "I think you know most of the Doms in our group prefer to make the first move."

She shrugged. "I'm just impatient, I guess."

He crossed his arms and stared at her until she dropped her eyes. "Are you here to serve or to be served, Rachel?"

"What?"

"Look at me." He waited until she met his gaze. "Are you here because you long to submit and serve, or are you here because you're looking for something you want?"

Her nose wrinkled as she thought about his question. "Aren't they the same thing?"

"No, they aren't. One is the heart of a submissive and one is not."

"I don't understand."

"When you approached me just now, were you truly thinking of my needs or your own?"

There was nothing but silence. "My own," she finally whispered.

"Do you see the difference now?" he asked gently.

"Yes, sir."

"Perhaps you should take a few minutes to think about why you're here tonight."

She mumbled her reply and he watched her walk back toward the main house. He could see she was dejected, but he knew her and felt with the proper Dom she could flourish into a wonderful submissive. That Dom just wouldn't be him.

On the other hand, if Julie turned out to be interested, he was certainly willing to help her discover her submissive nature. After talking with her yesterday, he desired nothing more than to take her interest and slowly transform it, first into want and eventually into need. He grew hard just thinking about being the one to introduce her to the pleasure to be found in surrender.

The steady rise of voices coming from the main house drew his attention. He scolded himself for being distracted by fantasy and hurried into the living room.

It was no surprise whom the two voices belonged to: Kelly Bowman, one of the group's few Dommes, and Evan

Martin, a Dom she was frequently at odds with. Kelly stood with hands on her hips, looking every bit the part of "Mistress K" in a skintight black leather bustier and skirt and boots that reached her thighs. Her long red hair was streaked with black.

Evan had a slightly amused look on his face and Daniel groaned. If he had to guess, the Dom had probably picked the fight with Kelly in order to get a response out of her. He thought about telling them to get a room and fuck it out like they both seemed so desperate to do.

"Mistress K. Master Martin," he said instead. "I'm three seconds away from throwing you both out. End it now."

Kelly broke the stalemate first. "Apologize to Master Covington, Martin."

"Suck my dick, K."

"I'd have to be able to find it first."

Daniel stepped between them. "Enough. You two know better. Evan, there's a petite redhead looking for a play partner. She needs a lesson in serving with the proper mind-set. Can I trust you to handle it?"

Evan winked at Kelly. "I'll take care of her. I love a feisty redhead."

"Asshole," Kelly quipped.

He blew a kiss over his shoulder.

Daniel waited until the other man left. "If I thought it'd do either of you any good, I'd suggest you help him. Force the two of you to work together."

"If you're going to lecture me, call Martin back so he

can hear it, too." She snapped her fingers at one of the group's male submissives. "You, there. Come here."

"Maybe I thought I'd speak to you since you're the more reasonable of the two," Daniel said.

The submissive had made it to where they stood. A look of excitement was evident in his expression. "Yes, Mistress K, how may I serve you?"

"My cane needs a workout. If you're amiable, go wait for me in the upstairs bedroom. The green one. I want you naked and kneeling in the middle of the room."

"Yes, Mistress K."

"You're excused." She didn't bother to watch as he left; instead she turned back to Daniel. "You're sorely mistaken if you think Martin and I will ever work together."

"At least keep it outside the group. You guys should be setting a better example."

"Outside the group? As in private?" She waved her hand. "Forget it."

Daniel decided to quit while he was ahead. At least he'd defused the situation. "If I find you both in the same room again tonight, I'll be asking you both to leave."

"Fair enough." She gave him a sadistic smile. "Anything else, Master Covington? I have a backside to cane."

"That's it for now."

She turned and flicked her hair back over her shoulders, high heels clicking across the wood floors as she made her way to the stairs.

Daniel took a deep breath. The situation between Evan

and Kelly would come to a head one day. He had the feeling all he'd done tonight was delay the inevitable for a short while. But for the moment, it'd have to be enough. He had a party to oversee.

He walked through the kitchen, nodding and speaking to a few people. The kitchen was a neutral area where no play of any kind was allowed. Groups of people stood around the kitchen's island, talking and laughing. If you ignored the way everyone was dressed, it could have been a party held anywhere to the casual observer, but he recognized the subtle undertone.

There was an underlying current of awareness between the paired-up couples. Every so often there'd be a certain look given and a flash of knowledge would cross from one partner to the other. Or there would be a barely noticeable touch: a hand to the small of a back, fingers lightly brushing the nape of a neck, or a gentle tug of hair. All very normal and yet used in this group to convey any number of things between Dominant and submissive.

Jeff waved him over.

"What's up?" Daniel asked.

Jeff was another senior Dominant. He was known for his expertise with rope bondage and was often sought after among the submissives of the group. He was an introvert who played with a variety of women, but never spent too much time with anyone in particular. At the moment, he was alone.

"Closed door in the bedroom off the living room," Jeff said.

He raised an eyebrow. "Who?"

Only approved members were allowed to play behind closed doors at a party. Even then, there was an understanding that the door could be opened at any time by a senior member. The rule was put in place to keep everyone safe and to provide security for those playing.

"William. I'd check it out, but I'm due to oversee Peter and Sasha, since it's his first demo."

William was approved for closed-door play, but he'd never done it before.

"Thanks, I'll go have a peek."

The mention of Sasha brought Julie back to his mind. He tried not to think of bringing her to a play party, but found the image kept returning. Would she be an exhibitionist? Some submissives were.

He shook his head. He didn't know for a fact that she was a submissive. Hell, she'd barely been able to admit she'd *thought* about being a submissive. He needed to take it slowly, one step at a time.

He stood outside the door listening for a few minutes. A few soft moans came from inside the room, followed by a low, deep voice and a sharp slap. He didn't know William all that well; he'd been recommended by another Dominant in the group. Daniel didn't want to bust into the room and disrupt the scene, but with William being an unknown, to him at least, he'd wanted to be sure everything was okay.

He turned the knob slowly and pushed the door open a few inches. The darkness of the room was the first thing he noticed. It took his eyes a few seconds to adjust and make out the shadowy figures inside.

A kneeling woman, hands bound behind her, had her back to him. William faced her and the door, and he nodded at Daniel.

"We have company, my pet," William said, swinging a flogger near her, but not striking.

Daniel couldn't make out who the woman was; the darkness of the room kept her anonymous.

"He needs to be sure you're okay. Are you? Answer honestly."

"Yes, Master Greene. I'm good." Her reply was soft and breathy.

Daniel watched for a little while longer. William shifted his attention back to the woman at his feet. With a measured and seemingly meticulous pace, he first worked the submissive mentally. He whispered how naughty she'd been and how he planned to punish her.

When he told her to bend over the foot of the bed, Daniel quietly closed the door. He felt confident William knew what he was doing and that the woman was safe and in good hands.

He walked back into the garage. Ron must have taken to the submissive introduced to him by Dena, as he had her bound to a wooden bench. Unlike William, Ron was using only his hands. Daniel planned to introduce toys at their next training session, so until then, he was restricted to working with his hands. However, judging by the sub's moans, he was doing well with his limited resources.

Daniel knew he needed to work his way upstairs, but he hesitated. Sasha would be up there with Peter and he knew his thoughts would drift to Julie if he saw her best friend and business partner.

Like your thoughts aren't already on her.

He didn't know Sasha all that well. What he knew came mostly from other Dominants who'd played with her. She was friendly, but had a slight insolence about her that would require a certain type of Dominant to control. He hoped Peter would be the type to do it.

Julie, though, while being strong-willed, wouldn't be considered insolent. There was a fine line between the two. Some Dominants enjoyed walking that line; he just wasn't one of them.

He stopped in the kitchen on his way to the stairs to have a glass of water and spent a few minutes chatting with the people hanging out. A young Dominant asked for advice on a scene he was planning and Daniel set up a time to talk with him early the next week.

After making it upstairs, he first checked on Kelly and her caning session. The Domme had finished, it seemed. Her submissive for the evening was kneeling at her feet and she had her hands in his hair, whispering something to him. He gazed up at her with worshipful eyes, seemingly oblivious to the massive erection he sported.

Daniel knew Kelly; he'd watched her play before. The caning might be over, but she was far from finished. Another night, he might have stayed and watched, but his Dungeon Monitor duties dictated he move on.

In the next room, Peter had Sasha bound to a padded table. She was on her back, spread-eagle, while Peter stood at her side with a crop. Jeff stood by observing, and Daniel joined him.

"All good with the closed door," he told him. "How's Peter doing?"

"Competent."

Daniel nodded and the two men watched the scene before them for a few minutes. More people trickled into the room, as part of the play at the party was being allowed to observe other couples. When it became more crowded, Daniel caught Jeff's eye and motioned his head toward the hallway.

Jeff followed him and they went downstairs.

"Listen," Daniel said. "I wanted to thank you for trusting me yesterday at the meeting. I know it wasn't totally by the book, but it was the best thing for the situation."

"I trust you know what you're doing." Jeff's voice was deep and rough. "But she was an unknown to me. I was looking out for you."

"I appreciate that, but I know Julie and I knew there wasn't anything to worry about." He wondered how much to share with Jeff. Technically, he didn't owe Jeff any explanations, but he respected the guy.

"She came with Sasha," Jeff stated.

"Sasha's her best friend and business partner. Julie is . . . *new* in her interest in our lifestyle. I feared having an unknown Dom listening to the conversation might be too much."

"That's why she's not here tonight?"

"Yes, but she decided on her own not to come. Probably a good thing since Sasha's busy and I'm DM."

Jeff gave a curt nod.

Maybe next month, though, Daniel thought. If everything went well and Julie was still interested, he would ask her to attend. He wouldn't be DM, so he could be by her side while she took everything in. He imagined whispering to her as they watched a scene. Maybe he'd take her back to his house after for some private time in his playroom. . . .

"Master Covington?"

He snapped back to attention at the sound of his name.

"Yes?" he asked the man who'd called out to him.

"There's a scene in the garage I think you need to check out."

"I'm coming." As he walked away, he looked over his shoulder to Jeff. "Might want to find a sub and play. Next month you've got DM duty."

FIVE

"So," Sasha said late in the morning on Saturday. "You're going out with him again?"

Julie had called her first thing when she woke up following a late night of Internet research. She finally felt ready to discuss submission with Sasha. Thankfully, even though Sasha had planned to spend the day with Peter, she'd rearranged her schedule to talk with her.

Sasha lived in a cozy, eclectically decorated apartment above the flower shop. Julie brought over muffins, since she knew Sasha probably didn't have anything edible in her kitchen. The only thing Sasha made on a regular basis was coffee.

"I'm doing more than going out with him," Julie answered, putting her blueberry muffin down and wiping her hands. They were sitting in Sasha's living room, spread out on her couch. "I'm going to have dinner at his house."

"Ohh . . . really? He has his own playroom, you know."

"He does? In his house?"

"Yes." Sasha hid a sly smile while she took a sip of coffee.

Something about the thought of that made Julie's belly quiver with excitement. She wanted to see his playroom and wondered if he'd show it to her. She'd like to see if she could imagine herself in it, because she had a feeling she could. As it was, the more and more she thought about it, the more and more she believed she might like to see if she was submissive.

"Wow," Sasha said.

"What?"

"No freak-out? I'm impressed."

"I spent hours online last night reading up on all this stuff. It's going to take a bit more than finding out Daniel has his own personal dungeon to freak me out." She had no idea there was such a wide variety of kink out there. Her research had definitely been eye opening. Kind of made her feel like a virgin all over again. "But before we talk more about me, I have a few questions for you. Like, how did you find out you were a submissive?"

A big grin covered Sasha's face and excitement filled her voice. "I'm so happy you're finally admitting you're curious. I've seen the way you look when I talk about it. I kind of thought you'd come around eventually."

"Yes, yes, yes." Julie waved at her. "You're always right. Now tell me how you knew."

"Honestly"—Sasha's forehead wrinkled—"I've known for a long time. The second guy I slept with restrained me with his hands while we had sex. I didn't know what it was called at that point, I just knew it really turned me on. After that, vanilla sex just didn't do it for me. I just drifted for a while, but finally found the group a few years ago and things got better after that."

"From the little I saw, it looks like a good group."

"Our group's dynamics are a bit different from most. We have the senior members, who oversee everything, but we're not like a club or anything. Mostly, it's just known as a group with members who abide by certain guidelines. For a submissive, it helps ensure safety, knowing a Dominant can't be a member unless they comply."

Julie nodded. "That makes sense."

"I guess it works that way for a Dominant, too. Knowing a submissive is serious about the lifestyle and follows group mandates."

"Daniel said you had a meeting for just subs?"

"Yeah, if you want, you can go to one. It's a good place for support and everyone's real open. Chances are if you're going through something, someone else has already been through it and can help."

"We'll see. I don't want to jump into anything. I'd rather take it slow."

"Slow is good." Sasha got an evil look in her eye. "Of course, hard and fast is, too."

Julie laughed, but images of the night in her hotel room with Daniel flashed in her mind. She was willing to bet Daniel could make both slow and fast incredible.

"You have that dreamy, faraway look again," Sasha said. "Are you thinking of Master Covington and hard and fast?"

It was Julie's turn to be a bit evil. "And slow, too. Can't forget about slow."

Sasha reached over and took her hand. "Can I say again that I'm so proud of you for admitting you're interested in at least exploring this part of yourself. Not everyone is brave enough, you know."

"If I don't, I'll never stop wondering."

"You're such a smart woman."

"That's why you keep me around." Julie hugged her. "Okay, personal question: What's your favorite part about submitting to someone?"

A serious look came over Sasha's expression and she stood and walked to the window. She stayed there for a few minutes, simply staring outside. When she turned around, she looked uncharacteristically vulnerable.

"We actually discussed that a few months ago at a group meeting for submissives," she said. "I didn't say anything then, but I've given it a lot of thought since. I enjoy the sex, of course, but for me, I think . . . I think it's being under someone's care."

Julie frowned. "That's not what I was thinking. I thought you'd tell me some hot bondage story."

"I know." She smiled before turning serious again. "For me, it's more than just *that*. On the surface it doesn't make sense, but the more I thought about it, the more it did."

"How so?"

"When you're with a Dom, you're under his control, sure, but you're also under his protection. For me, there's something liberating in knowing you can drop all your worries, cares, and inhibitions and just feel for a while. Trust someone else to take care of everything. To take care of you."

It shocked Julie to hear Sasha say that. Her friend had always been one to take charge. She forever seemed so self-reliant, it never occurred to Julie that under the tough exterior, under the spiky hair and snappy comebacks, lurked a woman who just wanted someone to take the reins for a short time.

Submission, it seemed, fulfilled that need for Sasha.

"Okay, but then where do the whips and chains factor into that?" Julie asked.

A smile broke across Sasha's face. "Now, that, *that's* simple. The whips and chains just turn me on. And when you pair that with a caring Dominant who knows what he's doing?" She flopped down on the couch, head thrown back and arms spread wide. "I'm done for."

"Daniel seems like a caring Dominant who knows what he's doing."

Sasha lifted her head. "I've seen him in a demo or two. He definitely knows what he's doing."

Julie really didn't want to think about Daniel playing with someone else. "If he's so good, how come the two of you never got together?"

"It's not like I've been with all the Dominants in the group. Maybe I just don't go for blond guys."

Sasha had never been dissuaded by hair color before. Julie cocked an eyebrow at her. "You've dated plenty of blond guys. Tell me the real reason."

"Now you just make me sound cheap and easy."

Julie threw a small couch pillow at her. "Spill."

"Okay, okay," Sasha said, holding her hands up. "I guess he just intimidated me a bit."

"Daniel? Really?"

"You met him first as a customer downstairs. When I saw him first, he was demonstrating how to use a cane in a punishment scene."

"Ouch." Julie had read about canes the night before. They sounded . . . interesting. But nothing she wanted to try anytime soon. "I guess that would cloud your judgment."

"And he's a senior member . . . and he's very wealthy."

"He's just a regular guy."

"Oh, please." Sasha rolled her eyes. "Even you don't believe that."

"You're right. I don't." She looked down at her watch. "Less than six hours until I see Mr. Not-So-Regular."

"He would be a good choice for you to get your kink on with. If you're still interested."

The quiver had returned to her belly. "I think I am."

"What about it interests you the most?"

"Time to talk about me now?"

"Fair is fair."

Julie trailed a finger along the edge of the couch. "I don't know if I can really say for sure. I think it's about trusting someone enough to surrender my body to him. Knowing he wants my pleasure as well."

Sasha's smile covered her face. "You're so done for. You're going to taste it once and never go back."

Julie had a feeling she was right.

Five hours later, she pulled into Daniel's driveway with her heart pounding and her body buzzing with excitement. Not because she necessarily thought anything would happen, but because she was finally going to talk about being submissive again. This time with Daniel.

Daniel's home was a large two-story farmhouse, set on ten acres, about fifteen miles outside of town. He told her it had been his grandfather's, complete with stocked pond on the property. It really didn't fit the image of the corporate banker, but somehow it fit Daniel.

He met her at the front door wearing worn jeans and a blue sweater.

"Glad you didn't change your mind," he said before kissing her cheek.

"You're not giving me enough credit," she said. "No

one forced me to go to the group meeting, you know. I went because I wanted to."

"Point taken."

He led her through the spacious house. It was tastefully decorated with a sprinkling of antiques, but just enough electronics to tell anyone entering that it was, in fact, a bachelor pad.

Several pieces, though . . .

She pointed to a table in the living room. "Is that Herter Brothers?"

"It is. Are you into antiques?"

"If by 'into,' you mean do I drool over them, then the answer is yes."

A wicked grin crossed his face and he dropped his voice. "You should see my bed."

Hands on her hips, she turned to face him. "I bet you say that to all the girls."

"So few appreciate an English Jacobean *lit à colonnes*."

She'd only seen pictures of that kind of huge bed with a heavy wooden canopy supported by four large, intricately carved pillars—and he slept in one? "No, I imagine few people do. But I've always dreamed of seeing one up close."

"Well, maybe if you're good . . ."

She punched him. "You know what I meant."

He caught her hand and brought it behind her back, stepping close, and trapping her. "I know exactly what you meant. And I want you to know it delights me that you know what the bed is, and if you're interested in seeing it after dinner, I'll be more than happy to show you."

She twisted out of his grasp, just because she felt like teasing him. "Promise?"

"Fire, Julie. You better be careful."

His words warmed her body and intensified the needy ache between her legs. She thought back to the previous weekend, how his body pounded into hers. The way her climax overtook her. The weight of him, satisfied and sated, heavy against her.

"Why? Will you burn me, Daniel?"

"Only if you don't consume me first."

They took their time talking over dinner, while eating the seafood stew Daniel had made. He kept the conversation light, talking about learning to cook from his grandmother, and how his sister was teaching her daughter how to make bread. What he didn't talk about was anything related to sex, the meeting two days before, or the playroom under their feet. She eventually realized he was waiting for her to start.

"How was the party last night?" she finally asked.

"Since I didn't have to throw anyone out, I would call it successful." He didn't show any surprise at her question. He simply leaned back in his chair, calm and relaxed.

"Do you often?"

"No, not often, but more times than I'd like. We have

rules in place, not only to protect our privacy, but also to keep our members safe."

She took a swallow of her water. Now or never. "I read the checklist. A lot of it sounds dangerous."

"It's not just the obvious things like edge play. It could be as simple as having a submissive tied too tightly, in the wrong position, or not realizing how deep they are in subspace."

"Sounds like a lot of responsibility. Makes you wonder why . . ."

"Why anyone would be a Dom?"

"Exactly."

"I can't speak for every Dom, but for me, having a submissive give herself to me completely, to grant me the right to control her pleasure, to allow herself to be used by me—it's the greatest turn-on there is."

"And those who say you're just in it for the power trip?"

"Don't understand the absolute devotion a Dom holds for his sub. How he protects her and holds her above all."

When he put it in those terms, and looked at her the way he was, his blue eyes so piercing, yet so gentle? It made her insides melt.

It also made her want to give herself to him. Completely.

She knew Daniel wouldn't push her, wouldn't make the first move. She just wasn't sure she was ready to strike the match.

"The other thing I wondered," she said. "In your relationships, do you expect submission all the time?"

"Do I want a twenty-four/seven submissive?" At her nod, he continued. "No, for me personally, I want obedience in the bedroom or playroom only."

"But last weekend?"

"Was wonderful."

"Yet I wasn't kneeling, or calling you 'Master,' or anything."

At once, his eyes grew dark and unyielding. "Think back, Julie. Remember. Was it a negotiated power play scene? No. But was it, perhaps, somewhat *more* than the sex you've experienced before?"

Well, when he put it like that.

"It was certainly something else," she admitted. She took another sip of water and wished for just a second that the glass contained something stronger. Finally ready, she met his gaze. "One last question."

"Ask me anything."

"Will you show me your bed?"

He didn't ask her if she was sure and he didn't clear the table. He simply nodded, rose to his feet, and held out his hand. Likewise, she stood and placed her hand in his.

As he led her through the house, he talked of the bed: where he found it, how he transported it, and the custom bedding he had to have made. She was thankful because it gave her something to think about besides what she'd just asked for. Even still, her mind couldn't focus on the details of the house.

Up the stairs and down a hall he guided her, all the while holding her hand. The room he led her to contained the most massive and beautifully made bed she'd ever seen. It was huge, with two hand-carved posts at the foot and a wooden canopy overhead. The delicate woodwork begged you to run a finger over it and she could only imagine the time it took the carpenter to create such a masterpiece. She was awed just thinking about how many centuries it'd seen.

"Wow. It's exquisite."

"Yes," he said, but when she looked at him, his eyes weren't on the bed. They were on her.

She felt very small in the midst of his room, next to his huge bed and him. His eyes were intense with desire and his voice was coarse when he spoke again.

"Stay with me, Julie." His arms came around her and his breath was hot against her ear. He nibbled her earlobe. "Let me show you the pleasures of my world."

His erection pressed hard and heavy against her and chills shot down her back just from imagining what he wanted to do. She'd known by asking to see his bed, she'd be taking a step into a place she'd never been. To be dominated, was that who she was? Who she wanted to be?

"I don't know." She took a deep breath, filling her lungs with air and taking in the all-male scent of the man whose arms surrounded her. "I'm . . . I'm a bit scared."

His arms moved to her shoulders and he tenderly turned her to face him. "Look at me."

His voice was gentle, but firm, and left her no choice but to look up and meet his eyes. "Daniel, I . . ." But she didn't know what she wanted to say.

He slipped a finger under her chin, keeping her head steady and her eyes focused on his. One look at his firm, unyielding expression was all it took for her to remember Sasha's claim that women dropped their pants after simply looking at him. She no longer doubted her.

"Nothing will happen tonight that you don't want," he said. "If at any point you want me to stop, just say 'red.' "

A safe word. She remembered from what Sasha had told her, that's what it was called.

Holy hell, she was actually going to do this.

"Will you hurt me?" She couldn't reconcile what she knew of Daniel with him inflicting pain on her. On purpose. But he was a Dom, wasn't that what they did?

His thumb stroked her cheek, traced her lips, and a soft smile crossed his face. "No, not tonight. For now, I only want to show you the pleasure I can bring us when you trust me with your body."

His words turned her knees to jelly and she swayed into him. *Us.* Funny how that made a difference. She felt wanting. Aching. Needy. She nodded.

"I need to hear the words, Julie." His tone was firm, tinged with a hint of desire. "Say, 'Yes, sir, tonight I'm yours.' "

Her throat felt dry, and she wasn't sure she could speak. She licked her lips.

He waited, the epitome of patience, but somehow looking as though he knew she wouldn't do anything other than what he asked.

"Yes, sir," she finally whispered. "Tonight I'm yours."

Joy, desire, and possibly relief flooded his expression, and then he pulled her gently to him. "Thank you. I'm humbled and pleased at your trust in me."

His lips traveled from her ear, nibbled across her cheek, and came to rest against hers. The kiss started slow and easy, and she let him lead. Simply enjoyed the feel of him exploring her lips, enjoyed tasting him as he slipped inside. As the kiss deepened, she knew that while she'd been kissed many, many times before, never had anyone kissed her with such authority.

All too soon, he pulled back, and she nearly moaned at the loss of him.

"For the rest of tonight, unless told otherwise, you only speak when told to. Unless, of course, you need to say 'red.'" His eyes had turned to blue steel once more. "Do you understand? You may answer."

She nodded. "Yes, sir."

A look of complete pleasure crossed his face and she knew she'd do damn near anything to keep seeing that expression. She felt herself swell with pride, knowing she'd addressed him correctly.

"Very nice," he said. "Move to your knees."

Her heart pounded so loudly, she was certain he could hear it. *This is nothing,* she told herself; *you've given blow jobs on your knees before.* But deep down, she knew it was nothing like she'd ever done before. Somehow the blow job she was about to give was completely different.

"Now, Julie."

She scurried to drop to her knees in front of him, gulping huge deep breaths of air as she did. *I can't do this. I can't do this. I can't do this.*

"Look at me," he said, and she realized she'd been staring at the floor.

The same pleasured expression filled his eyes and she felt herself calm under his steady gaze.

"You're doing great," he said, and an odd joy swept over her. "Are you okay? Shall we continue? You may answer."

"Yes, I'm okay."

The slight tilt of his head told her she'd done something wrong.

"Yes, sir, I'm okay," she mumbled out, ashamed at how quickly she'd forgotten how to address him.

"Much better," he said. "I can't wait to feel that sweet mouth around my cock."

Hot and damn. When he spoke like that, she couldn't wait to take him in her mouth. But did she take his pants off or wait for him to tell her? She really wasn't ready for this. How did women do it?

When you're with a good Dom, an experienced one, Sasha had said, *it's almost like he can read your mind. Downright freaky.*

Daniel's hands came to rest on her head. "You're thinking too much. Let yourself go. Trust me to take us where we both want to go." His fingers rubbed her scalp and it was as if he hypnotized her with his words. "Empty your mind until I'm the only one who fills it. Just me, Julie. For this moment in time, I'm all that matters."

She focused on the gentle tug of his fingers, the pull of his hands. Little by little, her worries and fears were swept away by his simple actions.

"That's it."

Ever so slowly, his hands dropped. She watched, mesmerized, as he undid his pants and pushed them and his boxers down, then stepped out of them.

She hadn't had time last week to look at him closely. Not so much a problem now, when his rather impressive erection stood inches before her. He looked longer and thicker than she remembered and she wondered briefly if she could actually take him.

"Suck it, Julie. Put my dick in your hot little mouth and suck."

Yes.

His words turned her on and she wanted nothing more than to do as he commanded. She licked her lips and leaned forward, easing her mouth around his tip, and took him deeply. Above her, he inhaled, his hands fisted her hair.

His hips thrust gently at first, a slight push and pull. She sucked him as he withdrew and swallowed when he pushed in. Ever so easily, he worked himself farther and farther into her mouth. She had a slight moment of panic when he bumped against the back of her throat. She'd never learned how to deep throat and didn't want to gag. Especially her first time with him.

He sighed and his hips stopped. "Much as I'd like to come in your mouth, I have other plans."

He took a step back and lifted her head. "I need you to answer me, are you okay?"

How did his eyes grow so intense? Had they been like that before?

"Julie?"

"Yes, sir. I'm fine."

Those intense eyes crinkled up at the corners as a smile covered his face. "Just fine? Answer, please."

She found herself smiling back. "Slightly better than just fine."

"Just slightly? Answer, please."

Who knew a Dom could be such a tease?

Surely she could tease, too. "Well, if you must know, I'm slightly disappointed you're the only one who's half-naked."

"All in good time, my sweet. Trust me."

She realized at his words that she did, she did trust him. It was both scary and reassuring at the same time. How was that possible?

"Are you thinking of something other than me again?" At his firm voice, her thoughts fled.

Her mouth opened and a "No, sir" almost slipped out

before she realized he hadn't explicitly told her to answer. She tightened her lips into a line.

He gave a husky chuckle. "Smart girl. Although for a minute there I thought you'd make a mistake, and I was looking forward to turning you over my knee and spanking your ass until it turned a beautiful shade of pink."

No one had ever spanked her before. She wouldn't have thought she'd have liked it, but his words left such an image in her mind, she couldn't help but wonder what it would be like.

"Would you like that?" He took a step toward her and circled her, like a lion teasing his prey. "Me putting you over my knee?"

He unbuttoned her shirt, and she shivered as he pushed it off her shoulders. "Spanking you?" He deftly unsnapped her bra and ran his thumbs over her nipples. "I don't even need you to answer, your body tells me all I need to know." Two steps and he was behind her, whispering, "I bet you're wet already, just at the thought of it." A strong hand cupped her ass. "Imagine me doing it."

She almost moaned, because suddenly, she wanted it. Wanted to feel his hand spanking her.

He remained behind her, his hands traveling across her shoulders, down her chest, gently cupping her breasts, and dipping to her waist before moving up her body and back down again. All the while his whispers were wicked. "I think I'd sit on the bed and watch you strip for me, but I'd keep my clothes on the entire time. That way when I commanded you to position yourself across my lap, you'd feel the roughness of my clothing against your bare skin."

One of his hands slid between her still-clothed legs and cupped her, his thumb pressed against her clit. She rocked into him.

He nibbled her earlobe and continued. "I'd play with your pussy while I situated you just so. Tease you, never quite giving you what you craved. All the time reminding you what a naughty, naughty girl you'd been. How naughty, naughty girls deserved to be punished."

She was practically at the point of begging him to take her. To do something. *Please.*

She let out a gasp when he landed a soft swat to her backside.

He chuckled. "I'd start slowly. Gentle pats to warm your skin. Make you sensitive. Gradually, I'd get harder and harder. Maybe spank your pussy a few times. Even better, I'd fuck you with my fingers. You'd like that."

Oh, hell, yes. She most certainly would. She wanted it right then and there.

But he wasn't ready to give it to her yet. "I'd spank that beautiful ass just up until you're about to come from my hand and fingers alone. And do you know what I'd do then? Answer me!"

Her voice trembled with need. "No, sir."

He moved to stand before her, made sure she was looking at him. "I'd put you on your back, so you could feel the sting of my spanking while I spread your legs and fucked you senseless."

She exhaled in a ragged gasp.

"You would like that, wouldn't you? Answer please."

"Yes, sir."

~~She would like it a lot. Guilt flooded her.~~

She dipped her head, but he wouldn't allow it. With one finger he lifted her chin.

"Look at me, Julie."

She could do nothing else.

"There's no shame in anything we'll ever do together." He traced her lips with his finger. "If we both agree to it and we enjoy it, there is no room for guilt. Understand? Answer me, please."

Anything resembling guilt or shame faded with his touch. "Yes, sir."

"Say it again."

"Yes, sir."

"Louder."

"Yes, sir."

His hand dropped to his side. "Don't ever feel badly for admitting what you need."

She stood, waiting for him to say or do something, and watching as he stripped his sweater off. He was just as breathtaking as he'd been the previous weekend. Maybe more so, because she knew more now.

"Your turn," he said. "Take the jeans off."

While she'd undressed in front of men before, somehow doing so under Daniel's watchful gaze made every
step of the act one hundred times more intense.

"What lovely panties," he said when she'd stepped out
of her jeans. "Did you wear them especially for me?"

"Yes, sir."

For several seconds the words hung in the air between
them. Daniel tilted his head and narrowed his eyes.

Damn it.

His voice was soft, but firm. "Did I ask you to speak?
Answer me."

"No, sir."

Her heart pounded in her throat. What was he going to
do? Laugh and say she was a sorry excuse for a submissive?

"And after I finished telling you what I'd do if you
spoke. It's almost as if you want me to spank you."

She trembled with excitement, dread, and anticipation.

He walked to the bed and sat down. "Take the panties
off and come sit down beside me."

Her jaw nearly hit the floor. Was he going to spank her
or not? And how strange would it be to just sit on the bed
with both of them naked?

"Now."

Strange or not, it's what he requested and she wasn't
nearly ready for the evening to be over yet. Slowly, she
reached down and stripped her panties off, all the while
aware of his intense stare. She would have expected to be
self-conscious, but she wasn't. She felt empowered.

She dropped the panties to the floor, walked to the bed, and sat down. He placed a hand on her upper thigh and squeezed.

"In a power play scene, there are rules. For example, tonight I indicated you weren't to speak out of turn. When rules are broken, there are consequences. I'm going to spank you for speaking, unless you want to stop. Which I will do, no explanation needed."

He was offering her a way out. She knew she could say "red" and he would stop, but he was telling her that wasn't even needed. She looked at him, met his gaze: calm, controlled, and filled with heat.

"You can speak freely now."

She wanted to taste this world; she wasn't about to stop now. Couldn't stop now. She glanced to the floor. "I don't want to stop, sir."

"Look at me."

The rough command of his voice caught her off guard. Was he angry? There didn't appear to be any sort of ire in his expression.

"You don't know how much hearing you say that pleases me. Never doubt that you're a strong, brave woman."

"Thank you, sir."

The hand on her thigh caressed her roughly. "Now there's the matter of your punishment."

Hell, it shouldn't turn her on so much when he said that.

"I want you to lie down over my knees. Wrap your arms around my calf. And lift your ass as much as possible."

He kept his hands on her while she positioned herself, almost as if he knew his touch would calm her. Even so, her heart pounded wildly.

"Have you ever been spanked before?" he asked, running his hands over her backside. "Spread your legs a bit."

She widened her stance and found doing so made her more stable. "No, sir."

"You're so brave. I'm proud of you." He ran both hands over her, dipping one between her legs. She knew he found her wet and waiting. "It won't be as hard as the spanking I'd give an experienced sub, but you'll feel it. You can stop me at any point by saying what?"

"Red, sir."

"Good girl."

She was surprised by how good his words made her feel. She wrapped her arms around his lower legs, fingertips brushing the hard muscles there. His hands swept over her backside and she closed her eyes when he gave her butt a gentle slap.

He didn't stop, but continued to rain light slaps over and over. It didn't hurt, but rather made the lower half of her body feel warm and tingly. She hadn't expected a spanking to feel so good but it really was turning her on.

There was a short break, and she wondered if that was all, when a sharp slap hit her backside and made her gasp. It stung, but then his hand covered the spot he'd struck and the heat melted into her body. She moaned. "Like that?" he asked.

"Yes, sir."

He chuckled. "You're such a naughty girl."

Another slap landed and again his hand covered the spot, allowing the sting to sweetly diffuse into need. A need for more, more of his touch, more of him. More.

He repeated the actions, following each swat with a gentle press of his hand. The spanks seemed to be getting harder, but the pain from them was somehow only intensifying her need for him.

"Your body is asking for more," he said. "You're lifting your ass up."

Was she? She hadn't realized.

His fingers drifted between her legs and brushed her. She jerked against him, trying to relieve the ache. He answered with a swift slap.

"Needy girl. You'll have to wait, I'm not ready to fuck you yet. I'm still working on this ass."

And work on it he did, raining swat after delicious swat on her backside. He didn't cover them with his hand anymore, but kept up a steady tempo, sweeping a finger lightly over her clit once or twice. She had never felt so turned on in her life.

"Three more and you're done. They'll be harder. Can you handle them?"

Her body pulsed with the need to come and she desperately wanted his hands back on her.

She lifted herself toward him. "Yes, sir. Please."

"So polite," he mused. "Such a good girl."

She gasped at the first slap, but didn't have time to process the pain before the second came. She squeezed her eyes tight against the third. No sooner had it landed than she found herself pulled into his arms and gently placed on the bed. He lay down beside her, breathing heavily and keeping her tight in his arms.

"Are you okay?"

Outside of the need to have him inside her, like NOW? "Yes, sir. Please."

"Please, what?"

She almost whined. He wouldn't do it until she asked. "Please, sir. Fuck me."

*D*aniel closed his eyes and forced himself to focus. It was taking all his considerable self-restraint not to bind her to his bed and do all sorts of wickedly perverse things. For all her insistence she had only wondered about BDSM, she was a sexual submissive through and through.

He just had to remind himself how new and inexperienced she was. He wanted to introduce her gently to the freedom to be found in submission, not scare the hell out of her. So, though he wanted her bent over his bed, blindfolded in his playroom, and offering herself to him in any way he wanted to take her, he wouldn't give in. She trusted him and he wouldn't give her reason to regret that trust.

She was on her side, looking at him with pleading eyes.

He pushed himself up to his knees, after donning a

condom. "You remember what I said would happen after I spanked you."

Her eyes grew wide, but the surprise in them couldn't hide the desire behind her softly whispered, "Yes, sir."

He swore his erection grew another inch every time she called him "sir" and he knew he'd do damn near anything to hear her call him "Master." How long had it been since he collared a submissive? Had someone wear the symbol of his dominance, proclaiming for all to see that her submission was to him alone? Years? It was so easy to picture Julie kneeling, naked, and waiting for him to claim her with his collar.

Focus!

He fisted his hands by his side. "Move up the bed. I want you on your back, knees spread and held to your shoulders."

She scooted up the bed, wincing slightly as she brushed her butt against the sheets.

"Sore ass?"

She situated herself the way he asked. In the requested position, she was open to him, and he could see the result of his handiwork.

"I asked you a question, Julie."

"Yes, sir. It's sore."

He moved between her legs and took hold of her hips. He teased her with the tip of his cock. "Feel how hard you make me. What you do to me."

He slipped his hands beneath her, so he could feel the

heat of the spanking he'd given her, but more importantly, so she could.

"I'm going to fuck you so well, you won't remember your ass."

She whimpered and tried to press him closer.

"Not yet," he said. "Take a second to anticipate it." He rubbed himself against her slit. "Think about how good it's going to be when I sink into you. Fill you up. Stretch you."

"Please, sir."

"I love it when you say please." He pushed just his tip in and pulled out, making her moan. "Say it again."

"Please, please, please." She trembled under him.

"Since you asked so nicely." He tightened his hold and thrust deeply into her.

He wasn't sure which one of them shouted; probably it was both. He took a second to relish the feel of being buried inside her tight, wet body before allowing his instincts to take over.

He unleashed his primal nature and pounded into her over and over. "Feet on the mattress," he ground out through clenched teeth.

She shifted, positioning herself so he could grab on to her hips better, aligning their bodies so she could take him deeper.

"Fuck, yes," he panted, as he started thrusting rhythmically.

Her back arched and he rocked into her harder. She was panting, too, but in time with his thrusts, and pushing to take more of him. She was close. A good thing, because he didn't think he would last much longer.

He slipped one hand to brush her clit. "Come hard for me, Julie."

One more hard thrust and stroke of her clit and he held still as she climaxed around him. Her head dropped back and she groaned with relief and satisfaction.

But when she tried to drop her hips, he stopped her.

"Not quite yet. It's my turn." He pulled out. "On your hands and knees and make it fast, or else I spank you again instead of giving you another orgasm."

She moved to all fours, ass in the air, and he swatted her pink flesh.

"Just because it's so spankable," he said, positioning himself behind her. With one swift thrust he entered her and started a rhythm that drove him closer to his own release.

Greedy Dom that he was, though, he wanted another one of her orgasms, so he slipped a hand between their bodies and circled her clit.

"Come again for me. One more time."

When she climaxed the second time, he allowed himself to follow. Finally sated, he pushed deep and held still as he exploded into the condom.

Not wanting to crush her, he pulled her into his arms and rolled them so she lay on top. Her breathing was heavy and her body shook slightly. He ran his hand down her back. "Are you okay?"

By his standards, it had been a mild scene, but it had been her first and her response was an unknown. Some women cried, others shut down. Then there were those who slept or talked incessantly. What response would Julie have?

She stirred, pushing up to look at him. "Okay is an understatement, sir."

He hushed her by putting a finger to her lips. "Much as I enjoy hearing you call me 'sir,' you can use 'Daniel' now."

"No more play?"

Her softly asked question caused his cock to stir. Whatever responses he'd imagined, having her ask for more wasn't one of them. He gently brushed her backside and noted her flinch.

"I think you've had enough for one night." At her frown, he added, "Trust me, if you want more, I'll be happy to oblige another time."

Her head dipped. "I'd like that."

He took her face in his hands. "Look at me. You did great. I'm so proud of you."

"Really?" She propped herself up on her elbow. "There's so much I don't know."

The way she'd situated her body exposed her breasts. He realized he'd been rather neglectful of them. He circled the nipple of one with his finger. "Knowledge will come if you want it. What you did tonight was yielding to me. Turning control over to another. And you did it beautifully."

"It felt . . ."

He circled the other nipple. "Yes?"

"Good."

Yes, if nothing else, that was what he wanted. For her to discover how good a submissive felt in a Dom's hand.

"There are so many ways I can make you feel good." He gave her nipple a gentle flick and grinned at her moan. "So many ways I can play your body and make it sing."

Her eyes were wide with desire and he knew he needed to get out of bed or else he'd take her again. Even knowing that, however, he stayed where he was, playing with her breasts until he was once more hard and she writhed against him.

He rolled them to their sides. "I want you again. Will you have me? I'll be gentle."

It would probably damn near kill him to be gentle, but he'd make himself for her. He could go slow and easy.

He hoped.

"Yes," she replied, and then, with a wicked grin, added, "Please."

"Naughty," he said. "You know what it does to me when you say 'please.'" He reached into the bedside table and got another condom. But looking down at it, he thought twice, then put it back in the drawer.

Julie looked crestfallen when he turned back to her.

"I'm afraid that sweet pussy of yours will impede my resolve to be gentle," he said. "So I'm going to fuck your mouth and if you're good, I'll return the favor."

Since she was already on the bed, he had her roll onto

her back. He straddled her face, keeping a grip on the head-board for support. Looking down, he lined himself up with her mouth. Her lips parted and he slid inside her warmth.

He started with short, shallow thrusts. He didn't know if she could take all of him in her throat, and he didn't want her to choke trying to find out. Her tongue circled him as she tried to suck him deeper.

"So good," he panted, speeding his thrusts up a bit. "Your mouth feels so damn good."

Typically, he could hold out for a long time during oral sex, but he felt his release building quicker than normal. He looked down and watched his cock fucking her mouth. Watched as it slid in and out.

She reached up and cupped his balls. He knew then it was a lost cause.

"I'm going to come," he panted, still thrusting. "If you don't want—"

She must have understood where he was going, because she clamped her arms around his hips and pulled him close.

"Fucking yes, swallow what I give you." He pumped a few more times, then held still as he shot his release in her mouth and down her throat.

From his position above her, he watched as she licked her lips when he pulled out. He swore he almost came again.

"Oh, Julie," he said, sliding down her body, trailing kisses as he went. "That was so good."

He pushed her legs open and knelt between them,

careful of her pink backside. Very lightly, he nibbled on her sensitive flesh, pausing a few times to lick her clit. He swirled his tongue around her opening, teasing, and then plunged inside her with a long lick and a gentle suck.

Her hips bucked upward, but he kept her legs firmly spread, and repeated the actions again. Over and over, he licked and nibbled until her legs trembled and her heavy breathing became cries of pleasure. Only then did he focus his attention where he knew she desired him most, sucking hard. Her body shook his with the power of her release. He gave her one last lick and her legs trembled as if an aftershock hit her.

He crawled up her body, suddenly exhausted. She was still panting when he took her into his arms and kissed her softly. There was so much to say, so much to discuss, but she kissed him back, snuggled deeper into his embrace, and fell asleep within seconds. Unable and unwilling to do anything else, he closed his eyes and joined her.

SIX

*J*ulie jerked awake immediately the next morning and looked around in confusion. Where was she? Sunlight poured in through a nearby window and she was in the middle of a huge bed.

Daniel's bed.

Oh.

She rolled to her side and found him awake and watching her.

"Good morning," he said with his charming smile.

"Morning." She looked around the room, and the scattered clothing and tousled sheets brought back memories of the night before. Had he really spanked her? And then she spent the night at his house?

He pushed her hair back and kissed her cheek. "What has you looking so troubled so early in the morning?"

"I didn't plan on staying last night."

"Is there someone you need to call? Will they have the police out looking for me?"

"No, I don't have a roommate, it's just . . . I didn't bring a change of clothes. And I don't want to be an imposition."

He pulled back and gave her what she was coming to recognize as his Dom stare. The one no smart person would argue with. "You aren't an imposition. Don't think of yourself like that. Besides, I'm glad you stayed last night."

"You are?"

"Yes, now I get to fix you breakfast."

"Can I help?"

He gave her a truly wicked grin. "Sure. Do you want to cook naked or should I see if there's a spare T-shirt sitting around?"

She threw a pillow at him. "I'm not cooking naked."

Before she could blink, she was on her back with him looming over her. "Careful now, you're still in my bed. And you're quite naked."

Her butt still ached slightly from his spanking the night before and there was a delightful soreness between her legs. She knew she'd think about him just about every time she moved. And she wondered when they could do it again.

He nibbled her ear. "Is someone thinking naughty thoughts?"

"Yes, she is. You're turning her into a wanton woman."

"Just the way I like my woman to be."

His woman. Is that what she was? She rather liked the sound of it. She had so many questions about submission, especially submission as it applied to him. But before she could decide which one to ask first, her stomach rumbled.

"Guess I better feed you before we go much farther on that wanton trail." He gave her a quick kiss and then rolled out of bed. He strolled about the room, unconcerned with his nakedness. She scooted back up in bed so she could admire him better. His body would make a sculptor weep; his ass alone was enough to make her want to suggest they skip breakfast.

He slipped on a pair of sweatpants and brought her a long-sleeved tee. "I'm afraid the pants are too big." He pointed to a door off to the side. "Bathroom's in there. I'll go start breakfast."

Fifteen minutes later, she stepped into the kitchen, which already smelled of bacon. She wore his shirt, though she'd had to push up the sleeves and the hemline hung almost to her knees. She stepped beside Daniel and took over making scrambled eggs while he cooked the bacon.

He smiled. "Thanks."

They worked in a comfortable silence. While freshening up in his bathroom, she'd feared breakfast would be strange. She'd wondered if it would be odd to sit at a table across from a man who'd turned her over his knee the night before. Surprisingly enough, it wasn't.

He watched her closely as she sat down, but then lifted the juice pitcher and poured her a glass. He was on his second helping of bacon before he asked, "How are you feeling this morning?"

"Great. Never better," she said, knowing it was damn near the truth.

"If you need anything, you'll let me know?"

She nodded and buttered another piece of toast.

"Julie."

His eyes were serious when she looked up.

"One of the most important things you need to know is a submissive must always be completely honest with her Dom."

"Is that what we are?" She wasn't sure she wanted a label yet. It had only been one night. Surely it took more than a night to make one a submissive.

He seemed to be examining her before he spoke. "There is no formal agreement between us, but I did serve as your Dom last night."

His words made her insides quiver. *Her Dom.* Just thinking it made her shiver.

"Do you still have the paperwork from the meeting?" he asked.

"Yes."

"If you want to explore submission more, I meant what I said, but I'll need you to fill out the checklist. I'll give you a copy of mine."

She put her toast down, suddenly not hungry. "Makes it sound more like a business transaction than a relationship."

He reached across the table and took her hand. "I like you, Julie, and I want to get to know you better. We can leave it at that for now. But"—he stroked her hand with his thumb—"if you're interested in exploring what you've always wondered about, we need to do it right."

She felt safe with him, felt secure in his hands. She'd enjoyed the previous night, and she had always wondered about BDSM. He was offering her a way to explore the part of herself she'd buried for so long.

"Do you have a blank checklist here?"

His gaze nearly burned her with its intensity. "I'll print one off."

Thirty minutes later she sat in his kitchen looking over a checklist, thinking to herself she had no business even attempting to fill one out. Daniel sat across from her, reading. He'd wanted to leave her alone while she completed the form, but she'd asked him to stay.

"Have you done all these things?" she asked.

"Not all, but I've done a lot."

He said it matter-of-factly, like he was talking about riding a bike, rather than kinky sex practices. She glanced down at the list trying to picture him doing some of the things to her.

"There's just, so much, you know?"

"Don't let it overwhelm you, but whatever you do, don't mark everything 'Like to try.' Everyone has limits. Establish yours."

"Trust me, I have several hard limits marked."

"No one should ever violate your hard limits. Discuss? Yes. Violate? Never."

She set aside her pen for a moment. "That brings up a question—what happens if a Dom violates someone's hard limit?"

"In our group, the individual in question would be forbidden to participate in anything we did and we'd inform others in the BDSM community as well. Depending on the offense, there might be other punishments inflicted." His expression and tone of voice underscored how seriously he felt about the matter.

"I have a feeling you mean something more than being put over your knee."

"By the time I finished with them, an over-the-knee spanking would be viewed as a reward." The corners of his mouth lifted again. "Speaking of limits and spankings and knees, how's the list coming?"

"Almost done."

She went back to work, finishing up the remaining items and sliding the list across the table. Daniel took the piece of paper that had been sitting beside him and handed it to her.

"I wanted you to fill yours out without looking at mine. I didn't want your list influenced by mine at all."

She tentatively picked up his list and looked it over.

Holy shit, he hadn't lied when he said he'd done a lot on the list.

Her eyes scanned the page for her hard limits to see

how they matched up with his. "You have fire play listed as 'likes a lot'?"

"Yes," he said, reading over her list. "And I'm not surprised it's a hard limit for you."

"I know it's not just lighting people on fire, I just—" She shivered. "No, thank you."

He chuckled. "Keep in mind, limits can change. We can redo and revise as needed." He spent a few more minutes reading over her list before speaking again. "If you're still wanting to play and explore, I'll look this over in more detail this week. You could come by next Saturday and we could play."

Every nerve in her body responded to his words. *Yes!* Her heart raced and her breathing came in shorter breaths. She realized in that moment she wanted nothing more than to submit to Daniel. She wanted to be the one yielding and she wanted to yield to him.

Even though he sat across the table from her, she felt his presence as clearly as she did the night before when his hands were fisted in her hair while she knelt before him.

"Do you exchange checklists with everyone you play with?" she asked.

He leaned onto the table so his body rested on his arms. "Yes, everyone. You should never play with anyone before talking about limits. And as a senior member of the local club, I strongly recommend you get to know anyone before entering into a serious relationship."

"Trust me. I'm all about the slow. I won't be asking for a collar or anything any time soon."

She meant for her words to put him at ease, to assure him she wanted to walk into the exploration with tiny baby steps. Yet when she mentioned a collar, his hands fisted on top of the table and then went back to normal so quickly, she wondered if she imagined it. She glanced up to his eyes. Calm and even, but something lurked behind them, she was certain.

"I think next Saturday is a great idea," she said. "But I was wondering one more thing for today."

He relaxed slightly. "Yes?"

"Will you show me your playroom?"

*D*aniel was glad he didn't have any liquid in his mouth. As it was, he nearly fell out of his chair. "What?"

She looked all innocent-like. "Sasha said you had one. I've never seen one. I thought I'd ask."

Yes, when she put it like that, it made sense. He supposed it wouldn't be unheard of for him to show a person interested in submission a playroom. His only fear was that once he got Julie in his playroom, he would never want her to leave.

He rose to his feet. Best to do something about his growing erection before showing her the playroom. "I washed your clothes from last night. I'll go get them and we can meet back here in ten minutes or so?"

After giving her the clothes, he spent the next ten minutes forcing his body into something resembling control. First, he took her checklist and firmly placed it on his nightstand. He wouldn't look at it again until she had left. Then and only then would he memorize it while planning for the weekend to come.

Secondly, he gave himself a stern talking-to. He reminded himself that Julie was extremely new to BDSM, had no prior experience, and that he was putting himself in a situation that required delicate handling. One wrong move and not only would he lose her, but he could damage the beautiful submissive he clearly saw buried within her, yearning to be free.

By the time he made it back to the kitchen, where she was already waiting, he thought he was in a fairly decent frame of mind. Julie appeared caught between nervousness and excitement, both underlined with a hint of lust.

He held out his hand. "Ready?"

Tentatively, she took it and he led her to the basement stairs. How did one go about this? he wondered. If he mentioned women were typically naked when they entered his playroom, would that only bring to her mind the fact he'd had other women? But of course she would know, he argued with himself. She knew him to be a Dom.

Still, he finally decided, knowing it and having him mention it were two totally different things.

He remained quiet.

When they stood before the closed door, he silently recited the pledge he always did before entering.

May I be found worthy of the submission given to me in this room.
May I remember it is a gift and not a right.

May I never punish in anger, speak without thinking, or act without knowledge.

May I never forget that in order to master another, I must first master myself.

Finally calm, he looked to Julie, waited for her to nod, and opened the door.

He tried to imagine he was looking at the playroom for the first time. Would she take in the beige walls first or the equipment?

Julie let go of his hand. "Can I look around?"

"Sure." He stuck his hands in his pockets so he wouldn't be tempted to hold on to her. "I'll just stay here. Let me know if you have questions."

She amazed him with both her curiosity and the easy way she took the lifestyle in stride. She walked around slowly, staring at the padded table, lightly running a finger on it. She stopped before his collection of floggers and didn't touch, but seemed to take note of each. He tried hard not to envision using one on her.

Later, he told himself. When she was more accustomed to identifying as a submissive. After he had more of a handle on what she liked, what she craved.

She shivered when she moved on to the wall where masks and gags hung. He didn't think it was a shiver of pleasure. The cane collection got a cursory nod and she tilted her head as she inspected the padded bench. She appeared so at ease with everything, it caught him off guard when she stopped short at the whipping post.

"What's that?" she asked in a whisper.

Her voice held a note of anxiety he hadn't anticipated. In less than two seconds, he was at her side, a hand on her shoulder. "Julie?"

"Is that a whipping post?"

He told her earlier a submissive had to be honest with her Dom. The reverse was also true. "Yes," he said.

There was no mistaking her shiver at his affirmation. "Where you whip people?"

Silently, he cursed himself for being so blasé about her exploration of the playroom. "You can also use it for flogging and less intense play."

"But you have a whip, like a bullwhip?"

He did, carefully tended to and practiced with weekly to ensure he stay proficient in its proper usage. "I think it's time we left the playroom."

"Show it to me."

"No."

"I marked the bullwhip as 'won't object' on my list. Then I saw the . . . post . . ."

He breathed a sigh of relief; her reaction made more sense after she said that. "Sometimes we think we're okay with something," he said. "But when actually faced with it, we change our mind."

"Just the thought of being strapped there, naked and exposed. Waiting . . . I want to change bullwhip to hard limit."

"Yes, of course," he said, but she didn't move her gaze from the post.

"Look at me." He took hold of her shoulders and turned her to face him. "Every submissive has a different need when it comes to sensation play. Some only desire a soft flogging, but others are hard-core masochists and require the bite of the whip. Part of play is to find where your need lies, but *you* get to be the one who ultimately decides how far you'll go."

Her body relaxed under his words and touch, which made him feel better.

"That's right," she said, though he realized she spoke more to herself than in response to him.

He took her hand and led her from the room. "Come with me."

For the next few hours, they bundled up and he showed her around his property. She didn't seem to be suffering any lasting effects from either the spanking or the playroom. In fact, she seemed more at ease around him.

He took her by the pond he'd spoken of earlier, showing her the place he would fish as a young boy. He pointed out his guesthouse and explained that he hosted play parties there. He even spoke of his parents, which was something he rarely did with anyone. How his mother died after giving birth to his sister and how his grief-stricken father had taken off and never come back.

He knew that, having lost her own parents, she understood. She simply took his hand and commented on how now it was even clearer why his grandparents were so dear to him.

Before she left, they made tentative plans to meet for lunch midweek and for her to come back to his house on Saturday. He wanted to ask her if she'd bring an overnight bag, but decided to wait until they met for lunch.

Sasha, of course, knew as soon as Julie walked in the door on Monday that something had happened.

"Tell me all about it, don't leave a thing out." She was hopping around the shop, way too hyper for a Monday morning.

Julie shrugged and tried to act all casual as she put her purse behind the counter. "We had dinner. It was nice. I spent the night."

"Did you?"

"Did I what?"

"Get your kink on?" Sasha said with a waggle of her eyebrows.

"Must we discuss every detail of my sex life?"

"Yes, we must. Every detail. So spill. Now."

"Not until I'm properly caffeinated. And what's gotten into you?"

Sasha talked while Julie prepared the coffee. She had rarely seen her friend so animated. Her eyes glowed and her entire body seemed energized. "I think Peter's going to collar me."

"Whoa. Really?" At first, Julie felt surprised to hear her friend was ready to take what she'd learned was such an important step. Although thinking about it, she realized Sasha had been with Peter longer than any other man in recent history. Which wasn't saying a lot, but still. Julie couldn't remember her ever wearing a collar.

"Yes! He hinted at it this weekend and I ended up staying at his place all day yesterday. And he's building a playroom, it's not anything like Daniel's, but it's still a room, right? And he's—"

"Damn, take a breath."

"Sorry." Sasha climbed onto the stool next to her. "It's just . . . I'm ready, you know?"

Julie nodded and took a sip of coffee. She was starting to understand. "How does that work, being collared?"

"Peter likes playing the entire weekend." Her forehead wrinkled. "I'm not sure about that. It seems like a lot, but we'll work it out. Besides, you've had coffee now."

"Half a cup."

"Surely that's enough. Now spill."

She wasn't sure she was ready to spill; she rather wanted to keep it to herself a bit longer. To take the memory of being on her knees before Daniel and examine it, piece by piece, until she unlocked the secret of why it felt so good.

But she knew Sasha wouldn't let it drop.

"He spanked me. I slept over. Had a mini freak-out in his playroom."

"You played in his playroom?"

"No, he let me look around."

"Okay. Whew," Sasha said. "I didn't think he'd play

with a newbie in his playroom. Not Mr. These-Are-the-Rules-and-You-Will-Follow-or-Else."

"That's what you think of Daniel?" She couldn't reconcile it with the man she'd spent so much time with the last few days.

"I don't know Daniel. I just know Master Covington."

Master Covington.

She would put that away to inspect later, too. Why the sound of it made her insides feel all wobbly.

Sasha was watching her closely. "What caused the freak-out?"

"And here this whole time I thought you'd ask about the spanking."

"We'll go there next."

Julie swirled her coffee. "The thing is, I'm not ready to talk about it. It made me feel things I didn't expect and I need to process that first."

Her words had the desired effect on Sasha; she straightened up a bit. "Sure, I get that. It's been a while for me, but I remember being new." The bell above the door chimed and Sasha went to greet the customers. "Just remember, I'm here when you're ready to talk."

Julie took longer than normal lingering over her coffee. Daniel had said he had the need to dominate only in the bedroom and the playroom. The playroom made sense to her, but how would it be to always give up control in the bedroom? Could she do that?

She thought back to the hotel, when she'd slept with Daniel before knowing he was a Dominant. No matter which way she looked at it, the night had been beyond anything she'd ever experienced. Well, at least until the night in his bedroom.

Perhaps, she decided, that was her answer.

*H*e met her for lunch Wednesday at her favorite deli. Though they had talked on the phone and texted a few times, there was something about seeing him in person that made Julie feel as giddy as a teenager.

He stood when she approached the table and pulled her chair out. Before she could sit down, he placed a soft kiss on her cheek.

"I'm so glad this worked out," he said. "That you were able to step away."

"Sasha owes me. She does lunch with Peter regularly and I'm left at the shop by myself."

"She's a lively woman. The group wouldn't be the same without her."

Julie placed her napkin in her lap. She didn't have to look over the menu; she knew exactly what she was going to order. "She's the people person of the shop. Never met a stranger. And she'll talk to a stone wall just to have someone to talk with."

"You're not exactly an introvert."

"No, I wouldn't call me that. I'd just say I'm guarded."

"There's a lot of wisdom in being that way." He stood up. "Do you know what you want? I'll go order for us."

She told him her sandwich order and watched as he walked up to the counter. There was such confidence and grace in the way he moved, she swore she could watch him forever. Even though he wore a suit and tie, it was easy to picture him the way he'd been over the weekend. She knew exactly what was under those clothes.

"This looks great," he said, when he came back with their sandwiches. "I decided to try what you ordered."

"It's one of my favorites." Chicken, Brie, and sun-dried tomatoes on ciabatta. She and Sasha ordered takeout here at least once a week.

They ate in compatible silence for a few minutes, though she was aware he watched her with careful eyes. When they started talking, they spoke about work and how the week was going.

"How are you feeling?" he asked at one point. "Any questions about last weekend or anything you want to discuss?"

"Here?" She looked around the crowded deli. Sure, people were wrapped up in their own conversations, but she didn't feel comfortable discussing kinky sex in public. He'd spanked her, for crying out loud.

"I could take you back to my place, but I'm not sure I'd be able to keep my hands off you long enough to talk."

That made her laugh. "It's just so public."

"I think we'll be able to discuss it without anyone knowing what we're talking about."

She pushed her chair forward and leaned close to him to ensure no one heard but him. "I feel conflicted. There's one part of me that says, what should it matter if I enjoy being spanked? I'm a grown woman fully capable of making my own decisions. Then the other part says, why would a grown woman let herself be spanked?"

He didn't show any surprise at her confession. "And in your mind you think a grown woman shouldn't want to be spanked or submit sexually?"

"I don't know if it's me who thinks that or if it's what society has told me to think."

"Then the question becomes, who do you listen to? Yourself or everyone else?"

She sighed and sat back in her seat, looking at the table. "You make it sound so simple."

"Do you think I never struggled with the nature of my sexual needs?"

Her head shot up. "You? Why?"

This time it was his turn to lean in close to her. "Do you think society at large finds it acceptable for a man to get off tying up his lover and spanking her? Forcing her to her knees so she can suck him?"

"That's different. You're the man."

"So where does that leave submissive men?"

She didn't have a reply for that.

"You have to treat everyone by the same rules," he said. "If you say men can be submissive or Dominant simply because they're men, you have to say women can likewise be submissive or Dominant simply because they're women. Fair is fair."

She offered him a small smile. "Everyone's equal?"

"Everyone's equal. Inside the playroom or outside the playroom."

"You make everything seem so easy." What he said made sense at the moment. She just wasn't sure if she'd still look at it that way when he wasn't sitting across from her.

"Not easy," he said. "Simple. There's a difference. Something can be simple and still be hard. It was simple for your body to react to me last weekend. It's hard for your mind to admit your submissive nature."

She picked at a bit of cheese hanging off her sandwich. "You think I'm submissive?"

"Look at me, Julie."

Her eyes met his before she could even process that he'd given a command she'd obeyed effortlessly.

"I'm not going to answer that," he said. "If I say 'yes' because I've been around enough novice submissives to know, it'll appear as if I'm trying to fit you into a defined box. If I say 'no,' it'll look like I'm trying to make you something you're not."

"But if I'm simply looking for your opinion?"

He shook his head. "I'm too personally involved. Besides, understanding and accepting your sexuality is a journey of self-discovery."

They spent the next few minutes eating silently. Daniel seemed at ease with the quiet. She appreciated that he allowed her time to think. Of course, she could always think more about their conversation when they weren't on a date.

"Tell me about your journey," she asked, breaking the silence. "How did you know?"

He put the remainder of his sandwich down and wiped his hands. "First of all, you should know it wasn't easy for me, okay?" At her nod, he continued. "While I was in college, I dated a girl who liked to be spanked. I kept telling her no, that I wasn't like that. Couldn't do that to her. She kept insisting, so I eventually did it. It had to be the most inept spanking ever, but it made me harder than I'd ever been before."

She nodded and picked up a potato chip. "And that's how you knew."

"No, that's when I broke up with her the next day and swore I'd never do anything like it again."

The potato chip fell to the table and he laughed at her expression.

"You're laughing about it?" she asked.

"Sure, *now*. Then I was scared shitless thinking I was some sort of deviant who should either be locked up or kept far, far away from women."

"So, what did you do?"

"I quickly learned that the more I told myself I wouldn't think about it, the more I actually thought about it. I was miserable. For a long time. Then one day I was online and saw a notice for a group gathering and I went. Met some like-minded people. Discovered I wasn't a freak." He winked at her. "Learned how to give a proper spanking."

She laughed.

"The point is, I've been where you are," he said. "From a different point of view, but one just as hard to come to terms with."

Knowing he'd dealt with his own demons while accepting his sexual needs gave her a sense of relief and hope. Just like Daniel, maybe she'd one day look back on this time in her life and smile at how far she'd come.

She reached across the table and took his hand. "Thank you."

*D*aniel was smiling brightly when she arrived at his house on Saturday. "Hello, Julie. I see you've brought your bag."

He'd asked her when they met for lunch if she'd stay overnight. At the time, she told him she'd have to check her calendar and make sure she thought the invitation through. At times, she felt everything was moving too fast and that she should take a step back. The funny thing was, though, every time she did think on it, she found herself wanting more of Daniel.

He leaned over to take her bag, and his lips brushed her cheek in the process. "You smell great."

She'd actually put on the body mist as an afterthought. As she'd gotten dressed, nervous about not knowing how to prepare oneself for a playroom session, her eyes had fallen on the mostly neglected mist and she'd thought if you had to be naked, you should at least smell good.

He placed her bag inside the front door, explaining they could take it upstairs later, and led her into his living room. She sat beside him on the couch, taking the hand he offered her.

"How's your weekend so far?" he asked.

She nodded. "Okay. Better now. Worked a bit this morning. How's your grandmother?"

"Tess is still fighting me on putting her in an assisted living facility. The thing is, I'm not home enough to care for her properly, so she can't move in here, and, well, Tess just found out she's pregnant with twins."

"Oh, wow."

"Exactly, like she wasn't busy enough with one." He shook his head. "A facility just seems to be the best thing right now."

She squeezed his hand. "You'll decide on the right thing."

"I sure hope so." He lifted her hand to his lips. "But we can talk about this later. You came to play, right?"

"Yes, but I also came to spend time with you. To get to know you better and because I like you."

"You have no idea how refreshing it is to be with someone who tells it like it is." He leaned so close she felt the heat radiate off him. "I like you, too."

His hand came up and cupped the side of her face, while his lips trailed lower to brush against hers. Softly. Nothing but a touch, but already she was hungry and aching for him. She clenched her fists in her lap.

He pulled away, but left an arm around her shoulders. "I thought we could spend some time in the playroom today. Nothing intense, just some basics."

She leaned closer to him, anxious for more of his touch. "Yes."

"Last weekend, I gave you 'red' as a safe word. There's also 'green' if you want more, and 'yellow' if I'm pushing too hard or you're approaching your limit."

Green, yellow, and red. Seemed simple enough.

"No one should ever hold the use of a safe word against you. And you should never, ever play without one." His arm dropped from her shoulder. "Make sense?"

"Yes, sir," she said, simply because it seemed the right thing to say.

He gazed at her with unconcealed hunger and then took her in his arms and kissed her with a breathless intensity. His lips were hard and so possessive that she was finally beginning to understand the warnings he'd given her in the past.

He moaned when he pulled back. "Julie." He took her hand and placed it on the bulge of his erection. "When you call me that . . ."

Something a lot like pride rushed through her at being able to affect him so.

"Are you ready?" he asked.

"Yes, sir," she said, stroking him through the material of his jeans. "Please, sir."

"My, my, my, you nearly purred when you said that."

He lifted his hips into her palm. "Does my playful little kitten want what's in her hand?"

She gave him another stroke. "Yes, sir."

He grabbed her wrist. "Then first she has to prove she can behave. Submissives are always naked in my playroom and as of right now, that's what you are. Meet me in there in ten minutes. You can undress in my bedroom."

It was funny the things your brain thought sometimes, she decided as she walked to the playroom minutes later. Like, if she got undressed in his room, where did he get ready? Did he even have to get ready? Would he be naked?

Then of course, there were the thoughts she expected. How odd it was to be walking around his house naked. The excitement with a touch of trepidation at the fact that she was naked and on her way to his playroom.

The door to the playroom was open, and though Daniel stood inside waiting, he wasn't where her eyes were drawn. Instead, she looked to the far corner where the whipping post had stood the previous weekend.

It wasn't there.

She glanced around the rest of the room, but couldn't find it.

"Come on inside, kitten, you won't find what you're looking for."

If someone had told her the day before that someone

calling her "kitten" would be a turn-on, she'd have called him a liar. Yet somehow, when Daniel said it, it made her feel sexy and strong.

"Punctual, I see."

She wasn't sure if the no-talk rule of the previous weekend still applied, so she decided to be quiet until told otherwise.

"Come stand next to me."

He had changed, she noted. Or more aptly, he'd taken his sweater and shoes off, but left his jeans on. His eyes traveled over her body as she approached.

"So beautiful without those clothes." The back of his hand brushed her breast and she leaned into his touch. "Mmm, you'll have to earn the pets, kitten," he said, removing his hands.

She almost whimpered; she wanted his touch so badly.

"Next time I have you meet me in here," he continued, "I want you kneeling, like this."

He dropped to his knees, butt resting on his heels. His hands each cupped a knee, and his head was bowed. He looked up. "You try."

She knelt like he had, trying to get her body in the same position. Daniel came behind her, straightened her back, ensured her shoulders were square. Then he stood before her and separated her knees a bit with his foot.

He was silent for so long, she almost looked up. In fact, she'd decided to do just that when he finally spoke.

"A submissive is not weak because a Dominant controls

her. A submissive is strong because she surrenders her power to him willingly." He rested his hand on the top of her head. "It is not a power a Dominant should take lightly. Rather he should guard it as he would his life and when he returns it, she should feel her power increased because of his care."

Kneeling before him like she was, it finally made sense to her. It did take strength to submit. While it was difficult on some level to be on her knees before someone, it also felt oddly right. She took a deep breath and allowed all the preconceived notions she'd held to disappear.

Daniel must have sensed a change in her somehow, because at her exhalation he simply whispered, "That's my girl."

His words washed over her body, spreading warmth, almost as if he'd touched her.

Then his hand stroked her shoulder and playful Daniel was back. "Stand up and come with me, kitten."

He led her to the padded table she'd looked over the weekend before. Interesting, but nothing scary. It looked rather like a twin-sized bed, covered with leather. He patted the surface. "Hop up."

Much like he did when she knelt for him, he positioned her the way he wanted her. This time on her back.

"There are straps out to your side. Reach out, grab, and hold on. Keep your legs here," he said, separating them slightly. "Your job is to not move. Understood?"

She took a strap in each hand and took a deep breath. "Yes, sir."

"Relax," he said, softly brushing her cheek, his thumb trailing along her eyelid. "Close your eyes and concentrate on the sensations and not moving."

His hands moved in an unexpected massage, lightly across her face, down her shoulders, and up her arms. Then back the other way. Over and over he caressed her as she sank deeper into the leather.

So caught up was she in the sensation of his touch, she jerked when his finger unexpectedly grazed her nipple.

"Tsk, tsk, tsk," he said, and his hands were gone.

She had to fight not to open her eyes in an attempt to find him. Surely he hadn't left. But he wasn't touching her and it was so quiet.

The seconds dragged on.

"Let's try again," he said, low and soft, and right by her side.

Once more he started his sensual massage and when he next brushed over a nipple, she remained still.

"Good girl." There was a flicker of warmth where he'd touched her and then his mouth replaced his fingers, sucking.

She whimpered, but remained still.

"Such a good girl," he said. "I think my kitten needs a reward." His lips trailed across her skin until he reached her other breast and he suckled that nipple. He teased her with his lips and tongue, gently palming one side of her while kissing the other.

Then he bit oh so slightly on her nipple and it felt so good, she lifted herself up for more.

He didn't say a word, but moved away and she was empty and alone and cold without him. She tried to feel his presence, but she had no sense of him, couldn't judge where he was. The very air in the room stood still.

Steeling her body, she willed him to return and vowed not to move again.

But there was nothing but silence.

Just when she'd convinced herself the session was over, he stroked her hair and she sighed.

"Better now?"

"Yes, sir," she said, thrilled to have his hands on her again.

He kept himself contained to the upper part of her body, never venturing past her waist, but setting every nerve ending she had aflame as he worked his sensual magic on her skin. It felt as if every caress reverberated between her legs, and she wondered if she could come from breast play alone.

"You're being so good, kitten," he whispered against her skin. "I'm going to keep going."

Though she pretty much knew what he meant, it still took all the strength she could muster up to stay still when he haphazardly dragged a fingertip from her belly button, down lower, tracing between her legs. The second pass was heavier. The third time, he dipped a finger into her.

She sucked in a breath, but remained still.

"Such a good girl."

He added a second finger and began stroking in and out of her body. Every stroke had him going just a bit deeper, and her body tensed with the effort to be still.

I can do this.

I can do this.

I can do this.

She had almost convinced herself of it when his thumb started brushing her clit with every inward thrust. Her legs trembled. She couldn't do it.

"Orange. Fuck, yellow."

She felt a little bad for saying it, but decided it was more important he knew.

His fingers didn't stop. "Open your eyes, kitten. Look at me."

When she met his gaze, he was smiling. "You're doing so well. Keep your eyes on me." His fingers moved deeper, his thumb brushed harder, and his eyes pierced her with their intensity. She couldn't look away. "Keep watching me. That's it. Good girl. A little bit more and you're going to come."

It built inside her, swirling, wave after wave, almost crashing. Caught between his gaze and his fingers, she let it come and sweep her along. He pushed three fingers inside and with a final rough swipe to her clit, she came with a yelp, her release made all the more powerful by the strain to be still.

As her climax passed, she closed her eyes and sighed. Bliss. Her entire body felt completely blissed out. She never wanted to leave the table. The feeling only intensified as Daniel started stroking her arms.

He gently pried her hands free from the straps. "Let go, kitten."

She had no idea she'd been grasping them so tightly until he helped her flex her fingers.

He placed a hand on her shoulder. "Can you sit up?"

She slowly worked herself into a sitting position and Daniel moved so that he stood at the foot of the table, between her legs. He lightly placed his hands on her upper thighs.

"How do you feel?" he asked.

"Mmm," she hummed. "Weightless and floaty."

He dug his fingers into her hair, massaging her scalp. She nearly purred.

"I lied, you know," she said.

She didn't realize the impact of her words until she saw the shock cross his face. Even then his voice was calm when he replied. "Lied about what, kitten?"

She turned her head into his hand and brushed her lips across his palm. "About not being putty."

He laughed. "Oh?"

"I'm complete putty in your hands."

He lowered his head and whispered against her lips, "I'd hoped that might be the case," before capturing her lips with his.

. . .

*J*ulie thought it might have just been her imagination, but something seemed off with Sasha. Maybe it was her relationship with Peter, though things appeared to be moving right along on that front. It just didn't seem normal for Sasha not to beg for every detail of Julie's weekend with Daniel.

Late Thursday afternoon, Sasha was making calls in the back when the front door chimed. Julie swallowed a groan. She wanted to get home, curl up on the couch, and talk to Daniel. They'd been chatting by phone every night and met for lunch on Tuesday. The more and more she got to know Daniel and spend time with him, the more she was willing to admit to herself that she was falling for him. When you paired that with what she was learning about her craving to submit? It made her shiver thinking about how everything seemed to be falling into place.

Unfortunately, before she could talk with Daniel, she had to deal with the late-arriving customer.

Julie stopped cold in the middle of the room when she saw who it was.

Dena, the submissive she'd seen at the group meeting, stood before her. The one Daniel was quick to call for help. The one who called him "Master Covington."

One look at the tall blonde walking into her shop proved she wasn't the only one who remembered.

"Oh, it's you," Dena said, with a thinly veiled curiosity and a tilt to her head. "I'm here to see Sasha."

"She's on the phone, but she'll be out soon."

Julie looked the willowy woman over quickly. She didn't have a collar on, and a glance at her wrist showed no cuff.

Dena smiled as if she knew what Julie was doing. "I'm unattached right now."

"Sorry," Julie said. "I didn't know I was that obvious. I'm new."

"Dena," the blonde said, sticking out her hand. "I didn't get a chance to introduce myself at the meeting."

"Julie," she said, shaking the offered hand.

The conversation died there and they stood in an uncomfortable silence. Too many thoughts were crowding in Julie's head all at once. What was the history between Daniel and Dena? Assuming there was history. Why was it Dena had never stopped by to see Sasha before?

And speaking of her friend, what was taking Sasha so long?

Dena still watched her with a curious expression.

"Have I grown a third head?" Julie finally said. "Because I'm pretty sure you've seen a submissive woman or two before."

Dena laughed. "Sorry, it's just—" She shook her head. "I had to see."

"See what?"

"We're a close group, those of us who've been around for a while. You'll have to forgive us if we gossip." She leaned over and whispered, "The Doms are the worst."

Julie lifted an eyebrow. Dena hadn't answered the question.

"You're gorgeous and you have spunk. No wonder he's so taken with you."

Dena's words hit her so hard, Julie actually took a step backward. "Daniel? Gossips?"

"No, not Daniel," Dena said with a wave of her hand. "But some of the others are like old women. Just don't tell them I said that, it'll be our little secret."

Julie smiled. She had a feeling she would get along just fine with Dena. "Let's start over. Hi, I'm Julie. Why don't we sit down and you tell me about yourself, because you obviously know everything about me."

Dena put her hands on her hips. "Damn, I like you."

Julie laughed and motioned to a bench.

"I went by Daniel's late Sunday," Dena said, walking over to the bench and sitting down. "Daniel's mentoring a new Dom and asks me to help out sometimes. We normally meet on Saturday, but *somebody* was busy and pushed the session to Sunday."

He had mentioned he had a meeting. Funny, Julie thought it had to do with bank business.

"There had been whispers after the last group meeting. About you." Dena shrugged. "So after the Sunday night session, I asked him."

Julie's hands felt sweaty and she pressed her palms against her thighs. "What'd he say?"

"That the next time I asked about his personal life, I'd

spend some quality time on his whipping bench. That's when I knew he was serious. Always before he'd shrug and say it was nothing."

Julie didn't know what to say to that. She'd only recently accepted that she was falling for the sensual Dominant. To hear he might feel the same . . .

"Sasha's coming over to my apartment for dinner," Dena said. "You should come, too."

"Say yes, Jules," Sasha said from the doorway to the back room, looking slightly flushed. "It'll be good. We can have submissive girl chats." Then she turned to their visitor. "Sorry to keep you waiting, Dena. That was Peter." She looked at Julie. "So, you in?"

It didn't take much thinking for her to decide. After all, she could talk to Daniel on the phone from anywhere.

*J*ulie wasn't sure what Dena did for a living, but the woman had excellent taste in wine. They breezed through the first bottle during dinner and opened a second while they sat around Dena's living room.

"Daniel's your first Dom?" Dena asked, returning to a conversation touched on during dinner. At Julie's nod, she continued. "Lucky bitch. First guy I submitted to was a grade A asshole."

"Then why did you do it?" Julie asked.

"Because as bad as it was, it was better than anything I'd done before."

Julie wasn't so sure nothing wouldn't be better. "At least you knew and admitted what you needed. You weren't like me, sitting around, wondering, and too afraid to do anything about it."

Dena patted her on the shoulder. "You're doing something about it now. That's the important part. Besides, look who you have for a teacher."

The wine had loosened her tongue. "I want him for more than a teacher."

"Don't they all." And with one swallow, Dena downed the last of her wine.

Julie wondered if that meant her assumption about Daniel and Dena was correct. "What?"

Dena sat her glass on the floor. "All the submissives in the group want him."

"I told you they all drop their pants, remember?" Sasha asked.

Sure, Sasha had told her, but to have Dena confirm it . . . it made her head spin. Before she could think of a reply, her phone rang. "It's him!" she said, and realized if either of the other two women had any doubt of how she felt about Daniel, her reaction to his phone call probably cleared it up.

Dena pointed to a closed door. "Guest bedroom through there. You'll have privacy."

"Thanks," she said, then answered the phone. "Hey."

"I thought for a second you were screening calls and I didn't make the cut," he teased.

Julie shut the door behind her. "Afraid I'd decided you didn't pass my test after all?"

"Yes and I'd be upset. Last I checked, I speak in complete sentences." There was a slight pause. "Most of the time."

She shivered, remembering what caused him to speak in phrases. Picturing him over her, his back arched in pleasure as he climaxed inside her.

"Mmm," she hummed. "Maybe complete sentence are overrated."

He laughed. "We better change subjects before I'm tempted to come pick you up and render you speechless."

"Tease."

"I'm completely serious," he said, and she didn't doubt him. "What are you doing tonight?"

"I'm actually at Dena's place. Sasha and I came for dinner." She took a second to look around. The room was tastefully decorated in a French country theme. Simple and uncluttered, much like the rest of the apartment. "I like her."

"I didn't realize Sasha and Dena were close."

"I didn't either. Today was the first time I've seen her, not counting the group meeting."

There was silence before he spoke again and when he did, his tone was flat, almost as if he were describing the weather. "She's a good person. And an experienced submissive. She'd be happy to answer any questions you have on the lifestyle."

"She mentioned she saw you on Sunday." She brought it up, not because she felt jealous, but because she wanted him to know.

"Mentoring session with a new Dom. She helps some-times."

She wondered what that would be like, training some-one. From what Daniel had told her, there seemed to be a lot to learn.

"I thought about asking if you'd like to stay and watch," he said. "But decided it might be too soon."

She respected both his decision and the thought that had gone behind it. He told her he'd been a Dom for over ten years; if he felt it too soon, it was too soon.

"Probably," she agreed.

"I won't keep you. I just wanted to call to see if you could come for dinner tomorrow?"

"Just dinner?"

"I was hoping you'd spend the night, too, but it didn't seem polite to ask you to dinner and then to stay after so I could tie you up in my playroom."

He chuckled after he said it, but she had a feeling he wasn't joking. He was going to tie her up and have sex with her. Her heart pounded with excitement and desire swelled between her legs.

"Julie?"

"Is it tomorrow yet?"

"Have a good time with the girls, kitten." His voice was low and sultry. "Tomorrow night you're all mine."

Minutes later, she walked back into the living room on weak legs. She didn't have to guess what her face looked like; Sasha's expression said everything.

"Damn, that must have been some phone call," Dena said.

Julie knew she could lie and say it was nothing, but instead she took her seat and smiled. "It was."

Sasha and Dena both waited.

"So, what were you two talking about while I was gone?" Julie asked.

"Is she always like this, Sasha?"

"Yes, it's annoying as hell."

They both looked at her and she sighed. There was no escaping. "If you must know, he asked me to dinner tomorrow night."

Sasha crossed her arms. "There is no way *dinner* would put that expression on your face."

"And then he might have mentioned what he'd do after."

Dena stood up and carried her wineglass to the kitchen. "I so do not want to hear this." She looked over her shoulder to Sasha. "Not worth the evil things he'll have his mentee do to me."

Sasha snorted. "You love it."

"Of course I do. It's just part of my game to pretend otherwise." Dena shifted her attention back to Julie. "If you tell us what he has planned, we could give advice."

Julie ran a finger along the rim of her wineglass. "I know you could and I'm sure there'll be a time in the future when I need your advice. But for right now, it's just Daniel and me, and it's new and we're getting to know each other, and, well, I just want to keep it to myself right now."

"Oh, wow." Dena was looking at her all strange.

"Told ya." Sasha just looked smug.

Julie didn't understand what they were talking about. She was missing something. "What?"

"It's basically what Daniel said Sunday." Dena sank into the couch. "You just squashed the hopes and dreams of damn near every submissive in the western hemisphere."

"And half the vanilla women, too," Sasha added. "It's clear Mr. Covington is no longer available."

*D*aniel hung up the phone with a smile on his face. If he guessed correctly, Julie would think of little other than his words until she came over the next day. Hopefully by the time they finished dinner, she'd be so needy with want, any trepidation she had at being tied up would be overshadowed by desire.

He was surprised to hear she was spending the evening with Dena. Though if his relationship with Julie continued on its current path, it only stood to reason that the two women would spend time together. Dena had taken several young submissives under her wing over the years; she enjoyed mentoring as much as he did. Daniel was relieved Julie now had two people other than himself she could talk with.

He decided to walk down to the playroom so he could start planning for the next evening. But halfway down, his doorbell rang.

That was odd. He wasn't expecting anyone. He checked his phone to make sure he hadn't missed a call. Nothing.

He opened the door and smiled when he saw who waited.

"Cole Johnson, you bastard," Daniel said, pulling the scruffy man into a hug. "How long has it been? Don't you have a phone?"

Cole laughed and returned the hug. "Too damn long and yes, but by the time I figured out where I was going, I was already here."

Daniel led him inside with a shake of his head. Some people never changed. He had met Cole when they were both in graduate school, though Cole left before getting his master's, opting to return to his homeland, England, to finish school there. He currently lived Stateside and was a well-known award-winning journalist. They typically spoke every few months, but it'd been at least a year since they'd spent any time together.

They settled into the living room after Cole passed on a drink and Daniel got his first good look at his old friend. It appeared as though Cole hadn't shaved in days and fatigue laced his features.

"What brings you to my doorstep?" Daniel asked. "And you look like hell, by the way."

Cole scrubbed his fingers through his dark hair, making it look even worse. "I haven't slept in over thirty-two hours. I was hoping I could crash here."

"Sure, for as long as you need."

"It won't be long. I'm on my way to India for a few months. I leave in a few weeks."

Which meant there would be no playroom with Julie the next night. He'd have to call and tell her about the change in plans. He wondered if she'd even want to stay. Even though he hadn't seen Cole in over twelve months, he wished his friend had picked a different weekend to stop by.

Daniel stood. "Why don't you take a shower and crash? You can sleep here for now and move into the guesthouse over the weekend."

"Thanks, much appreciated."

After Cole made his way upstairs, Daniel went to his bedroom and sent Julie a text asking for her to call him when she got home. His phone rang less than an hour later.

"Miss me that bad?" she teased when he answered. "Or were you afraid of what I learned from Dena and Sasha?"

He laughed. "Both, if I think about it long enough. But I was actually calling to let you know about a wrinkle in our plans."

Her breath hitched and her even tone belied the desire he knew she felt. "Wrinkle? For tomorrow night?"

"Unfortunately, yes. An old college friend of mine stopped by unexpectedly and needs a place to stay. I'll move him into the guesthouse, but the cleaning crew won't have it ready until Saturday. I knew it'd probably be uncomfortable for you to play knowing he was in the main house."

"Thank you, yes, I'm not bold enough to go there yet." Her voice had lost its teasing touch.

"I'd like for you to meet him, so the dinner invitation stands. And you can still stay over if you'd like. We'd have the whole day to spend together." He added the last statement to try and bring back her teasing side. "You know, if you're not otherwise tied up."

She laughed. The low seductive tone never failed to make him hard.

"There's only one person going to tie me up," she said.

He felt unexpectedly pleased at her reference and an overwhelming feeling of something that felt almost like possessiveness burned through his body. "You got that right."

She sighed. "I guess a little bit more anticipation won't hurt me."

Probably not, he thought, but his erection wasn't especially the most pleasant feeling in the world. Might as well do something about it.

"Talking about tomorrow night has me hard," he said. "Let's build that anticipation a bit more."

From the other end of the phone came a low moan and he smiled. "I believe the correct response would be, 'Yes, sir. If it pleases you.'"

Her reply was a whisper. "Yes, sir. If it pleases you."

"Good girl, kitten. Now put the phone on speaker and undress for me."

While she followed his order, he took time to slip out of his own clothes and put his phone on speaker.

"Okay, I'm finished," she said.

"Okay, I'm finished, *sir.*"

"Okay, I'm finished, sir."

"Thank you. Now for neglecting to call me sir, you get a punishment," he said. "I'm not there to spank you, so instead take a picture of yourself naked and text it to me."

Silence from the other side of the phone.

"Julie?"

"Yes, sir?"

"You have words if this is too much." He felt the need to remind her; asking her to take a naked picture and send it to him might be more than she could handle at this point.

"Yellow."

"Thank you for being honest, kitten. What's wrong?"

"I know you're not going to post pictures of me on the Internet. I know that. It's just, once it's out there, it's out there."

"I promise you as soon as this call is over, I'll delete it. I won't download it anywhere or show it to anyone. If you still don't want to do it, say 'red.' We'll say our good-byes and good-nights and have a wonderful day tomorrow. Otherwise, send the picture and we'll continue. It's up to you, so take your time deciding."

He waited patiently while she thought. He knew he had to give her the time and space to make her own decision. Needed her to realize she was the one who decided the next step.

He'd prepared himself for her to say "red" when a soft chime alerted him to an incoming text. *I trust you*, it said, followed by a picture of her naked from the chest down. He felt the enormity of the gift she'd just given him.

"I'm honored and pleased by your trust, Julie," he said, swallowing around the lump in his throat. "It isn't something I take lightly."

"Thank you, sir."

"Now I want you on your back in bed with your knees spread." He pictured her situating herself. "One hand on your breast, the other checking to see how wet you are."

"Wet, sir."

"Good girl, now palm your breast, gently pinching a nipple, but gradually and gradually get harder."

One day in the future he'd put nipple clamps on her. He had a feeling she'd like them. It was so easy to imagine her in his playroom, decorated for his pleasure.

From the other side of the phone came a short gasp.

"Did you pinch hard, kitten?"

"Yes, sir."

"Good. Now, see if you're wetter."

"I know I am, sir."

"Such a naughty kitten, getting off on pinching her nipples."

"What about you, sir?" she asked in that sultry voice that drove him wild. "Are you hard?"

He loved her playful side. "I'm so hard it hurts," he said, stroking himself. "If you were here, I'd have you suck my dick to take the edge off. Then just before I came in your mouth, I'd pull out so I could finish in that tight pussy."

She groaned again. "I wish I were with you, sir."

"You will be tomorrow night."

"But your friend will be there."

"We'll have time together, don't doubt it."

"I'm horribly impatient."

"Don't tempt me to withhold orgasm from you," he warned. "I can teach you patience."

She knew he could do it; it'd been on the checklist she'd filled out. It hadn't been marked as a hard limit.

"I'm patience personified, sir."

He chuckled and decided not to call her bluff. He'd already pushed her by having her send the picture. Now it was time for him to reward the trust she'd given him.

"Are you still in position?" he asked.

"Yes, sir."

"Good girl. Now take your finger and circle your clit, but don't touch it."

He listened carefully for her sharp intake of breath, smiling when it came.

"Ready to come, kitten?"

"Yes, please, sir."

One day soon, he'd have to work on delaying her orgasm, stretching it out so she could take more of the pleasure he had to show her.

"I'm going to stroke my cock in a steady rhythm," he said. "You follow along with me, however you wish."

He took himself in his hand. "Ready?"

"Yes, sir."

Stroking his cock, he started slow. "Now. Now. Now. Are you following me?"

"Yes, sir."

"Let me hear you."

She followed each of his "now's" with a "yes" of her own and together they kept up his tempo.

"Now."

"Yes."

"Now."

"Yes."

He gradually went faster and she went with him, until he finally felt his climax rushing forward. "Whenever you want, kitten."

She came in a rugged sigh and he followed, spilling in his hand.

"Mmmm," she said.

"Did that help ease your anticipation?" he asked.

"No, sir. I think it only made me want you more. My fingers are a poor substitute for the real thing."

Her honesty was enchanting and he found himself laughing. "Trust me, kitten, I feel the same. I'll take you over my hand any day."

"I'll see you tomorrow. I guess that's not so long."

He thought briefly about telling her she couldn't come again until he gave her permission, but decided against it. If everything went the way he planned, there would be plenty of time to claim ownership of her orgasms.

"Long enough, Julie. Long enough."

They spoke for a few more minutes, revising their plans

and saying good-nights. Not long after hanging up, he made his way down to the playroom to plan.

*D*aniel decided to work from home the next day, so he heard Cole trudge into the kitchen around noon.

"Feel better?" he called from his home office.

Cole gave a grunt that might have been an affirmative reply.

Daniel sent the e-mail he'd been working on and went into the kitchen. "Sleep well?"

His friend looked better after a shower, a shave, and a decent night's sleep, but there was still an underlying fatigue in his eyes. "Like the dead."

"Ready to talk about why you're going halfway around the world for months?"

Cole took a deep breath. "Kate left me."

The news was so unexpected, Daniel sat down. Kate had been Cole's girlfriend and submissive for years. "No. Cole, I'm sorry. When she wasn't with you last night, I just assumed she'd be following later. What happened?"

"There was only one thing we ever argued about on a regular basis."

"The baby issue." It had been an ongoing battle between the two for almost as long as Daniel could remember. Kate wanted children and Cole didn't.

"It's not an area you can compromise on," Cole said.

"You either have kids or you don't. She eventually decided kids were more important than me."

"I'm sure it wasn't exactly like that."

"Trust me, it was exactly like that."

Daniel chose his next words carefully. Cole was hurting, but Daniel wouldn't be much of a friend if he didn't tell the truth. "You know that if you're in pain over losing her, you can't escape it by running."

"Maybe not, but I can sure as hell avoid it for a while."

"You know you're always welcome here."

"Thanks." Cole smiled, but it looked forced. "How about you? Did you and Dena ever, you know?"

Cole had always thought Daniel should make more of a move with Dena. No matter how often Daniel insisted they were and would always be just friends and occasional play partners, Cole had the idea stuck in his head.

"No. I'm actually seeing someone new. She's coming for dinner tonight, you can meet her."

"New woman? Nice."

"She'll probably be spending the night."

"Ah, hell."

Daniel knew what Cole was thinking. Could only imagine how he felt. "I'm sorry. I invited her before you arrived."

"Don't worry about it. I'll be okay." He stood up. "I'm going to go for a run. Clear my head."

Daniel nodded. "Trail hasn't changed." The pond had

always been a favorite spot of Cole's to run when he visited and needed time and space to think. Daniel was under no misconception that one run would aid Cole in exorcising his personal demons, but maybe it would be a start.

The first thing Julie noticed about Cole was his eyes. They were a stunning bluish green, and though his mouth smiled, his eyes didn't. She wondered what made him so sad and if his warm smile fooled most people.

"Julie," he said, shaking her hand and speaking in a smooth British accent. "So good to meet you. Cole Johnson."

"Cole Johnson," she said. "Daniel didn't give me your name. I love your writing. Especially your piece on the diamond mines."

His eyes widened with shock and then he playfully pushed Daniel aside and took her arm. "Daniel vastly underestimated your many charms. Come sit beside me at dinner. We'll talk."

She laughed and threw a smile over her shoulder to Daniel.

He shook his head. "She's much too smart for that game. There's no way she'll sit through three hours of 'Cole Johnson, Man of Adventure and Intrigue.'"

"That's okay," Cole whispered, patting her arm. "I'll condense it down to one. I'm a little low on intrigue lately anyway."

Daniel served a hearty meal of steak and potatoes, and

the wine and conversation flowed freely. Cole actually did keep her fairly entertained retelling some of his many exploits, and if the certain sadness lingering in his expression never quite went away, it seemed he tried not to let it cloud the conversation. Daniel added enough groans and snorts for her to understand that Cole was embellishing his tales rather well.

"Tell me, Julie," Cole said when their plates were empty. "Are you new to the area?"

"Me, no. Why do you ask?"

"I visited last year. I didn't see you. . . ." Cole looked over to Daniel, and from the corner of her eye, she saw Daniel shake his head. "I just can't imagine him never mentioning you."

"We just met recently," she said, not sure what the interaction between the two friends meant, but deciding to question Daniel about it later. Something seemed off.

"That explains it, then," Cole said a little too easily.

Daniel cleared his throat. "Let's go to the living room. It'll be more comfortable."

"Nah." Cole stood up and stretched. "I'm still beat. I'm going to head on up to bed."

Daniel and Julie wished him a good night, but because it was too early for bed and the house was too crowded for playroom activities, they curled up on a couch in the living room after cleaning up the kitchen. A movie was playing, but between small talk and wandering hands, neither of them paid much attention to it.

"What was that look between you and Cole at dinner?" Julie asked during a quiet moment.

"Saw that, did you?"

"Mm-hm."

"Cole assumed we'd met in the group. He thought you were new to the area since he went to a meeting when he was here last year and didn't see you."

"Cole went to a meeting?"

"He's a Dominant. I didn't think you'd want to discuss your sex life during dinner."

She felt like she was on information overload. Learning Cole was a Dom and even imagining talking about sex with him threatened to crowd her brain. Something tickled on the edge of her mind, though, and she struggled to grasp on to it.

"He thinks you'd only go out with a submissive woman," she finally said. "Why else would he assume we knew each other from the group?"

"I typically only date submissives, yes," he said, but his words sounded calculated.

"So if I wasn't . . ."

"You are, so it doesn't matter, and if you weren't, it wouldn't have mattered."

She snuggled deeper into his arms, overjoyed he would still want to be with her if she wasn't interested in submission.

"You could look at the reverse, too," he said. "You could have not dated me because I'm a Dominant."

She turned around in his arms and kissed him. "What a mistake that would have been."

He didn't answer, but ran a finger along her jaw.

"Is something wrong with Cole?" she asked. "He looks sad."

"His longtime girlfriend and submissive, Kate, recently left him."

The pain Cole must be experiencing hit her hard. She wondered what had happened between them.

"Must have been horrible for him if he's leaving the country," she said.

"The bond between a Dominant and submissive is intense on many levels. Cole loved Kate. A part of him always will. But I don't know the details of what happened. He hasn't been able to talk about it yet. He just wanted a safe place to stay for a while, and we've been friends a long time."

The sadness of the situation moved her to silence. Daniel tightened his hold on her and kissed the top of her head. They watched the rest of the movie without speaking.

Late the next morning she knelt in the playroom, trying to calm her mind. The cleaning crew had finished with the guesthouse earlier and they'd seen Cole settled. Julie had enjoyed spending time with him and was glad he'd be around for a few weeks before heading to India.

Daniel's footsteps helped her refocus and she shifted,

trying to perfect her position. She was naked, and on her knees, having carefully positioned herself as Daniel had instructed her.

"Good morning, kitten," he said, the smile evident in his tone.

"Good morning, sir."

"You look so beautiful, kneeling, and waiting for me."

Before being with him, she'd never thought of kneeling as beautiful. Somehow when he said it, it made sense and she felt beautiful.

"Stand up for me, kitten. Let me see that body."

She rose to her feet, acutely aware of him watching her. She felt powerful.

He ran a hand down her side. "I missed this last night. Had to make do with fantasy and dreams."

With Cole in the house, when they went to bed, they'd only slept. Though she'd ached for Daniel's touch, she'd not comprehended how much until he touched her intimately now. He brushed her nipple and she moaned.

"Yes, kitten. I'm going to touch you in all kinds of ways today and I want to hear all your noises." He playfully slapped her butt. "Go hop up on the table. On your back."

The leather of the table felt vaguely comforting. Soft and supple against her skin. Daniel looked almost predatory as he approached. He slipped something from his pocket and within seconds, black silk stole her sight.

"You're going to be tied up and blindfolded at my mercy. What do you say if you want to stop?"

Her heart pounded and she was willing to bet he saw every beat. "Red, sir."

His fingers traced her lips. "Very good. And if I need to slow down?"

"Yellow, sir."

"You can also use 'orange,'" he teasingly whispered in her ear as he blindfolded her, and she smiled.

She had expected to be tied with scratchy rope, so it was a surprise when a soft, thin coil circled her wrist.

"I'm using black rope today," he said. "It contrasts so nicely with your skin."

He continued speaking, low and deep, all the while working to bind her to the table. Any fear she had slipped away under his expert touch and smooth-as-sin voice. He told her how good she looked, how much she turned him on, and how he couldn't wait to do all sorts of wicked things to her body.

Before she knew it, she was bound spread-eagle. His hands were absent just for a moment and she had a quick sensation of panic. She was all tied up and blindfolded. She sucked in a breath.

"Everything okay, kitten?" His hands were back, stroking her shoulders. Calming. Soothing.

"Yes, sir."

"I'm not going anywhere. I'll be right here beside you. Understand?"

She did. "Yes, sir."

"Good girl." He was no longer touching her, but she

could sense he was nearby. "Today's all about sensation. I just want you to feel and experience. It works better when your sense of sight is deprived."

Something lightly tickled the hollow of her throat, trailed downward between her breasts, circled them, and made its way back up.

"Can you guess what this is?" He flicked it against her nipple.

"Feather?"

He tickled the other. "Is that an answer or another question?"

"It's a feather, sir."

"Good girl. It is a feather." He lightly trailed it down one arm and then the other, teasing her in places she'd never considered erogenous before. Her nerve endings came alive under his touch and subtle teasing. It didn't seem possible to be so turned on by a feather.

"How about this?" he asked, and something soft and furry stroked her arm.

"Feels like fur, sir." Warm and soft and comforting.

"It is fur. It's also a flogger. A rabbit fur flogger."

She tensed at the word "flogger," but Daniel kept on with the fur strands, dragging them along and across her body until she was once more relaxed.

"A lot of people associate floggers with pain," he said. "And there's certainly a place for that. But with this type," he murmured as the soft strands flicked her chest, "it's more about sensation."

Tied as she was, she could do no more than relax her body and allow Daniel to elicit responses she never knew were possible. Starting at her shoulders, the rabbit fur swiftly pelted against her skin with light breezy strokes. He left no portion of her body untouched by the flogger. It felt delicious when used on her breasts and her nipples hardened with desire.

Along her belly, it felt more ticklish. She almost giggled, but with the next stroke, several strands hit her between the legs and she moaned instead.

"Like that, kitten?" he asked, and when the flogger came again, more of its tails landed against her wetness.

Her hips jerked, desperate for friction, and her body ached, longing to be filled. "Yes, sir."

"Would you like something harder?"

The fur struck her again, but it wasn't enough, could never be enough. She needed more. "Please, sir."

He spanked her there with three quick strokes and she moaned in pleasure.

"Please," she said again because it hadn't been enough.

"Poor kitten," he said. "It's not time yet. We have more toys to explore before you're allowed to come. And when you do come, I'm going to be buried inside you."

His footsteps sounded as he walked away from her. She tried to hear what he was doing, but it wasn't until she heard the telltale clink that she had any idea why he had left. Once she did, her body tensed in anticipation.

"I think my kitten needs to cool down, she's too hot."

She shivered at the touch of ice to her shoulder and groaned as he trailed it along her collarbone. So cold when the rest of her felt so heated. The ice continued moving lower, but in the second before it reached her breast, his mouth was on her skin. Then the ice was in his mouth and her skin was enveloped in the most surreal combination of frozen heat.

She strained against her bonds with a whimpering moan of pleasure.

A chuckle was his only reply. He suckled her, and then he slipped a finger inside her. A cold finger.

Her hips jerked. "Fuck!"

His finger was so cold, it might as well have been ice. As he worked it in and out of her, his skin gradually grew warmer. The ice in his mouth melted, leaving tiny wet paths along her body. Her every nerve stood at attention.

Slowly, he ran his hands down her right leg and untied her ankle. He repeated the action for each limb. Taking the newly untied arm or leg and massaging it gently before placing it back on the table. Any other time, his attention would have relaxed her, but at that moment all it did was serve to entice her more.

He moved leisurely, his seductive touch teasing every bit of anticipation possible out of her. A soft towel was draped over her body and those same hands gently dried her off. With tiny swirls, he circled her breasts, pressing rougher and rougher while he worked his way lower and lower.

The towel slipped from her body and heat once more

surrounded her, but it was him. He was above her, on her, and he kneed her legs apart, and seconds later, he was in her. The familiar sweet stretch of him pushing inside made her lift her hips in a desperate attempt to draw him deeper.

He was slow and tender, and shattered any lingering misguided impression she had about domination. Fast or slow. Hard or gentle. He would take what he wanted in any way he wanted. And she would let him, because she knew there was only freedom to be found in placing herself into his keeping.

His hands slid to her face and the blindfold fell from her eyes. She saw her own desire reflected in his gaze. And as he drove them both toward an encompassing climax, she saw something deeper. It was her strength that made him strong, and his command that made her complete.

*D*aniel looked to his right at Julie as they drove to the assisted living facility later that day. She had her head back on the headrest, eyes closed, and her fingers played a staccato beat against the doorframe. At her feet was the flower arrangement she insisted on putting together. Wildflowers. He smiled at the thought of her remembering his grandmother's favorite.

"What are you thinking over there, all relaxed and smiley?" he asked.

She lazily peeked through one eye at him. "I'm willing to bet you have a fairly good idea."

They had already talked about their morning. She indicated her enjoyment of sensation play, and even more so, he believed she had a breakthrough of sorts, though she hadn't said it in so many words.

He dropped a hand to her thigh and squeezed. "Stroke my ego and tell me anyway."

"How about I stroke something else?"

Damn, but she was always throwing him off guard by saying things like that. Two could play at that, though. He put his hand back on the steering wheel. "That would be an excellent idea."

She smiled in assumed victory and turned toward him.

"Unzip your jeans, kitten."

"What?" she asked, sinking back into her seat.

"You suggested stroking something and I'm agreeing. Unzip your jeans."

"I meant—"

"I'm well aware of what you meant. Now unzip the jeans or the shirt goes next." He was pushing, he knew, playing in such a new way for her. Outside the safe confines of his house, would she still be willing to bend to him?

He kept his eyes on the road, allowing her space to make her decision. Seconds later, he was rewarded with the sound of a zipper being pulled down.

"Good job, kitten. Now slip a hand inside your panties and tell me if you're wet."

Again he waited.

"Yes, sir. I'm wet."

"Excellent. Now I want you to stroke yourself. You have until the next stoplight to reach orgasm."

She sucked in a breath. "Honesty, right?"

"Always," he said, pleased she felt comfortable enough to be truthful with him.

"I tried once, with an old boyfriend, and couldn't do it. By myself, I'm fine, but with someone watching?"

He was willing to bet the old boyfriend did nothing more than to sit, watch, and jerk off. What Julie needed was someone with a bit more authority.

"I appreciate your honesty, kitten, but the truth is, that old boyfriend isn't here. I am. And you're going to fuck yourself with your fingers, in my car, with me watching, and you're going to orgasm before we get to the next stoplight."

He turned his head slightly to watch. First she looked out the windows. He pressed down on the accelerator and when she turned her gaze to him, he gave her a sly grin.

"Close your eyes. No one's watching."

She looked out the window again, but closed her eyes before he could say anything else.

"Now slip your hand between your legs and feel how wet you are for me."

Out of the corner of his eye, he watched as she obeyed.

"That's it. Pretend it's me. Those are my fingers parting you, slipping into you."

Her body was still tense, almost as if she was fighting herself.

"Except my fingers are bigger than yours, so you need to use two. I'm pumping them into you, going deeper each time, giving your clit a little stroke right before entering."

Her knees fell to the sides as she worked her fingers in and out.

"That's it. Feel how deep I'm going. Harder."

Before long, she was writhing in her seat, making little moans. He was so hard, he wondered why he thought having her masturbate in his car was a good idea. She rocked her hips into her hand and let out a whimper of release right as he stopped at a red light.

He smiled at her self-satisfied grin. "Good job, kitten. I knew you could do it. Now give me your hand."

"I'm sorry, sir. What?"

"Your right hand. That orgasm was mine and I want to taste it."

He took her offered hand and sucked one finger at a time. By the time he finished, she was shifting in her seat again and his erection was so painful he almost had her go with her original stroking plan.

Instead, he pressed a kiss into her palm and enjoyed her flushed face. "I wonder sometimes . . ."

"About?"

"How you denied for so long what you so desperately need."

She took his hand from where it rested on her thigh,

and drew light circles on it. "Maybe I was just waiting for the right man."

At her words, something inside his chest grew tight. He found that he couldn't speak, so instead he simply squeezed her hand and hoped she somehow knew what her spoken words did to him.

"Is that someone with you, Daniel?" his grandmother asked, peeking around his shoulder. Daniel had only visited the facility once before and that had been when he and Tessa were making their final decision. He was anxious to see how his grandmother was settling in.

"Hello, Mrs. Covington," Julie said, and stepped to his side.

"I know you, young lady."

He was shocked she remembered. Her dementia had been growing steadily worse, especially her short-term memory. Though she had good days, there were times she appeared to reside solely in the past.

"Yes, ma'am, at the floral shop. You were looking for something for your great-granddaughter. I'm Julie."

"That's right, you said pink roses instead of wildflowers. You were right, though I never did understand why people are so taken with roses. Compared to wildflowers, they're just plain." She turned to Daniel. "Come on inside, don't stand there in the hallway."

"Speaking of wildflowers." Julie stepped inside while

he held the door. "I brought you these as a housewarming gift."

His grandmother took the flowers with a wistful smile. "How beautiful. My husband used to bring me wildflowers. It was all he could afford when we first went out. To this day I'd rather have wildflowers than all the roses in the world."

Daniel caught Julie's gaze and mouthed a "thank you" to her. She had been the one to insist he stop at her shop so she could put something together. It'd touched him at the time, but at that moment, as he watched his grandmother, flowers clutched tightly in her hands, lead Julie into the small kitchen for coffee, the tightness in his chest grew.

He followed the ladies, but his grandmother shooed him out.

"I know you want to inspect every inch of my new home to make sure no one left a hair out of place. You go do that while I talk with your Julie."

His Julie. He really shouldn't think of her like that yet; it was much too soon. But all he had to do was remember her sighing into his touch, bending to his will, and the look of amazement that covered her face when she discovered something new, and he knew it was a lost cause. He was already thinking of her as his.

He walked around the apartment, making sure everything was in place as he had requested. The locks and alarms, call buttons and phones. He checked them all. But he kept one eye on the couple in the kitchen. They were sipping coffee and talking intensely about something.

"Everything looks good, Grandma," he said, walking into the kitchen. "What are you two ladies discussing?"

"We're talking about men. You in specific."

Julie raised an eyebrow at him. "Stories of your childhood. How you used to torment your sister."

He placed his hand on his heart and sat down at the table. "Me?"

"He was awful. Just awful," his grandmother said. "But just when I thought they'd be enemies forever, they'd crawl under the table and he'd read to her."

"Shel Silverstein," he whispered. "I remember that."

"The poems, yes." His grandmother's forehead wrinkled. "Wish I remembered where those books got to."

"I have a set I can bring you," Julie said.

"Oh, no, dear. I couldn't ask you to do that."

"You're not asking, I'm offering."

His grandmother lightly patted Julie's arm. "You're such a fine lady. Now, Daniel, you treat her right."

"He does, Mrs. Covington, I promise." Julie's face was the tiniest bit flushed. Her breathing just a bit hitched.

"He better. You let me know if he doesn't."

"Yes, ma'am," Julie said, and then turned the conversation to the upcoming spring season, suggesting a few flowers she thought would work well in a patio garden.

While she talked about it, Daniel had the most vivid

picture of Julie working in his garden naked. He decided he was particularly ready for spring to come as well.

"The next group meeting is the weekend after next," he said hours later, when they were back at his house, lounging on the couch. "Will you go with me?"

"Can I wear a red bracelet?"

His heart threatened to beat out of his chest in happiness. He'd wondered if she would want to turn in her white for red, but thought it best it was her idea. He circled her wrist with his fingers. "If you show up with me, wearing a red bracelet, everyone will assume you're my submissive. Will that bother you?"

She leaned back and he could tell she was thinking through her response. He was glad she took time to ensure her answer was honest and didn't spout off what she thought he wanted to hear.

"No, it won't bother me," she finally said. "I'm realizing I am a submissive, so it makes sense I'd wear red. And I'm not interested in being with anyone other than you, so I don't mind if people assume I'm yours."

His Julie, his grandmother's words came back to him. But now he added his own: *his kitten.* "I do enjoy your rational side."

Her eyes grew dark. "I'm sure if given enough time, you'd enjoy all my sides."

"Trust me," he whispered. "I plan to."

She sank deeper into his arms. "Can I think out loud for a bit?"

"Of course."

"Sasha said she thinks Peter wants to collar her. I guess I'm just worried for some reason. She's never had a collar before."

He ran a finger along her neck, unable to stop himself from picturing her wearing his collar. "For me, it signifies the bond between Dominant and submissive. When I have a collared submissive, it represents my commitment to her, and hers to me. I would hope it holds the same meaning for Peter and Sasha."

She was silent. He imagined she was thinking about Sasha. As far as he knew, Peter had never collared anyone before. His own thoughts were so focused on Peter and Sasha, her next question surprised him.

"How many submissives have you collared?"

His finger dropped from her neck. "Three."

"Is that a lot?"

"I was too young when I collared the first. Didn't know enough to know what I didn't know. I waited a few years before the second. We were together the longest, but she moved away. Job promotion." He paused, remembering her words that she couldn't pass up the opportunity. It wasn't until later he realized it was for the best. "The third wanted something more permanent than I was willing to offer. We went our separate ways two years ago."

"I'm not sure if that's a yes or no to my question."

"I'm not sure there is a yes or no to your question." He twirled a strand of her hair around his finger. "Some Doms have more, some less. Some have more than one."

"Would you? Have more than one?"

"No." He gave her hair a tug. "That wouldn't work for me. When a submissive wears my collar, I want all my attention and care dedicated to her. I've never been one to share my affections."

"Yet you haven't collared anyone in two years."

He had not. He hadn't found anyone he wanted to collar. Not from lack of offers. Several submissives in the group had subtly expressed their interest. His response had always been a kind but firm no.

That was all before Julie, though.

"No, not in two years," he said. "To echo what a smart woman told me earlier, perhaps I've just been waiting for the right person."

SEVEN

*F*or Julie, the next two weeks were some of the happiest she had ever experienced. She spoke with Daniel every day and they met for lunch several times a week. Friday nights were spent in his bed and Saturday in his playroom.

She looked forward to that time in the playroom, when she became his and he introduced her to the pleasure to be found under his control. On her knees waiting for him to instruct or tease her, she discovered she never felt more at ease. It seemed the world and all its problems floated away at the sound of his command or the touch of his hand.

Thursday night she was at home, researching new distributors for the floral shop business, when a knock on the door interrupted her.

Puzzled, she got up and looked out the peephole.

Daniel.

She unlocked the door with a huge grin on her face. "Hey, you."

"I hope you don't mind me stopping by." His smile was easy and light.

"Come in," she said. "Is everything okay?" It occurred to her maybe something had happened to his grandmother, but surely he wouldn't be smiling so if that were the case.

He followed her into her living room, shrugging out of his coat and draping it casually over his arm. "Everything's fine. I was just hanging out at home when something hit me."

"Sit down." She waved to her couch. "What hit you this time of night?"

He glanced at his watch. "Nine o'clock. It is a bit late. I'd apologize, but I'm not sorry at all."

She loved the way he could combine a gentle tease with the honest truth. "I never said I wanted an apology. Unless, of course, you want to apologize for not stopping by this time of night before."

He cupped her face and gave her a soft kiss that whispered of more buried just under the surface. "Trust me, kitten. If I didn't have to be at work so early, my nights wouldn't be spent jerking off to fantasies of you. They'd be spent with my cock inside you in any way possible."

Damn, what he could do to her with a few softly spoken words. Just like that, he could make her visualize everything he said. And more than that, make her want it.

But instead of moving forward, he pulled back. "Before I forget why I came here, the group meeting is tomorrow night."

Due to their schedules, time together beforehand would be limited. He would be picking her up right after she closed the shop and they'd drive to the meeting, where she would be seen by most people in the group as Daniel's submissive. Afterward, she would spend the night with him and in his bed, and she would once more act as his submissive.

She couldn't wait.

"I brought you a little something," he said. "Thought it might be a good idea for you to have it for a while beforehand. Get used to it."

He reached into his pocket and pulled out a red bracelet.

*D*aniel left not long after giving her the bracelet. She tried to convince him to stay, but he insisted he had to get up early for work and promised he would make up for it the following night. She watched the taillights of his car disappear and then turned off her computer, knowing there would be no more researching distributors in her current state of mind.

The red band dangled from her fingers and she spun it around, taking in what it meant. The following night she would put it on and attend a meeting where it would identify her as a submissive. Not only that, but she would show

up with Daniel and everyone would know she submitted to
him. When she spoke to him, she would have to address
him as "Master Covington."

The thought made her knees wobble and she dropped
into a chair.

"Master Covington," she said out loud, to test the
words. She found she liked them a lot.

She took the band and slipped it over her wrist. The red
looked so vivid against her skin. No one would have any
trouble seeing it. Probably wouldn't be a good idea to wear
it to work; she'd never noticed Sasha wearing hers. But she
decided she'd wear it to sleep.

She'd just taken the bracelet off to shower when her
phone rang.

Probably Daniel.

But an unknown number flashed on the display. She
answered with a frown. "Hello?"

"Julie Masterson, please," someone said, speaking over
a large amount of background noise.

"This is Julie Masterson."

"Ms. Masterson, this is Hope from Northeastern General Hospital. You're listed as the emergency contact for
Sasha Blake."

She pressed a hand against the wall to steady herself.
Sasha. "Is she there? Is she okay?"

"She's been admitted and is currently listed as stable."

"I'll be right there. Where's she at?"

"In the Emergency Department, waiting for a room."

Julie whispered thanks and hung up with trembling hands. She had to get to the hospital. Where were her keys? She fumbled in her purse, repeating over and over again that Sasha must be okay, because the caller said she was stable.

It wasn't until she was halfway to the hospital that she remembered Sasha had said she was spending the evening with Peter.

*T*hey'd moved Sasha to a room by the time Julie made it to the hospital. Running around, first to the ER and then up to the floor to Sasha's room, left Julie feeling harried and even more upset. Turning the last corner, she stomped to the room they told her Sasha was in and took several deep breaths to calm herself before pushing the door open.

It took her eyes a few minutes to adjust to the dim light and when they did, they settled on the blanket covering the fragile-looking bundle in the middle of the bed. Sasha. But her positioning looked odd and it took Julie a second to realize it was because she was on her stomach.

Julie wondered for the two hundredth time what had happened. She tiptoed forward, unable to tell if her friend slept or not.

"Sasha?" she whispered.

The bundle shifted slightly. "Jules?"

She rushed forward and stopped only when she saw

Sasha's red-rimmed eyes and wet cheeks. "What? What happened?"

A silent sob shook through Sasha's frame and she hissed in pain. "I can't . . . not yet . . . just sit with me?"

Without saying anything, Julie took her friend's hand and sat in the chair beside the bed.

Julie was there for hours, but she didn't sleep at all. It seemed like nurses were in and out of the room every hour, checking blood pressure, seeing if Sasha needed pain medication, and one time asking Julie to step outside while they changed dressings. Still no one told her what had happened and every time the nurse left, Sasha faked sleep.

Even with every imagined reason she came up with for why Sasha was in the hospital, she was unprepared for the two police officers who knocked and entered the room at six o'clock the next morning. She was even less prepared for the person she saw entering behind them.

She stood up. "Daniel?"

He didn't look shocked to see her; he looked resigned. Nodded in her direction. "Julie." Then he breezed past her and bent down to talk to Sasha. He whispered, but standing so close, Julie couldn't help but hear. "Tell them what happened in as much or as little detail as you want. Press charges if you wish. Just know that, regardless, this *will* be handled."

What the hell happened?

"Ma'am," one of the officers said to Julie. "Can you step outside? We need to speak to your friend alone."

She jerked a thumb toward Daniel. "Does *he* get to stay?"

"No." Daniel put a hand on her shoulder. "Let's wait outside."

She slipped out of his grasp and stomped to the door. Angry tears threatened to spill from her eyes and she steeled herself. She would not cry.

When the door closed behind him, she spun to face him. "Will you tell me what the fuck is going on and what the hell you're doing here?"

He raised an eyebrow. "She didn't tell you?"

"Don't answer my question with a question."

"I think it best she tell you herself. It's not my place. I'm here because Peter called me."

She'd come to the realization Peter was involved around two o'clock in the morning. Nothing else made sense.

"I knew that piece of shit was involved. Where is the asshole?"

He leaned close and whispered, "I'm going to give you five seconds to drop the attitude and clean up the language."

She crossed her arms. "Don't even think about pulling—"

His hand clamped around her wrist. "Best decision you can make right now is to not finish that sentence. I understand you're upset. I'm upset. But Sasha needs your support, probably for longer than you realize, and your outbursts aren't going to help."

Three deep breaths and she bit back the response dancing on her tongue. "Maybe I could be supportive if I knew what happened."

He shook his head. "It's best you hear it from her."

She wiped her eyes. Damn tears. "I've been sitting by her bed listening to her gasp in pain every time she moves the wrong way and you have the nerve to stand there and not tell me what happened?"

He closed his eyes and sighed. When he looked at her again, his expression was flat. "The short version is, Peter took a scene too far and used equipment he had no business using."

She didn't understand. "Did she use her safe word?"

He pursed his lips into a line. "He didn't give her a way to safe word."

Shock, then rage, coursed through her body. How could something like that happen? "You knew this and you had the nerve to tell me to watch my language? Just wait until I get my hands on him, I'll rip his—"

He took her shoulder, guided her down the hall, and spoke through clenched teeth. "Watch it. Last warning."

He led her to a private waiting area and nodded to a chair. She sat. He stood before her, arms crossed, looking down at her.

"Did I or did I not tell you that nothing happens to a submissive without their consent?" He held up a hand when she tried to speak. "I'm not saying Peter is blameless. I'm just saying Sasha isn't either. She should have never started the scene."

Julie didn't quite know what to make of that. But after

a few minutes, she did remember that he had always said she was the one who decided how far they went. Then it started to make sense. "I still don't know exactly what happened."

"Sasha will tell you when she's ready."

He wasn't going to tell her. Even so, she still had plenty of questions she could ask him. "What did you mean when you told her it'd 'be handled'?"

His eyes grew cool, colder than she'd ever seen. Something inside them scared her. "You remember asking me what happens when a Dom in our group violates a sub's hard limit?"

She remembered him saying an over-the-knee spanking would seem like a reward. She nodded.

"I suppose," he said, "it'll be a lot like that."

*T*he policemen had left by the time Julie collected herself enough to make it back to Sasha's room. Unable to feign sleep any longer, her friend was sitting up and eating. She gave Julie a wary smile and set her spoon down.

"Daniel leave?"

"Yeah, said he had things to take care of." Like letting everyone know the meeting had been postponed to another week. Just as well, she supposed; she doubted anyone would be in the mood.

"He tell you?"

Julie sat down in the chair she'd spent the night in. "Not much of anything. He said it would be better coming from you."

Sasha looked past her, tears still in her eyes. She pushed the breakfast tray away. "It started out so wonderfully. Peter said he was ready to collar me, wanted to know if I felt the same. I said 'of course' and we agreed to make it official at the meeting."

Sometimes, Julie remembered Daniel saying, couples would have a collaring ceremony, often following a group meeting. It had made her curious at the time, wondering if her relationship with Daniel would ever progress to that point. She'd fantasized what it would be like to have him place his collar on her. Unbidden, her hand stroked her throat.

"He said that to celebrate he'd like to try something new and I agreed."

"Did you ask what it was?"

"No, but we'd gone over our checklists. He knew my limits." Her fist tightened, tangled in the sheet. "I trusted him."

The door opened and a nurse's aide nodded to the tray.

"Take it," Sasha said. "I'm not hungry."

Julie decided it probably wouldn't be a good idea to tell her she really needed to eat. Food wasn't going to help Sasha's gaunt look.

"Anyway," Sasha continued, once the door closed. "He gagged me."

Unable to help herself, Julie shivered. She recalled the gags in Daniel's playroom. They didn't look fun.

Sasha didn't notice or acknowledge her shiver. "Always before when I've been gagged, I've been given a bell. To drop or ring as a safe word. Peter didn't give me anything. I knew better, but I . . ." She shook her head.

~~Just like Daniel had said.~~

"You what? Why wouldn't you say something?" *Make me understand,* Julie wanted to say, *why you would deliberately ignore one of the first rules Daniel taught me.* The one he made sure she remembered every time they started.

"Look, I know it was stupid, but at the time, it was like I was high or something. I was going to wear his collar. I wanted to please him. I thought he would be able to tell how I felt. I remember thinking it was so touching he knew me so well, we didn't need safe words anymore."

No, that wasn't touching, Julie wanted to say; it was stupid. But she refrained. Sasha hadn't even known Peter that long.

"He has chains suspended from his ceiling. That's where he bound me. We'd done it before. I enjoyed it. This time, he decided to blindfold me, too."

Julie recalled being blindfolded and bound. She'd liked it. Aside from the gag, part of her understood where Sasha was coming from.

And that scared her.

"He started with a flogger. One of my favorites, but it takes me a while to reach subspace." She looked at Julie with a raised eyebrow.

"Yes." Julie nodded. "I know what it is, just not by experience."

Subspace, that mysterious feeling submissives craved. The place a Dominant could take them that felt so good, it almost became addictive. The state where a rush of endorphins sent a submissive into a trancelike frame of mind so deep, pain was nearly nonexistent. She'd longed for the day she could experience it firsthand.

"He knew it took me a long time," Sasha whispered. "He knew."

She was quiet for such a long time, Julie wondered if she felt well enough to continue. "We can finish later if you want."

"I told them I didn't want to press charges."

"Are you regretting that now?" Julie asked. "Do you want to press charges?"

Sasha shook her head. "I don't think so. How can I when it was my fault, too?"

"What happened after the flogger?"

"I hadn't made it into subspace yet. I was close, I think." She sighed. "So much I've blocked. What I remember next was the pain. Searing. Like I was being burned over and over. All up and down my back. I tried to get away, but I was bound so tightly, I couldn't move. And I kept yelling 'red' over and over . . . gagged . . . he couldn't hear." She spoke through little hiccuping sobs and she kept closing and releasing her fist.

It took Julie a second to understand she was safe wording, releasing an invisible bell over and over.

Sasha blew her nose and continued, apparently through the worst part of the story. "They told me I passed out. Next thing I remember is waking up in the hospital. Apparently, my back's in pretty bad shape. I'm afraid to look at it."

Julie took her friend's hand and squeezed. "Oh, Sasha."

"I'm not even sure where he got it. I know he doesn't have any experience in using one."

"What did he use?"

"A bullwhip." Her lower lip started to tremble and Julie knew whatever bravado she'd briefly put on had reached its limit.

Julie went about getting Sasha into a comfortable position, all the while trying to keep her own feelings at bay. Nothing worked; in her mind she kept seeing Sasha bound, gagged, and desperately trying to safe word. After a while the image morphed and she was the one struggling to break free.

*A*n hour later she was still sitting beside Sasha's bed when Daniel came back. He didn't say anything; he simply walked across the floor to stand beside her. His hand rested lightly on her shoulder.

"When was the last time you slept?" he asked.

"I can't remember." She didn't remember anything except Sasha's fingers fluttering uselessly for a man who wasn't paying attention.

The hand at her shoulder tightened. "You can't be strong for her if you don't take care of yourself."

"I'll sleep later."

"She told you."

"Yes." Her body shook, remembering.

"Come here, baby."

He barely had the words out when she pushed the chair back and flung herself into his strong embrace. In his arms, she finally let her guard down and allowed the tears to flow. He held her, whispering things she couldn't make out, but that soothed her just the same.

"Why?" she asked when she could speak. "I don't get it. You said a Dom cherished his sub above all, guarded her with his life. How could he do that to her?"

"I don't know. I haven't had a chance to discuss anything with him in detail yet, but I will."

She didn't miss the sharp edge of determination in his voice.

A knock on the door caused her to jump, but she stayed in his arms when the nurse entered.

"Time to change the dressing," she said.

"I don't suppose I could convince you to leave while they did this?" he asked in a whisper.

"No way. They had me leave last night, but since I'll be the one changing it for her at home, I need to stay."

Standing across the bed from them, the nurse gently

roused Sasha and repositioned her. With the utmost care, she folded the sheet down, and removed the dressing. Daniel slipped his hand into Julie's.

Angry red marks crisscrossed Sasha's back. Many of the lines bled.

"Fucking hell," Daniel said under his breath.

Julie swayed against him and slid into her chair. It looked even worse than she'd imagined.

"That bad, Jules? You look green," Sasha said, so clearly trying to be brave.

Much too late she noticed Sasha's gaze on her. "Sorry, it's just . . . I didn't . . ."

"No need to apologize. You didn't do it and I know it looks bad, I can feel it." Sasha's eyes drifted shut and she started breathing slow and deep, though she jerked occasionally. Julie knew she was on a painkiller, and she was glad her friend could sleep through the discomfort of having the dressing changed.

The nurse worked quickly and silently. The entire time, Julie was acutely aware of Daniel's presence beside her—his power, his strength, his *being*. And for the first time, that power and strength scared her.

Sasha was released from the hospital the next day. Julie insisted she stay with her, at least through the weekend. And when Sasha brought up working Monday, Julie told her it was out of the question.

By Sunday, Julie could clean and dress Sasha's back without breaking into a cold sweat. The sense of fear she'd had in the hospital hadn't returned. Of course, she hadn't seen Daniel since Friday either. He'd called a few times, but between caring for Sasha and working out the schedule for how to run the shop alone, she hadn't been able to see him.

She wasn't ignoring him, she told herself; she was busy.

And if she put the red bracelet in her top dresser drawer, it was only because she didn't know when the next meeting would be.

She didn't quite know how to reach Sasha. Her once happy-go-lucky friend had sunk deep inside herself and refused to be drawn out. She answered questions with a "yes" or "no" and otherwise kept her conversation to as few words as necessary. Dena called on Sunday afternoon, but Sasha refused to talk to her. Instead she told Julie to tell her she was sleeping.

Julie didn't want to leave her alone on Monday, but she had no choice—the shop had obligations to meet. Someone had to be there. Fortunately, it was a busy day, so she was able to keep her mind occupied with thoughts other than her hurting friend and Daniel.

Her cell phone rang right after she closed the door behind the day's last customer. She looked at the display and sighed. Eventually, she would have to face the turmoil she was trying to ignore.

"Hey, Daniel."

"Good to hear your voice, how are you doing?"

"Busy." She eyed the clock on the wall, trying to judge how long it would take to get home and fix something for her and Sasha to eat. "Doing everything by myself is a bit much, you know?"

"I imagine it is, and once you get home, you'll be tending Sasha." His voice dropped. "Who takes care of you?"

She closed her eyes, knowing he probably heard her distancing herself every time they spoke. "I've been taking care of myself for a long time."

He didn't have to say anything; she could feel his displeasure through the phone. Something deep inside started to hurt.

"I'm sorry," she finally said. "I'm just so tired." It wasn't much of a lie.

"I need to stop by your place tonight and speak to Sasha," he said.

"We'll be there. About what time?" She hated the way they were talking, as if there was nothing between them. It just wasn't possible for her to do anything else at the moment.

"Seven."

"Okay, I'll make sure she's awake. See you then," she said, and hung up with a softly spoken good-bye.

I'm so sorry, Daniel.

· · ·

*D*aniel hung up the phone with a muttered curse. He was losing her. When Sasha was in the hospital, he'd felt it, although he'd hoped once she was released, it would be better. And maybe it would get better. It hadn't been that long. He just needed to give her space.

He raked a hand through his hair. Damn Peter and whatever the hell had been going through his mind Thursday night. Even after talking with him, he still wasn't exactly sure what transpired, but he would get to the bottom of it. He had a meeting set up with him before he needed to head out to talk to Sasha.

Sasha.

He knew it wasn't his fault and that there was nothing he could have done to prevent it, but he still felt guilty. She was a submissive in his group and he should have protected her. Had he missed some sign in Peter? He'd replayed in his mind all the times he'd seen him with a submissive and nothing stood out as being off.

Even still, whenever he thought of Sasha, he remembered the mass of welts and cuts on her back and it made him sick. As the recognized bullwhip expert in the group, he knew the training and practice its use required. Likewise, he recognized the handiwork of one who didn't know what he was doing. His only question was how Peter hadn't ended up in the hospital himself from the whip coming back to hit him.

He both dreaded and looked forward to seeing Julie. But even with all the turmoil he felt about their floundering relationship, he forced himself to focus on his upcoming conversation with Sasha. His heart was heavy when he pulled into Julie's driveway hours later.

Julie wasn't smiling when she opened the door. She simply pushed it wide open to let him pass. Sasha sat on the couch, her head down. He knew he was there for her, but he couldn't ignore Julie.

He cupped her shoulder. "I can only imagine what you're thinking and feeling, but don't shut me out. Please."

There was a particular sadness in her reply. "I'll try."

It was the best he could hope for.

Sasha stood up as he walked into the living room. "Ma-Ma-Master Covington."

He flinched and waved to the couch. "Please. Have a seat and call me Daniel."

"Can Julie stay?"

Typically, he liked to have a third person present for conversations like the one to come. However, he'd be lying to say he thought it a good idea for Julie to be that person. Regardless, she was the only one available, she had some knowledge of the lifestyle, and she was fiercely loyal to Sasha.

"Of course," he said. "Julie, will you join us?"

By the look on her expression, Julie didn't think it a good idea for her to be present either. That she nodded and took a seat beside her friend spoke volumes about her character and fortitude.

"First off," he said, "I want to apologize for what you've been through. I feel quite protective of the group's submissives and for something like this to happen on my watch? 'I'm sorry' just doesn't convey my feelings."

"You weren't there," Sasha said. "You shouldn't feel guilty."

"That's the funny thing about guilt. It's rarely reasonable."

That at least got him a half smile from Sasha. He said it intentionally to lighten the mood but also because it was true. If he knew anything about human nature, Sasha was probably dealing with her own guilt over the situation.

"The other senior members and I met with Peter earlier," he said. "I don't know if you're interested in his account, but I can tell you if you want."

Sasha nodded warily. "Okay."

"He claims he forgot the bell. Completely unacceptable for a Dom of any experience level. It's probably overkill, but we'll be stressing the importance of safe words, and how to use them when playing with gags, at every group meeting, every breakout, and every play party going forward."

"I don't think there's such a thing as overkill when it comes to safe words," Julie said. "For either party."

He looked to her in surprise. She'd so staunchly stressed her dislike for Peter, he wasn't prepared to hear her even suggest Sasha shared some of the blame.

I'm proud of you, kitten.

"Agreed," he said.

"What else did he say?" Sasha asked.

"He has no excuse for the whip and admits it was a

mistake. He'd watched a few demo scenes and thought he could handle it."

Sasha's expression drifted to somewhere else and her fist opened and closed repeatedly. Julie took her hand and whispered something to her with no response.

"Sasha," he commanded as gently, but firmly, as possible. "Right here with me. Focus on me. On my words. Nothing else."

Something inside the wounded submissive flickered to life and her gaze focused on him. She looked surprised for a second, but then she frowned and slipped her hand out of Julie's.

She was in a worse frame of mind than he'd thought and he decided to edit the remainder a bit.

"Peter thought you had gone into subspace. It was only after he realized you were bleeding and had gone slack in your bonds that he checked and discovered you'd passed out."

Julie kept her hand on Sasha's and she whispered to her friend. Sasha nodded.

Daniel cleared his throat. "While he did the right thing by taking you to the hospital and calling me, that the scene even progressed to that point is reprehensible. And as a submissive, you should have never let the scene start in the first place. The principal group members have called for a discipline session for you both to be held at my house on Friday."

Sasha simply nodded, but Julie's head jerked up in surprise. "For them both? What?"

"Sasha is dealing with the consequences of her misjudgment. I can't imagine the group to call for any action against her."

"But they might?" Julie's eyes grew big. "Are you serious?"

"It's standard procedure for us to at least speak with the parties involved."

"I can't believe—"

Sasha cut her off. "I understand. I'll be there."

"And I will be, too," Julie said.

He thought that would be a horrible idea. "Julie, I'm not sure—"

"Is there a group rule preventing my attendance?"

"No, but as your . . ." One look in her eyes told him not to finish the sentence. If he said he could forbid her as her Dom, he had no doubt that in her current frame of mind, she would tell him where he could shove his playroom. On the other hand, he feared if she attended the session on Friday night, she might tell him the same anyway. It was a lose-lose situation no matter how he looked at it.

"No," he said. "There's not a group rule preventing your attendance. I would just ask you to make sure you think it's the best idea for you to attend."

He'd known her to be a stubborn woman, but never had that been clearer than with her next words. "Just because something isn't good for you doesn't mean it isn't good for me."

She was drifting farther and farther away and there was

nothing he could do about it. For a moment he wished he could command her to stay by his side, but reason soon replaced that thought. He wanted her to be with him of her own free will. And if her free will took her elsewhere, he had to accept that.

No matter how much her leaving would crush his heart.

EIGHT

*F*riday night, Julie drove Sasha to Daniel's house with a heavy heart. Sasha was doing better physically and mentally, but Julie felt as if her own being were falling apart. Everything had seemed so simple before Sasha's incident. A week later nothing made sense.

She'd avoided answering Daniel's calls and had not returned any of them. For the last day, he hadn't even attempted to call. She told herself she needed time to think, to reassess her need to submit. Was it really a need, or had it been desirable only because it had been Daniel she was submitting to?

And even if she had a need to submit sexually, would it be wise to give in to that need? In giving someone that much power over her, would she be placing herself in a situation to be harmed like Sasha? People denied themselves daily. It was called self-control. She had lived thirty years without submitting; she could do it again.

She pulled into Daniel's driveway and her gaze fell on her bracelet. She had chosen not to wear the red one, but instead put on the white. Undecided. Just observing.

Or perpetual state of denial?

Guessing by the number of cars present, they were some of the last to arrive. Beside her, Sasha was silent as they made their way to the front door. But then again, she had been silent all week. The best thing Julie could say about Sasha was that she didn't open and close her fist in a silent safe word as often as she had days ago.

Daniel opened the door at their knock. Dark circles rimmed his eyes. He looked tired but resolved. He didn't look surprised to see her, but he did flinch when he saw the white bracelet.

"Sasha," he said. "If you would go on downstairs, please. The room to the right of the playroom. I need a word with Julie."

Sasha nodded and left her alone with the man she'd been avoiding for days. Julie and Daniel remained in the foyer, each watching the other, as Sasha's footsteps grew quieter and quieter.

Julie couldn't help but think back to the Friday nights she'd been welcomed into his house, but how very different they'd been. Before, she'd been excited and aroused. At that moment, she felt fear and sadness.

He waited until Sasha was out of sight before speaking.

"I need you to understand I would have been well within my rights to deny you entrance tonight. In fact, I came very close to doing so."

She started to speak, but he held a hand up.

"No," he said. "You've refused to talk to me for days. You're in my house now, so you can listen. I decided to let you come tonight because I won't hide what I am. If you're going to be with me, you have a right to know. I live by a set of rules and when those rules are broken, there are consequences. And you can wear that white bracelet if you think you can convince yourself in doing so that you're something you're not, but—"

"That's not what I'm doing."

His expression grew hard. "Don't interrupt me. The fact remains, you were born submissive and you know it. The only question is, what are you going to do about it? Because as much as you may try to tell yourself otherwise, you were never more content and at peace than you were on your knees before me."

She shouldn't argue with him. Deep inside, she knew he was right.

Shouldn't argue, but she did anyway. "Sometimes we have to deny ourselves in order to survive."

He opened his mouth as if to disagree, but instead he shook his head. "There's a time and a place for this conversation. This isn't it. You want to be here. Fine. Just know there is no safe wording tonight. You may get up and leave, but you can't stop what the group decides."

Before she could even attempt to process what he meant, he was speaking again.

"Downstairs. Room to the right of the playroom."

Though she had walked down the stairs to his playroom numerous times before and experienced a multitude of emotions while doing so, walking down the stairs to meet with the principal group members was unlike anything she'd done in the past. There had been fear the first time, but even then, it had been tinged liberally with an underlying desire. As she opened the door beside the playroom, all she felt was fear.

Fear for what was about to happen. Fear that Daniel was right about everything. And fear that she would never again experience the joy she'd felt at his feet.

The room she entered was a sitting area of sorts with plush chairs situated in two facing lines. Sasha sat on the far left facing her, Peter on the far right. There were three chairs between them. Dena sat next to Sasha, and Jeff, the Dom who wanted to question her at the group meeting, the one Daniel had all but thrown out so he could speak to her privately, sat in the middle. The chair next to Peter was vacant.

Julie took the last empty seat in the opposite line and wished she were anywhere else, doing anything else. She only recognized Cole sitting in her row. He showed no reaction to seeing her and she wondered what, if anything, Daniel had told him. In addition to Cole's, she counted two other black bracelets, as well as one green, and two red. She couldn't remember if Sasha had hers on, but a quick glance confirmed the red band was in place around her friend's wrist. Peter had no bracelet.

The door behind her closed and she jumped.

"Jeff," Daniel said, walking into the room. "Everyone's here, why don't you start?"

She'd assumed Daniel would run everything, but instead he sat in the vacant seat and turned to Jeff. He didn't look her way at all.

Though she didn't know what the meeting would entail, the strict sense of protocol didn't come as a surprise to her. Everything about the group she'd seen or heard so far had been firmly structured. Perhaps that was partially why what had happened with Sasha shocked her so much. She'd not expected a Dom in this group to act out wildly.

After opening the meeting, Jeff nodded to Sasha. In a soft, but captivating voice, she recalled the events of the night she got hurt. Julie was proud of her; only once did she make her safe word signal with her hand. When she finished, Dena leaned close and whispered something to her, then patted her shoulder.

Jeff then asked Peter to recount the events of that night from his point of view, and Julie balled her hands so tightly, her nails dug into her palms. She'd never understood what attracted Sasha to him. He was the most nondescript guy she could imagine. Average height. Average build. Average appearance. When he started speaking, he sounded and looked resolved, but as he spoke, his voice lost that resolution. When he described Sasha's unresponsive body, his voice broke.

He finished and sat down, head hanging down.

"Thank you, Sasha. Thank you, Peter," Jeff said. He addressed the row Julie was sitting in. "Both parties have been questioned previously and we believe what they have told you tonight is a true and accurate representation of what occurred last week."

Julie kept her eyes on Sasha. She looked okay, but Julie was glad Dena was beside her.

Jeff continued. "It's been decided both parties will be allowed to remain as active members following their reprimand with these provisions: Peter, you will be reenrolled in the mentee program. We've assigned you to Master Greene." He nodded to the man sitting at Julie's right. "In addition, you are not to engage in play with a submissive in our group without an approved member present for a period of two years. Do you understand and accept?"

That's it? Julie wanted to yell as Peter agreed. That was a slap on the wrist. She bit the side of her cheek so she wouldn't say anything.

"Sasha," Jeff said. "You will give a presentation at a future group meeting on safe words and why you should never play without one. Do you understand and accept?"

"Yes, Master Parks," Sasha said.

Julie gave silent thanks Sasha would still be in the group and that all she had to do was give a presentation. She was still mulling over how unfair it was that Peter got off so easily when Jeff started speaking again.

"Peter, your required reprimand is thirty lashes with the bullwhip. You will be gagged to ensure your silence, as you silenced the submissive who gave you her trust. If you accept, Master Covington will administer tonight."

Julie's mouth dropped open and she shifted her gaze to Daniel. His expression was grave and she realized in that moment he'd known what would be required of Peter. What would be required of him. He'd probably tried to persuade her to stay away because he remembered her panic in the playroom. But because she insisted on coming to the meeting, she would have to witness her fear, her hard limit.

She swallowed a moan.

"Sasha," Jeff said, and Julie straightened her back, scared anew for her friend. "It's the agreement of all involved that you have suffered enough for your poor judgment. Your only additional requirement is that if Peter agrees to submit to the whip, you will watch."

All the color drained from Sasha's face, but she nodded.

"Do you need time to decide, Peter?" Jeff asked.

"No, sir," Peter said, and Julie noted he'd turned as white as Sasha. "I'll submit. But if I may, can I address Sasha privately?"

Daniel answered. "No. If she wants to talk, you can go to the far corner, but you'll remain where you can be seen."

Sasha didn't look like she particularly wanted to talk with Peter, but she nodded as Dena whispered to her. "I'll talk," she said.

Julie didn't miss the look that passed between Daniel and Dena. He didn't seem overly pleased with the blonde, but Dena basically lifted her chin and gave him an I-couldn't-care-less look.

He stood up and Julie thought he'd go scold Dena, but instead he walked toward her.

"Julie, I need to talk with you, in the playroom. Jeff, keep an eye on those two," Daniel said with a nod at the corner where Peter was now talking quietly with Sasha. Sasha stood with arms crossed, shoulders slightly hunched.

"Will she be okay?" Julie asked.

"Yes, Jeff will ensure it."

She nodded. The stern-looking Dominant appeared to have everything under control.

Daniel led her to the playroom. Again, her feelings upon entering this room were so different from what they had been before. The other times there had been excitement and desire between them. Walking into the playroom that Friday night, all she felt was empty.

He opened the door and she gasped as she entered. The whipping post was centered at the back of the room.

"You need to get it out of your system now so you can be strong for Sasha."

She nodded. He knew how she'd react and he'd brought her in here so she would be prepared. "Thank you."

His eyes were sad. "I care a great deal for you, Julie. I hope you know that."

"I know." She cared a great deal for him, too. That was why everything hurt so much.

He looked like he wanted to say something else, but instead he walked farther into the room. "Everyone will stand here. Peter and I will be in the back. I need space when working with a whip."

Her knees wobbled. Fuck, she hoped she could do this.

"My entire concentration will have to be on what I'm doing," he said. "I need to know you'll be okay. Take deep breaths. Close your eyes. Leave if you have to."

She filled her lungs and exhaled deeply. "I'll be okay."

He walked to his cabinets and took something out. Silently, he passed it to her.

"What's this?" she asked. It looked like a diamond-shaped piece of Styrofoam.

"It's part of how I practice. This was a rectangle earlier today."

She traced her trembling finger down one neatly cut edge in awe of his strength and accuracy. "You did this with a whip?"

"I'm the single-tail expert of the group."

"It'll hurt him?"

"Yes."

His gaze was filled with questions when she looked up at him. Unfortunately, she had no answers. Not the ones he needed and not the ones she wanted. She handed the foam back to him. "Thank you for bringing me here."

"If you want to leave, I'll have Cole drive Sasha home," he said. "You don't have to stay."

But she did. She had to stay for Sasha and for herself and, for a tiny part, for Daniel. "I'm okay."

He brushed her cheek with the back of his hand. "My brave, brave girl."

She closed her eyes, lost herself in his touch, and tried not to think about how it hurt he didn't call her "kitten."

"I'm not so brave," she whispered.

"Look at me," he said, capturing her face in his hands. "I never lie. You're braver than you think. When you finally realize it for yourself, that's when everything will make sense and you'll lose that confused feeling."

He tipped her head forward and placed a soft kiss on her forehead. "I need a few minutes to prepare and get in my headspace. Let me take you back to the group."

He left after taking her back to the meeting room. From the corner of her eye, she saw Cole slip out as well. Glancing around the room, she noticed Sasha was no longer speaking with Peter, but stood surrounded by Dena and other submissives. Peter was in deep conversation with Master Greene.

She closed her eyes, still feeling the touch of Daniel's lips on her forehead, and only opened them when Jeff instructed everyone to move into the next room. Dena caught her eye and motioned for her to join her. In unspoken agreement, they led the way with Sasha between them.

Daniel stood beside the whipping post, his arms crossed. Julie recognized his expression immediately and shifted her eyes to the floor. It took all her self-control not to drop to her knees in supplication. Her belly twisted at the realization she still craved it. Still needed it.

Cole stopped them from moving any closer. "Stay here. We don't want anyone to get too close or accidentally move within range."

Sasha swayed against Julie and stumbled forward.

Cole caught her, placing his hands on her shoulders. "Easy there, little one. Are you okay?"

Sasha nodded and glanced down at his bracelet. "Yes, sir."

"Look at me. Do you need to sit? Should I get you a chair?"

"No, sir. I'm fine."

Cole didn't look convinced. "Inhale deeply through your nose for me. Good girl. Now out through the mouth. Good job. Again."

Julie had respected Cole as a writer, but watching him with Sasha, she realized she respected him as a Dom, too.

"Feel better?" he asked Sasha after she'd settled.

"Yes, sir."

"Don't lock your knees." He looked to Julie. "Good to see you again, Julie."

"Likewise."

His lips tightened into a thin line and his accent was clipped. "Address me properly, sub."

She stared at him in shock. At the moment he didn't

look at all like the easygoing journalist who'd entertained her at dinner weeks ago. Instead he looked hard and unyielding.

"My bracelet's white," she said.

His eyes were cold. "Let me assure you of two things. One, my eyesight is perfect; therefore, I know exactly what color your bracelet is. And two, you don't want me to ask you to do something twice."

She believed him, adding "scary" to the list of adjectives to describe him. "Good to see you again, too, sir."

He nodded and went to stand beside Dena.

A hush descended on the room as Peter and Jeff entered. Peter's shirt was off and Jeff kept a hand on his upper arm as though he feared the other man would flee. Julie's stomach dropped to her knees when the pair reached Daniel and he buckled Peter to the post with his back facing the crowd.

Daniel placed a hand on Peter's shoulder and spoke quietly to the bound man. Peter nodded at whatever it was Daniel said and even from where she stood, Julie saw Peter's body flinch. Jeff took a gag, buckled it around Peter's head. Then Jeff moved to stand in front of him, facing the crowd, but his attention was on Peter.

It was as if the entire room held its breath when Daniel stepped forward, coiled whip in hand.

Sweat dripped down Julie's shoulder blades and she tried to reconcile the whip-wielding man in front of her with the one who'd pressed a sweet kiss to her forehead less than thirty minutes earlier. She wanted to close her eyes, but found herself mesmerized as Daniel swung the whip over his head and brought it down across Peter's back.

One.

Beside her, Sasha jumped and Julie didn't have to look down to know she was giving her silent safe word.

The whistle of the whip once more broke the stillness, followed by the unmistakable slash of its tail meeting flesh.

Two.

By five, Sasha was mumbling under her breath. By ten, Daniel was breathing heavily. By fifteen, Julie would have given damn near anything to leave the room and she knew they were only half-done.

Daniel became another person in front of her. She didn't doubt his claim at being an expert with the whip. In his hand, the implement became an extension of himself. He was more than an expert; he was an artist. But her stomach felt sour as she saw the welts appear on Peter's back, because she realized Daniel's canvas was flesh.

When the count became twenty, she started counting down. Ten more and she could leave. Nine. Eight.

She moved her gaze from Daniel to Peter and though she knew nothing about whips, she could tell the difference between Sasha's back and Peter's. Where Sasha's had been a mess of crisscrossing lines, the marks on Peter were evenly placed and completely symmetrical.

Three.

Two.

One.

Had she been paying attention to Sasha the way she should have been, she would have anticipated her fall. As it was, Cole caught her seconds before she hit the floor.

"Easy, now," he said, scooping her up as if she weighed nothing. "Dena, blanket please."

"Is she okay?" Julie asked Cole, feeling rather weak herself.

"Master Greene," Cole said, still holding Sasha. "Bring me two chairs."

Seconds later, Julie was being helped into a chair by the Dom she recognized as Peter's new mentor.

"Are you okay?" he asked, one hand on her shoulder.

"Yes, sir," she said, the simple act of sitting down making her feel better.

Beside her, Cole sat holding Sasha in his lap, a blanket tucked around her legs. He looked slightly uncomfortable, but he held her all the same, and when she started to fidget, he murmured softly to her.

Julie risked a look at Daniel.

Peter had been released and the gag removed. He stood near the post, shoulders shaking, while Daniel dressed his back. In her mind, though, she still pictured him with the whip, his face hard as stone, and his arm moving back only to strike again.

Her stomach rolled once more.

"Master Greene," Daniel said as he finished taking care of Peter's wounds, and his voice was rough and deep. "Bring your mentee his shirt."

Once Daniel had helped Peter into his shirt and talked to him face-to-face, he turned and walked across the room with long, quick strides. He breezed past Julie's seat, and she wasn't sure if she was hurt or relieved he didn't look her way, but his face was focused only on the exit.

"Should I go to him, sir?" Dena asked Cole.

"No," Cole said. "He has to handle it his own way. Let him be."

"Red," Sasha said, eyes blinking. "Red."

"Shh, little one," Cole said, rubbing her arms. "You're safe. It's okay."

Sasha's eyes flew open and she struggled to break free. "I'm fine. Let me go. Please, sir. Please."

Cole gently unwrapped the blanket and helped her to her feet. "Are you sure?"

"Yes, thank you, sir."

Julie felt cold taking in the scene around her. From Peter, hunched and hurting at the front of the room. Sasha, troubled and trembling while trying to be strong. Even Daniel, who'd left the room as though the demons of hell were following behind him. Nothing spoke of wholeness or completeness. All of it spoke of danger and darkness. And in that moment she decided once and for all that BDSM was not for her.

NINE

aniel wasn't surprised when Cole found him in his office hours later. The house was empty and quiet, all the group members having left, showing themselves out. Or maybe Cole had done it. Daniel wasn't sure. He swirled the scotch in his glass. He wasn't sure he cared.

"Knock. Knock," Cole said, stepping inside the office.

"Go away."

"No. It's been three hours and that's your limit. One hour to sulk, one to jog, one to think."

"It wasn't a normal scene." Daniel took a sip of scotch.

"Which is why I allowed you to sit in here and drink. Now it's time to talk."

"Fuck you, Cole."

"You know he deserved every lash you gave him and then some."

Daniel snorted.

"Just what I thought," Cole said. "This isn't about Peter."

"Of course it is. It's his damn fault. If it weren't for him, I'd still have her."

Cole poured himself a glass of scotch and sat down in the chair facing Daniel's desk. "I don't think so. If it wasn't Peter, it would have been something else. She's second-guessing, but she'll eventually find her way back."

Daniel shook his head. "You didn't see the look she gave me. Like I was a monster."

"That look wasn't for you. It was for Peter."

"Bullwhip is a hard limit for her."

"Did you give her the option to leave?"

Daniel nodded.

"Then it was her choice to stay."

The room was silent for several long minutes. Daniel swirled his drink, watching as the faint light bounced off the glass.

"Do you ever wish you weren't a Dom?" Daniel asked.

"No, but sometimes I wish I wanted kids."

"Not the same."

"Exactly the same. You can't help being a Dom any more than I can help not wanting kids. It's woven into our being." Cole downed his scotch and took Daniel's glass, set it on the far end of the desk. "Know who else has this problem?"

"Every damn person here tonight."

"Every damn person," Cole repeated. "Including one confused submissive."

"She was confused when she arrived tonight. Now she's scared. Confused I can deal with. Scared is something else entirely."

"You can deal with scared, too. Trust me, it's best she works through all this now, because when she does, she'll be yours one hundred percent."

It was too much to hope for, too outlandish to imagine. Daniel pushed his chair back and opened the bottom drawer. He put the plain white box he took out on top of his desk. "Open it."

Cole didn't look like he wanted to open it, but he pulled the box to his side of the desk and opened it with a resolved sigh. He stared at the contents for several long minutes.

"It's been two years?" Cole finally asked.

"Julie and I had a conversation before all this happened with Sasha. She wanted to wear a red bracelet to the group meeting. I explained that would label her as my submissive. She didn't care." Daniel nodded to the box. "I had that commissioned the next day. It arrived this afternoon."

The "that" in question was a platinum choker made of two delicately woven bands, one of which had diamonds running its entire length. On the clasp was a tag engraved with "Master Daniel's kitten" on one side and "Beloved" on the other. The collar fastened with a lock, worked by the key also in the box. "Kitten's Master," the key had on one side. The other side was blank in the hopes Julie would have her own words added.

"That's quite a collar," Cole said.

"She's quite a woman."

"She didn't know you were going to offer it to her?"

"I was going to surprise her."

Without saying a word, Cole got up and poured Daniel another glass of scotch.

*F*or the next five days, Daniel put off doing what he knew he had to do. Perhaps, he thought, part of him hoped Cole had been right and Julie would come around. As the days went by, though, and she didn't take his calls or return his messages, he knew he had to take the next step.

He had to set her free.

She looked surprised when she saw him at her door, but she opened it and let him inside. Dena had told him Sasha had moved back to her own place over the past weekend.

"How's Sasha?" he asked anyway.

"Good. She came back to work on Monday." She nodded toward the couch, but he shook his head.

"I'm glad she's recovering well."

"Dena's been by a few times. It helps Sasha to talk to her. Are you sure you don't want to sit?"

"I'm fine standing. How are you doing?"

She glanced at him and then looked to the floor. "You

told me once to be honest, so that's what I'm going to do. I'm scared. I know I'm a submissive, but I don't know what to do with it."

Just as he expected. "I can understand you're scared, but what I don't understand is why you're avoiding me."

She looked up, blinking back tears. "Because I look at you and I get all confused. I make up my mind to do one thing, but I look at you and second-guess myself."

It took all his strength not to touch her, to gently stroke her cheek and tell her it'd be okay. But that would be a lie and he never lied.

"I need you to remember two things," he said. "If you forget everything else I say today, I need you to remember this: my feelings for you run deep and strong and true. Second, having you give me your submission means more to me than I can express with mere words and I am honored you trusted me with it for a time."

"For a time?" Her forehead wrinkled. "I don't understand."

"I've been waiting for you to decide what you wanted, but you can't seem to figure it out. That tells me you're not ready."

"What?"

"I'm deciding for you," he said, crossing his arms. "It's over, Julie."

She sank into the couch. "You're breaking up with me?"

"I'm doing the best thing I can for you. I'm setting you free."

"It feels like the same thing."

It felt like metal bars encircled his heart. Sitting on the couch, she looked so small and fragile. He wanted nothing more than to sit beside her and take her into his arms. He was supposed to be her protector, not the one to cause her more pain.

"I know it does," he said. "Believe me when I say I'd rather cut my own arm off than hurt you in any way, but this is the only option that makes sense. The only option that allows you the type of safety you feel you need."

"Safety I *feel* I need?"

He sat beside her so they could talk on the same level. "You're a submissive. You will never feel safer than when you're under a Dominant's control."

She wiped her eyes. "How can you say that with what happened to Sasha? She wasn't safe with Peter."

"We're not talking about Sasha. We're talking about you."

"That's semantics."

"It's not semantics, Julie, and you're forgetting one very important difference."

"What's that?"

"I'm not Peter."

Her breath caught and he gave her a sad smile. He should feel insulted she thought for one second he could ever treat her the way Peter had treated Sasha. Instead, he just felt sad. Sad she let her fear rule her. Sad she didn't fight him. And sad for the fact that everything they could have been together was slipping through his fingers.

"I know you're not Peter."

He wondered if her words sounded as empty to her as they did to him.

"We both know that's not the truth or else we wouldn't be having this conversation." He stood up, suddenly tired. "Good-bye, Julie."

*J*ulie went to work the next day, but she was only going through the motions. Inside she felt like a robot. A windup robot, threatening to run down at any second. Her feet were like lead and it took too much energy to function. Sasha was still too wrapped up mentally in her own thoughts to notice, but when Dena stopped by to bring lunch, Julie moaned. There was no way she could hide what had happened from the sharp-eyed woman.

"I brought sushi," Dena called, gliding through the store, carrying bags into the break room in the back.

"Not really hungry," Sasha said.

"Me either," Julie echoed.

"You, too, Julie?" Dena stuck her head out of the break room door. "You're supposed to be on my side."

"I'm just not hungry, is that a crime?" She tried to make her voice sound as normal as possible, but it broke at the end.

"You okay?" Dena asked, stepping into the main room, her teasing gone.

Even Sasha looked her way.

Julie gripped the back of the chair in front of her. They were going to find out anyway. The normal group meeting was being held Thursday night. When she didn't show up, Dena would know something had happened. Wouldn't it be best if she heard it from her? If she heard it from Julie, maybe there wouldn't be any gossip. Daniel deserved more than to be relegated to gossip fodder.

Julie took a deep breath. "Daniel broke up with me yesterday."

They both spoke at once.

"He did?"

"Oh, Jules."

"It's okay," Julie said, blinking back new tears. "It's like he said, it's for the best. It's the best option for me."

Dena rolled her eyes. "Ugh. I hate it when they get all Dom and decide what's best for us. Hello? I have a mind."

"But part of me thinks he's spot-on. I was being all wishy-washy. And he was right to step in. That's just being a good Dom." She looked to where the two other women stood. "Right?"

The corner of Sasha's mouth lifted. "Count me out on judging someone as a good Dom."

Dena put an arm around the petite woman. "We all mess up. Don't let it get to you." She looked up at Julie. "You either."

"It's not so much letting it get to me." She nodded. "It's accepting Daniel was right. He is who he is and he accepts it. I am what I am and I choose not to act on it. That makes us incompatible."

She glanced over at Sasha, who was still embraced by the tall, willowy blonde. Her friend had told her the day Daniel walked into the shop that they weren't compatible. Even looking back, though, she wasn't sure if she was happy or sad she went against Sasha's advice.

In dating Daniel, she'd learned things about herself she'd never imagined. She'd met an incredible man. And, if she was totally honest, she'd admit that she had fallen in love with that incredible man. No, she decided, in looking back, she knew she couldn't allow herself to be sad with her choice to have a relationship with him. She could only allow sadness at how it ended. That it ended at all.

"I'm free now," Julie said. "That's important."

Dena removed her arm from Sasha's shoulder and walked back into the break room, without saying anything. Julie had the strangest suspicion she'd said the wrong thing and followed her.

"Did I say something to upset you?" she asked, watching while Dena went around the table setting up for lunch.

"I'm sorry." Dena placed the chopsticks down and took a deep breath. "I just don't know if you're ready to hear what I think."

Julie's heart started pounding like it did when she realized she'd done something very, very wrong. "Tell me," she whispered.

She hadn't known Dena long. Probably less than two

months. But in all that time, she'd never seen her more vulnerable than she seemed at that moment. Dena was the epitome of self-confidence, but right now she looked uneasy.

"I've been collared twice," Dena said. "The first was to the asshole. That was a mistake, but it lasted less than a year. The second . . . the second was wonderful."

Something a lot like grief lurked behind Dena's blue eyes and Julie couldn't help but ask, "What happened?"

Dena shook her head, blond hair tumbling across her forehead. "I don't want to talk about it. I only brought it up because I wanted you to understand."

"Understand what?"

"I'm unattached right now—I told you that when we first met—but I'm not *free*." Her fingers brushed her neck as if stroking an invisible collar. "I make do. I play with Doms and I help train the new ones, but *free* isn't how I would describe my life. The day he took his collar back was the day he sent me to the darkest, deepest prison imaginable."

Her words struck Julie in the center of her chest. She held a hand out, as if to touch her, but Dena shrank back.

"Dena, I'm sorry."

Dena closed her eyes. "It's okay. Most days I can deal with it. I just . . . always thought we'd get back together. But each time I see him, we drift farther and farther apart. I'm starting to think it'll never happen. Pretty soon we'll be strangers."

"You see him? He's in the group?" Julie's mind spun,

picturing the different Doms, trying to figure out which one still held Dena's heart.

"I said more than I planned to," Dena said. "Who he is doesn't matter. The important thing is you and Daniel. Regardless of what he said, you've got to come to terms with who you are yourself. But do me a favor and take some advice from someone who's been there. When the right Dom collars you, when you become his? That's when you find your wings. That's when you'll be so free, you'll fly."

*J*ulie gaped at Sasha. "You're going where?"

It was the next Thursday night and she'd just invited Sasha over for pizza and a movie. Julie still felt unsettled after Dena's advice a week earlier and had been looking forward to getting wrapped up in a movie. She'd guessed Sasha would feel the same. Sasha, though, had other plans.

"I'm going to the group meeting," Sasha said after they finished eating.

"That's what I thought you said. I just wanted to make sure." She wanted to take Sasha by the shoulders and shake her. How could she even think about going back after what happened with Peter?

"Don't look at me like that," Sasha said, and Julie noticed her lower lip trembled.

"Just give it a little bit. No one expects you to jump right back into it."

"I'm just going to a meeting. Dena's talking about legal issues within the community. It'll be safe. I'm not going to the party tomorrow."

"It'll be safe," Julie repeated, hands on her hips. "Always the measure by which I pick my weekend plans."

"Don't judge me."

"Don't give me a reason to. You've barely said four words all week and I'm just supposed to smile and nod when you walk back into what could trigger a panic attack?"

"At least I'm honest about who I am and what I need."

"Yeah, well, what you need put you in the hospital. You can hardly hold it against me if I'm a bit worried."

Sasha lifted her chin. "I'm doing this for me. Proving I can do it. I know I'm not ready to go back to a play party yet, but surely I can handle sitting and listening to Dena go on and on about legal matters."

Julie eyed her friend warily. It looked like Sasha had found her stubborn side again. Yet Julie still pictured her hunched over talking to Peter. "Will he be there?"

"No," Sasha whispered. "He's not allowed yet."

"I thought Jeff said he could remain in the group?"

"Master Greene's his mentor and he told him he couldn't attend yet."

A small smile tickled Julie's lips. "I knew I liked that Greene guy."

"You could go with me," Sasha said, a glimmer of uncertainty showing for the first time. "I'd feel better with a friend."

Julie reached out and put a hand on her shoulder. "I'll make you a deal. I won't say anything else about you going to the meeting as long as you don't say anything else about me not going."

Two hours later, Julie sat on her couch, not paying any attention to the movie on her television. Her mind ran trails this way and that, trying to guess what was happening at the group meeting. She pictured Daniel, sitting near the front, and hoped there wouldn't be any small talk about why she wasn't with him.

Daniel was strong, though; a little bit of gossip wouldn't bother him. But it might, she decided, send signals to unattached submissives that he was on the market. That he was available and looking. After listening to Dena, she no longer entertained thoughts the vivacious blonde had her eyes on him, but there were plenty of other single women in the group.

With a sigh, she turned the movie off and walked into her bedroom. Almost unbidden, her feet carried her to the dresser, and without stopping to think twice, she took out the red bracelet and slipped it on her wrist. Holding her arm out, she twisted it one way and then the other before taking the plastic band off and putting it back in the drawer.

She sat down heavily on her bed. She'd thought it best to keep her thoughts of being submissive separate from Daniel, but found it to be impossible. In her mind, the two were intertwined. If only she could decide if that was a good thing or a bad thing.

Grabbing a pillow, she rolled to her side, her mind drifting back to Daniel and the last time she'd been in his playroom.

He'd been evil.

Evil in a horribly pleasurable nightmarish game of bringing her right to the edge, only to jerk her back down.

He hadn't bound her. Instead, she'd been on her back, knees bent with feet flat against the padded table. Her hands had been fisted tightly at her side while she fought to obey the one command he'd given her: don't orgasm without permission.

He'd been doing wicked things to her body. His mouth had been hot, sucking her nipples just to the brink of pain and then scraping the sensitive tips with his teeth. And his hands . . . holy hell, his hands had been working a dildo in and out of her. Alternating short, shallow passes with deep, penetrating thrusts.

The entire time he'd been whispering.

"Can't wait to fuck you."

"Feel so good pushing my dick inside."

"Going to ride you hard."

Then, right when she thought she couldn't hold out anymore, right at the second before her body betrayed her and disobeyed him, he stepped away. Her breathing had been choppy and ragged, but his kisses were sweet and his praise generous as he told her how well she was doing and how proud he was. Her heart didn't have a chance to slow, though, before he once more worked her eager flesh into another frenzy. . . .

Julie opened her eyes and squinted at the lamplight in her bedroom. Her body burned, remembering Daniel's touch and command. It'd seemed so simple that afternoon. Everything about their time in the playroom seemed simple. In that room, there were only two people and the rules were easy to remember: he spoke and she acted. Why was it when she stepped outside everything got muddy?

She flipped to her belly, remembering the rest.

Her body quivered in restrained need. She'd been certain she'd come if he even breathed on her. His hands stroked her skin and she amazed herself by arching into his touch, but holding out once more. She was putty in his hands, his to command, and his to pleasure at will.

He gently pulled her from the table, only to bend her over it, and inside she rejoiced at the sound of his zipper being pulled down and the rip of a foil packet. Then his body was warm against hers and he'd whispered into her ear.

"Brace yourself, kitten. I'm hard and horny as hell." His fingers slid inside, ensuring she was ready for his cock. "This won't be soft or gentle, but you can come when you want and as often as you're able."

She gasped when he entered her fully with one powerful thrust. As promised, he rode her hard and long, and she lost count after her third climax. He'd been unrelenting in his quest for pleasure, unashamed in his use of her, and his cock drove mercilessly toward one goal. But as he stilled deep inside her body, breaking the silence of the playroom with the roar of his own release, she realized the truth of who she was. Who she is.

She is his.

Julie jerked, remembering. Had she really thought that?

She must have, the memory was so clear. Likewise, she remembered it running through her head while Daniel gathered her, afterward, in his arms and kissed her trembling flesh, calming her overly sensitized skin. He drew a warm bath and washed her with a careful touch.

She recalled brushing his rough cheek with her hand and how he pressed a kiss into her palm.

Her eyes burned, as she remembered that days later she got the call. How quickly she'd forgotten everything when she heard Sasha was in the hospital.

What if the call had never come? What if nothing had happened between Sasha and Peter? Where would she and Daniel be today?

Her concentration shattered with the sound of her doorbell.

Troubled, she jumped off the bed and ran to the door. Looking back at her through the peephole was Sasha. She'd been crying.

"Julie," she sobbed as the door opened. "Can I stay here tonight?"

Julie ushered her inside, grabbing tissues, and guiding her into the living room. "Yes, of course. Are you okay? What happened?"

"You were right." Sasha wiped her eyes and dropped onto the couch. "About everything."

"Oh, no."

"Yes, it was way too soon. And I don't care what anyone says, I'm never going back." A shudder ran through Sasha's body. "Ever."

     *A*s the last remaining members trickled out of the room, Daniel slowly filled his lungs with air and exhaled. His back ached and he was tired, but even still he knew what sleep he did claim in a few hours' time would be punctuated with dreams of Julie.

There had been some raised eyebrows and questioning glances when he showed up alone, but no one said anything to him directly. Both the blessing and the curse of being a senior member.

Jeff stood watching him. "You okay?"

"Yeah." He glanced at his friend. "Just thinking about Sasha. She didn't look too good when she left."

It was partially true. He'd also wondered briefly if he should call Julie and have her go by Sasha's house. Just as quickly, he knew he couldn't call Julie; it was much too soon and entirely too late. And if experience taught him anything, Julie wouldn't answer.

"I was surprised to see her back so soon," Jeff said.

Daniel pushed back from the table and took his phone out of his pocket. "I'll text Dena, have her reach out to Sasha."

Jeff gave him a curt nod and then added, "I was even more surprised to see Sasha here alone."

Daniel had been, too. Not that he ever imagined Julie showing up with her; he knew that wouldn't happen. Had Dena not been giving the talk, he was certain she'd have sat with Sasha. And several of the other group members had spoken with her, but they had been tentative and too careful.

"Julie's not up for discussion tonight," he said in response to Jeff's earlier statement.

"She's a strong woman, but she's hurting. She's going to need someone patient and resilient to help her heal," Jeff said. "To help her find herself once more."

Daniel stood up, steeling himself to go home and face his lonely bed. "Sasha's been a member for years. She'll find her way."

Jeff's gaze pierced him. "I wasn't talking about Sasha."

*D*aniel walked through his house an hour later. Dena had finally replied, texting back that Julie had answered Sasha's phone. While he was glad Sasha had such a supportive friend, the selfish part of him couldn't help but wonder how much further this would push Julie away from her submissive needs.

Jeff's words echoed in his mind. *Patient and resilient.* He felt certain he'd been both, but had he been patient and resilient enough? At one time he thought so. Had he, in fact, been self-serving and too quick to call everything off? When he was with Julie, hell, when he just thought of her, every emotion he experienced seemed magnified. But what was done was done.

His phone vibrated in his pocket and for the quickest of seconds, he thought it would be Julie. A quick glance told him otherwise.

"Cole," he said with a half smile. "How's India?"

"It smells."

Cole must not have arrived at his final destination yet. Usually when he was on assignment, Daniel didn't hear from him at all.

"Everything else okay?" Daniel asked.

There was a long silence from the other end of the line and he wondered if they'd been disconnected when Cole answered simply, "Kate sold the house."

He could only imagine how much that hurt. The final blow. The last good-bye. "Sorry to hear that."

"It's for the best. Neither one of us wanted it."

Neither one of them wanted it alone and without the other person, in other words. "Still . . ."

"Yes. Well," Cole said. "How was the group meeting?" he asked as if desperate to change the topic of conversation.

"Julie wasn't there. Sasha was."

"Certainly would have been better the other way around."

Daniel snorted.

"Still nothing from her?"

"No," Daniel said. "Still nothing."

"Don't beat yourself up. You did the right thing."

"If you love something, yada yada?"

"There's a lot of truth in that."

Yes, Daniel supposed, there probably was. Deep inside, he knew he'd made the right choice in doing what he had. Knew that as much as it hurt, he'd make the same choice again.

Then Cole surprised him. "Give her time. I have a strong suspicion she'll come back. Deep down she knows the truth about her submission."

Daniel almost dropped his phone. "What? How?"

"The night you whipped Peter, I made her call me 'sir.'"

"You what?"

"I greeted her and she replied with some flippant remark. You know what that does to me."

"Cole," he groaned. He knew his friend had a certain reputation in the playroom. The Badass Brit. Hell, he'd watched him scene before; he knew he could be a bastard. Honest and fair? Yes. Just harder than Daniel.

"I won't apologize."

"Wasn't asking you to."

"Just wanted you to know, deep down she knows."

It was too much to hope for. He had to change the subject. "Cole?"

"Yeah."

"You did the right thing, too. It wouldn't have been fair to you, Kate, or your child for you to have given in on something you feel so strongly about."

"Thanks," Cole said. "Sometimes you just need to hear the words."

*S*asha threw herself into work the next Monday. Julie thought she was trying to keep her mind busy so she didn't have to face whatever it was that had upset her at the group meeting. Sasha refused to talk about it, though, simply stating she was done with being a submissive.

Since Sasha had the shop covered, Julie decided to stop by Daniel's grandmother's place after lunch. While cleaning house on Sunday, she'd come across the books she'd promised the older lady. A weekday afternoon would be a safe time to go take them, she thought. After all, Daniel would be working.

Except he wasn't.

"Daniel," she said, taking a step backward when he opened his grandmother's door. "What . . . why . . . ?"

Daniel covered his surprise quickly and opened the door to let her inside. "I had to take her to the doctor's. We just got back and I've convinced her to nap." He nodded to the books in Julie's hand. "Wanted to swing by when I wouldn't be here?"

She lifted her chin, refusing to feel guilty. "Can you blame me?"

"No." His expression was sad. "I can't and I'm sorry, I didn't say it to be cruel."

The truth of his words—the truth that he wasn't a cruel man—made her feel warm inside. He cared for his sister and his niece, and took his grandmother to doctor appointments. She knew he'd asked Dena to check up on Sasha after the group meeting Thursday night.

Even in his playroom, where obedience was expected without question, he'd never treated her cruelly. He'd been patient, slowly introducing her to the unexplored side of her sexual nature.

She tentatively touched his arm. "No, I'm the sorry one."

She thought he looked tired and wondered if he tossed and turned the way she did. Did he lie in bed remembering their time together? Did those memories haunt him, too?

"Let me take those for you." He reached for the books. "You know you didn't have to bring them."

"I wanted to."

"I know and she'll love them." He walked into the sitting area and placed them on a table beside the couch. "Would you like to sit down? I'll get you a drink."

She was torn. Like before, being in the same room with him left her confused. One look at him and she felt lost in need and desire. A glance at his hands and she wanted them on her. She missed his smile, his wit, and his easygoing manner.

"Or if you need to get back," he said, misinterpreting her silence.

"No, it's fine." She sat on the couch, not ready to leave him just yet. "Sasha's got it covered."

He sat beside her. "How is she?"

"Overcompensating. Throwing herself into work. Refusing to talk."

"Do you think it'd be a good idea for her to talk with someone? Professionally?"

"At this point I'd suggest anything."

"That bad?"

"I just hate to see her hurting."

"I know how you feel," he said. "It's difficult to see someone you care about in pain."

She couldn't face the intensity of his gaze, knowing he was talking about them, so she dropped her head and played with a loose thread on her shirt. "I know you told me it was over, but I haven't stopped wanting. Needing."

"Julie," he said, softly. "I only did what I did to ease your internal turmoil. To give you what you thought you wanted."

"I know, but you can't command my mind the way you did my body."

"You just didn't give me enough time."

Her head shot up. "What?"

"A Dominant-submissive relationship takes time to build, especially when one of the participants is new." He scooted forward. "Do you remember that last day? When I commanded you not to orgasm?"

"Frequently," she confessed, earning a smile from him.

"Do you understand that, yes, part of the scene was taking control away from you, but it was also me learning you and your body?"

She shook her head.

"Learning what turns you on, what you like, what you love. How your face, body, and breathing look when you're about to come." He leaned toward her and her body answered in kind. "Your forehead wrinkles and your left eyebrow twitches, by the way."

She couldn't hold back the laugh. "What?"

"Right before you climax, your forehead wrinkles and your left eyebrow twitches."

He would know, of course, because he was an excellent Dominant. Exactly like he'd told her once before. And still, even after what happened to Sasha, to be in the same room with him left her achy and needy.

Perhaps, she wondered, that was because her body accepted what she was and refused to deny itself that need.

And in that moment she knew. She could pretend all she wanted that she wasn't a submissive, but pretending would never make it so. Daniel had helped her discover her true sexual self, and now that she knew the truth, she could never again deny it.

The only question to answer was, what would she do with that knowledge?

• • •

*D*ena nearly squealed when Julie asked her to come by for a talk the following weekend. Seeing Daniel again had ignited something inside her. Even watching Sasha deal with her own demons didn't deter it. During the day, Julie forced herself to focus on work, but at night she allowed the memories to wash over her. Memories of time spent in Daniel's playroom and in his bed, yes. But more important, memories of him.

"I've decided it doesn't matter," she told Dena over dinner Saturday night.

"What doesn't?"

"That I can't separate thoughts of being submissive from thoughts of Daniel."

"That sounds like progress."

They were sitting at Julie's kitchen table, eating chicken salads. Julie had thought of asking Sasha to join them, but decided at the last minute that Sasha wasn't in the right frame of mind yet. If Sasha were with them, Julie feared she wouldn't be able to speak freely with Dena.

"Really?" Julie asked. "Progress?"

"You've only been submissive to Daniel, so of course you find it difficult to separate them. And, frankly, until you do, you might not be able to."

Julie's fork slipped from her hand and clanked against her bowl. "Submit to someone else? That isn't where I saw this conversation going."

"Then you have to ask yourself if it matters." Dena shrugged. "Sounds like you've made up your mind it doesn't."

They ate in silence for a few minutes. Julie knew there was no way she'd even entertain thoughts of submitting to someone else.

"You know, I'm thinking," Dena said. She took a bite of salad and chewed before continuing. "What if you watched?"

"Watched what?"

"A scene. I could arrange it." Dena's face lit up as she talked. "I can get a Dom to play and let you watch. Could you do that, you think? Watch me in a scene?"

Julie found it hard to believe she was even having this conversation. More than that, was she seriously considering it? "I don't know."

"I think before you go any further, you should explore the dynamics a bit more. It could be very helpful to actually see what it looks like for a submissive to place herself before a Dominant. For a Dominant to control that submissive. Pretty hard to do when you're the one on your knees and if you're like me, you have no desire to be the one in control."

It made sense when Dena put it that way. Julie shifted in her seat. Didn't she owe it to herself to make an informed decision? Even if that meant watching?

*T*he next Saturday night Julie rode to Jeff's house with Dena. Dena's mood was somber, though she tried to hide it with little smiles and subtle teases. As they drove closer to their destination, she gave up and stopped talking altogether.

"You know," Julie said, "you don't have to do this."

Dena's expression went from borderline anxious to resolved in a flash. "I do. You need to see it before you make your mind up. See that it's so much more than kinky sex. It's more than a physical need—it's emotional and mental, too."

Julie decided not to think too much about the fact that she'd be watching her friend and a man she barely knew engage in BDSM play. Dena said she needed to see a scene from both perspectives and that the best way to do that would be to watch.

"Why Jeff?" Julie asked. Whenever she thought about the dark Dominant, she remembered his commanding voice as he presided over the meeting and his dispassionate manner as he spoke about Peter's punishment.

"Why not?" Dena asked. "He's available. He's an excellent Dom. Besides, Cole left, and even if he hadn't, I wouldn't pick him—"

"Why not?"

"Cole is, um . . ." She seemed to be having a hard time finding the word she wanted. "He's an excellent Dom, too. He's just a bit *intense* in the playroom."

"Intense?"

"He's known as the Badass Brit. Just don't ever call him that to his face."

Julie remembered the way he made her address him as "sir" the night of Peter's punishment. "I believe that."

"Which is fine. It's just not what I want you to experience right now. That leaves Master Greene, who's busy with Peter, and, well, I couldn't ask Daniel."

Julie squirmed in her seat, not wanting to go anywhere near Daniel playing with Dena.

"Not that he would have taken me up on the offer," Dena continued. "He hasn't played since you."

"Really?"

"He might have spoken the words to let you go, but his heart hasn't processed them yet."

Julie sat back in her seat, turned to the window, and smiled. Maybe all hope wasn't lost after all.

Jeff lived in a cabin-style house, set back in the woods. Dena had told her he owned a security company. A small two-man operation that did well enough to support his modest lifestyle. He'd turned outside lights on, which was helpful, Julie thought. Without them, they would be in complete darkness.

"Little bit scary, don't you think?" Julie asked. She couldn't even see if he had neighbors.

"Maybe a bit. Just until you get used to it." Dena's eyes were on the front door. Her demeanor had relaxed somewhat, and if anything, she looked full of anticipation.

Jeff met them at the door and let them into his house. The cabin look was continued inside with exposed wooden beams in the ceiling and spotless hardwood flooring made from wide planks. Though she'd thought the outside to be scary, inside it felt warm and inviting.

He greeted them both kindly and while he made small talk, Julie took a few minutes to get a good look at him.

He was just as dark as she remembered: dark wavy hair, dark eyes, and though his voice was pleasant enough, he didn't seem to smile often. She couldn't help but compare him with the woman at his side. With her blond hair, blue eyes, and lively personality, Dena appeared to be his polar opposite.

He led them into a spacious living room and motioned for them to sit down.

"Julie," he said, in the same deep, commanding voice she remembered. "This is an odd request for me. Normally, I don't invite people to my home to watch me play, but I'm doing this as a favor to Dena and to Daniel."

Her heart raced and she wondered if Daniel knew what she was doing tonight. "Thank you, sir."

"Daniel's a good friend of mine, but he needs a woman strong enough to take what he has to give." Jeff's gaze grew even more intimidating. "If you have no interest in being that woman, I suggest you leave now."

Julie met his gaze, hoping to show how serious she was. "I'm here to watch. Hopefully what I witness tonight will help me make certain."

He studied her quietly for several long seconds, as if attempting to discover the truth of her words. She hoped he didn't find her lacking. Finally, he nodded and stood up.

"Ten minutes, Dena. Julie, down the hall to your left, second door on the right. There's a chair. Make yourself at home."

"You don't have to do this," she told Dena once more after Jeff left.

"I know," Dena whispered. "I want to."

A little over ten minutes later, Julie sat in a chair in what appeared to be a spare bedroom turned playroom. It was smaller than Daniel's, but well stocked with equipment she recognized. Dena knelt, naked, in the middle of the room and Julie's heart ached as she remembered how she would wait in a similar manner for Daniel.

Jeff strode into the room with such quiet authority, she sat up straighter and fought the urge to mimic Dena's downward gaze. Instead, she watched as he came to a stop just in front of the pale submissive. His eyes burned with intensity so strong, she almost wondered if she imagined it.

His voice was gruff when he spoke. "It's been a long time, Angel."

Dena's breath hitched, but she calmly answered, "Too long, sir."

"Did you think I'd go easy on you if you brought a friend?"

"No, sir."

"What's your safe word?"

Dena hesitated, just for a second. "Wings, sir."

"Noted." With one hand, he reached out and stroked her head. "How does it feel to be kneeling before me again, Angel?"

Dena's reply was almost a sigh. "It makes me feel happy, sir."

"I almost said *no* to your request. How would that have made you feel?"

"Sad, sir."

"Sad for your friend?"

"For me."

He stood still and seemed to be weighing her words. Julie sat mesmerized at the emotion flowing between the two. She jumped when Jeff snapped his fingers.

"Show me how grateful you are I said yes."

Dena didn't hesitate, but slid gracefully to her forearms. Her long blond hair hid her face, but Julie knew she was kissing his feet. His eyes were closed and he was breathing rather heavily.

"Kneel," he said when she'd finished both feet.

Dena went back to her waiting position and Jeff turned away to take something from the tabletop nearby. A riding crop swung from his hand when he stood before Dena again. He trailed it down her thigh, giving her knee a flick with the tip. She spread her legs wider.

"Someone's gotten lazy."

He walked behind her, all the while running the crop along Dena's body, adjusting her posture this way and that. "Tsk. Tsk. Tsk. Are you this sloppy kneeling for everyone or is it just me?"

"I'm sorry for being sloppy, sir."

"That didn't answer my question, Angel. Look at me.

You remember what happens when you neglect to answer a question?"

"Yes, sir," Dena said, meeting his gaze, but she didn't seem upset or worried. She looked peaceful and calm.

"Go," he said, and Dena stood to her feet and walked to an odd-looking bench. He nodded toward Julie. "For the benefit of our guest, tell me what the penalty is for not answering a direct question."

"Five swats with the implement of Master's choice," Dena said, draping herself across the bench.

"Plus five more for the improper use of the title 'Master.' Only my collared submissive addresses me as such in this room."

Dena winced. "Sorry, sir."

Jeff walked to stand at her side and ran a hand over her exposed bottom, trailed a finger between her legs. "Doesn't feel like you're sorry at all. Feels like you're looking forward to my punishment. Count, my naughty Angel."

Julie didn't know if it was because she'd never seen anything like what played out before her or if it was just the magnetism of the couple involved, but she found herself unable to look away. Julie had thought Jeff to be hard and abrasive before. She had been partially correct. Jeff pushed, tormented, and teased Dena. Yet the entire time, his expression showed fierce concentration—though at times, she thought she glimpsed something more desperately trying to break through.

For her part, Dena looked hungry, eager to please and serve. In front of Julie, her friend transformed into a picture of satisfied contentment. When Jeff bent her over his padded table and bound her, Dena complied with a devotion that spoke of absolute trust. When he worked her with a flogger, Dena filled the room with sounds of pleasure and needy desire. Even when he finally took her, hard and harsh from behind, there was a look of pure bliss on Dena's face.

But it was after, when the bonds were loosened, and the room silent, when Jeff sat on the floor with Dena held tenderly in his arms, that she knew. For Jeff and Dena, Julie was no longer in the room. Jeff whispered something to Dena and lightly kissed her cheek. Dena turned her face toward him and their lips met briefly.

Somehow, Jeff and Dena entwined in each other's arms, whispering and sharing stolen kisses, became exponentially more intimate than all the things they'd done before. Julie no longer felt comfortable watching, so as quietly as she could, she stood up and slipped out of the room. It wasn't until she made it back into the living room that she realized she'd been crying.

*I*t was almost an hour before Jeff let them leave. Even then, he made Julie drive. Dena argued with him, but he wouldn't be moved. The dark, dour Dom was back, replacing the affectionate lover of an hour before. But Julie took his secret and tucked it away so she could study it later.

They were halfway back to her house before Julie turned to Dena. "So, uh, you and Jeff, huh?"

Dena gave her a dreamy nod.

"So does this mean you're back together?"

"No," Dena said. "But let me bask in the aftermath a bit longer before making me face reality, okay?"

Julie had a plethora of questions she wanted to ask, but out of respect for Dena, she kept them to herself. As they drove into the night, she glanced to the side and watched a single tear make its way down Dena's cheek.

Julie still noted a lingering sadness in Dena's expression when the blonde came to talk with her the next day. They sat around Julie's table, sipping coffee, and chatted about a little bit of everything before the conversation turned to the previous night.

"Is it odd, playing in front of someone like that?" Julie asked.

"I've done it so often, I don't think about it much. Maybe it was the first few times." Dena's gaze grew wistful and Julie imagined her to be thinking about Jeff. "The thing is, when I'm there, in the moment, my attention is so focused on him, there's no room for anyone else."

Julie had expected her to say as much. It was obvious in watching the pair the night before that Julie's presence had not been acknowledged above the bare minimum.

"What did you think?" Dena asked.

"It was"—Julie searched for the right word—"intense. So much more than I thought it would be. But it also reminded me of a dance, though that doesn't seem right either. It's just the way your bodies moved. Together. How he would make a move and you'd somehow know just how to respond. Is it always like that?"

Dena placed her coffee on the table. "No, not always. Remember, Jeff and I have played many, many times and I wore his collar once. There's more intensity to be expected in a relationship like ours. Emotions don't have to be involved, of course, but I've always found play to have more of an edge when they are. That's why I picked Jeff. I wanted you to see the emotion."

"The emotion you still won't talk about?" Julie asked, figuring it wouldn't hurt to try again to find out what happened between Dena and Jeff.

"Nice try, but no. Besides, we're talking about you."

"One day," Julie promised, "we're going to talk about you."

"Not if I can help it."

"You didn't see what I saw. You didn't see the emotions I saw between you and Jeff."

Dena grew even more serious. "That's the thing, don't you understand? The emotion between you and Daniel would be the same."

Julie thought about that. It hadn't occurred to her while watching or even as she thought back on the scene later. Yet, there was truth in the statement and she shivered, imagining Daniel watching her the way Jeff watched Dena.

Across the table, a self-satisfied smile covered Dena's face and she sipped her coffee.

"Ask yourself this," Dena said. "Have you ever felt more safe or protected than you were under Daniel's command?"

Julie didn't have to think too long to know the answer to that one. She hadn't. Whenever she knelt at his feet, she knew he would guard her with his life. Just thinking about it made her yearn for that feeling.

"No," Julie finally answered. "I haven't."

"I've known Daniel for years and if there's one thing I know about him, it's this: he protects what's his. And if you're in his playroom, for that moment in time, you're his."

Julie swirled her coffee, trying to ignore the ache in her heart. She didn't want to be his just in the playroom. She wanted to be his everywhere and all the time.

"He'll push you," Dena continued. "That's what a good Dom does, but he'll never take you too far. And, Julie, trust me on this: if you let him, Daniel could be the one to give you your wings."

Friday night Julie drove to Daniel's house, her heart racing the entire way. She'd thought about calling and letting him know she was coming, but only entertained that thought briefly. It would be better if she surprised him. She couldn't even think about what she would do if he wasn't at home. It was doubtful she'd be able to work up the courage to come again.

She stood on his front porch, her heart pounding so hard, it echoed in her head. Her hand trembled when she rang the doorbell. It seemed to take forever for the door to open, but surely it was mere seconds.

Daniel's face was a combination of shock and surprise when he opened the door and saw her.

"Julie?"

The nerves that made her hand shake took over her entire body. Even her toes trembled. "Can I come in?"

"Sure." He stepped out of the way to let her in, but she only cleared the threshold. He closed the door. "Is everything okay? You look—"

He stopped talking when she knelt in front of him.

"Julie?"

She kept her eyes on the floor. "I've made my choice, sir."

He didn't say anything. He didn't move. Her head throbbed with one unwelcome thought.

What if he didn't want her anymore?

TEN

*D*aniel stood dumbfounded at the sight of Julie on her knees at his feet. It was more than he'd thought possible, but first . . .

"Stand up, Julie." His voice sounded rougher than he intended.

Slowly, she came to her feet and when she met his gaze, he saw uncertainty. It pained something inside to see her look at him that way. He wanted to erase her unease and get to the bottom of why she'd said and done what she had.

"Come sit down and talk," he said, taking her hand and leading her inside to a couch. Once they were seated, he kept her hand in his. Clasped his other around it. "Tell me what happened."

"I can't do it anymore." Her eyes pleaded with him. "I

can't be something other than what I am. You opened a door inside me and it won't close. I need it and I want you to be the one to give it to me."

He squeezed her hand, struggling to control the emotions she stirred within him. "You're sure? You've thought about this?"

She nodded. "Dena's helped a lot. I watched a scene with her and Master Parks, and it showed me so much." She shivered. "I can't imagine not experiencing submitting to you again. I need it. I need you."

He was only slightly shocked Dena talked her into watching. What shocked him more was her use of Jeff's title. After Sasha's accident, Julie had referred to the other Dominants by their first names. He trailed a finger down her cheek, rested his hand on her shoulder so his fingers gently encircled her throat. "You want to be my submissive? To be mine to control while in my bed and in my playroom?"

Her lips curved into a wicked smile. "And occasionally in your car."

She wanted to be his! His laugh came easily. "Oh, yes. And occasionally in my car."

They shared a smile of anticipation at the things to come. A joint understanding that though they had different needs, those needs were only satisfied in the other.

He thought of the times they'd spent together and how empty everything seemed without her. She needed to understand his expectations.

"I don't do short-term, Julie. If I take you again, I won't easily let you go."

"I'm not running anymore." Her voice was low, seductive, and whispered a promise of shared pleasure.

Their lips brushed lightly. He pulled back and gazed into her eyes before slipping his arms around her and capturing her lips in a kiss that left them both panting and anxious for more.

He couldn't wait to give it to her.

*T*he soft chime of the shop door opening sounded ten minutes before closing. Julie frowned. She'd hoped no one would show up. Sasha had left earlier than normal, claiming she had a headache and needed to lie down. In the last few weeks since Julie had gotten back together with Daniel, Sasha had been distant. Julie was worried about her.

But now she had a customer. She took a deep breath, walked into the main room, and stopped short.

Daniel stood at the door, facing away from her. He flipped the sign in the window to CLOSED and locked the door.

"Am I closing early?" she asked.

His eyes were dark and sultry when he turned to face her. "I'll make it worth your while."

She moved toward him and kissed him softly, her hands locking around his neck. "Is that a promise?"

"Should I make it a threat?"

"You can make it anything you want."

He growled. "I'll take you up on that."

Her heart raced just at the thought of it.

"As soon as I buy some flowers."

Her hands dropped from his shoulders. "You came here to buy flowers?"

"It *is* a floral shop." He nibbled her earlobe. "And I told you I'd make it worth your while."

"What flowers are you looking for? Anything specific?"

"Very specific. Close the blinds."

He'd been nuzzling her neck. She almost didn't hear him. "What?"

"Close the blinds. I don't think you want an audience for what I have planned. But if you'd like to put on a show?" He shrugged. "You can leave them open."

Her head spun. Here? In her shop? "Are we going to . . . ?"

He placed a finger over her lips. "Do you trust me, kitten? Nod if you do."

She looked into his eyes, so confident and sure, filled with both desire and need. The warmth from his finger heated her entire body and traveled to that secret part of her she'd kept buried for so long. She nodded.

"Thank you." He moved his finger. "Now, do we entertain your neighbors?"

"No, sir."

He tilted his head and she quickly closed the blinds. She couldn't believe she was going to have sex in her shop. It sounded so wanton, so wicked, so wild. She loved it.

Since the shop only had a few windows, it didn't take her long to ensure they were adequately covered. When she turned around to Daniel, she noted he'd taken off both his winter coat and his suit coat. He watched her walk toward him, rolling up his shirtsleeves as she came closer.

"Very nice, kitten," he said when she stood before him. "Tell me what you say if you need me to stop."

"Red, sir."

He palmed her cheek. "Good girl. And if I need to slow down?"

"Yellow, sir."

He drew her close and whispered against her lips, "It makes me so hard when you call me 'sir.'"

Being with him like she was, in her shop, knowing there were people walking by outside, made her feel more playful than normal. She slipped her hand between their bodies and cupped his erection. "Is that right, *sir?*"

He captured her wrist, immobilizing it. "Someone's being naughty tonight. Does my kitten need a spanking?"

Would he spank her in her shop? So people walking by could hear? She found herself surprised by how much the idea turned her on and decided to push him.

"Maybe, sir."

"Maybe?" He took her wrist and pushed it behind her back. "Where I come from, 'maybe' is what people say when they want to say 'yes,' but something's keeping them from saying so. I think you deserve a spanking for the wandering hand *and* the wishy-washy response to my question."

Damn, she wanted him inside her right the fuck NOW.

Daniel, however, appeared to be in no hurry whatsoever. "I'm going to go in the back to look for the flowers I need. I want you to undress and wait for me right here. Completely naked, kitten. While you wait, I want you to think about how your naughty little ass is going to feel as I spank it."

He kissed her cheek and left, leaving her alone with her thoughts. Of course, since he'd talked about it, the only thing running through her mind was the fact that he was getting ready to spank her. In her shop. She fumbled with her clothes, excitement making her fingers more clumsy than normal. A soft giggle slipped from her. If someone had told her six months ago she'd be undressing in the shop, she'd have laughed at them. Finally naked, she dropped her khakis and polo in a messy pile, shoving her bra and panties in the middle.

She stood and waited. No noise came from the back room. Daniel must have found what he was looking for. He was probably planning exactly how he was going to spank her. Would he put her over his knee again, or perhaps over a table?

The sound of laughter from somewhere outside drifted in, reminding her of how close they were to people passing by. She felt even more naked, more excited. Then she thought of Daniel placing her on her belly over his knee, holding her in place with one hand, spanking her with the other, and she grew even more excited. She shifted her weight in a desperate attempt to alleviate the ache between her legs.

"Not yet, kitten."

She stilled. She hadn't heard him enter the room.

He moved across the floor and stood in front of her. A quick glance and she saw he was still dressed. In one hand he carried both a red rose and a white one.

"Hold this." He handed her the white rose, which was really little more than a bud. The red one, however, was almost in full bloom.

"You once asked me about collaring a submissive. There is a ceremony done sometimes involving roses. I thought this would be the perfect place to tell you about it."

He held up the red rose, passed the petals over her breasts. "The Dominant is represented by the red rose. It's almost fully open to show his experience and to symbolize he possesses the maturity to have a submissive. Not in complete bloom, though, for he can always grow." He turned the rose so the thorns scratched her skin and she couldn't stop her moan as one particularly sharp one hit her nipple. "The rose is red to show the Dominant's willingness to shed his own blood in order to protect his submissive. That he would lay his life down for her, should the need arise."

He placed the rose down and took the white one from her. "What does a white rose symbolize, Julie?"

"Purity, sir."

The petals trailed down her cheek. "Yes. In this case, the purity of a submissive's submission. Unsullied." He passed the rose under her chin and she met his eyes. "Unashamed. Without fault. And white as a symbol of a submissive's pure desire for her Dom. You'll notice it's a bud, for a submissive is always growing, always becoming better. Always learning how to better serve her Master."

She thought it a beautiful representation of this world she was becoming engrossed in. Loved how two opposites came together and formed a more perfect whole.

"What are you thinking?" he asked.

She spoke with an ease that hadn't seemed possible mere weeks before. Each day it became easier and easier to share her thoughts. "About how unexpectedly beautiful it is."

His smile spoke his approval. "And for me, the expected beauty. For that is what you are. That is what you give me." He pulled her close and kissed her softly.

She could have stayed in his arms, kissing him, all night. Daniel, however, seemed to have different plans. Ever so slowly, he trailed a hand down her back so his fingers danced along the top of her backside.

"We'll talk about this more a little later," he said. "Right now I want to spend some time working on this naughty ass."

Her heart pounded. It was only the second time he spanked her. He'd told her he went easy on her the first time. She was both excited and nervous to see what he had planned for the second.

There wasn't a couch in the store, not even a chair she thought suitable for what he probably had in mind.

"I want you leaning over your worktable. Arms stretched out."

She froze for just a second. Her worktable? Then she grinned, knowing she'd never look at it the same way again. As she walked toward the table, she swayed her hips, knowing he was watching. A low growl confirmed her suspicion and seconds after she situated herself, she felt him behind her. His hands were on her backside, cupping, rubbing, and pinching.

"I love the feel of your ass in my hands," he said. "Almost as much as I love the feel of your sweet pussy." He gave her a sharp smack. "Spread your legs more so I can see it."

She obeyed and moaned when he slipped a finger inside her.

"Nice, wet, and ready for me," he said, adding a second finger. "Brace yourself."

She barely had time to process his words before his fingers started a slow pump in and out of her while his other hand began a steady rhythm of swats to her backside. The sensations made her gasp in excited pleasure. Ever so slowly he increased his speed and as his fingers moved faster and deeper inside her, the swats to her flesh became harder.

"Oh, god, fuck," she said, scratching her fingernails against the table, while at the same time pushing back toward him.

Two sharp slaps struck her ass. "Naughty, *wicked* girl."

She squeezed her eyes tight against the ever-growing

sensation he was causing inside her. If she tried hard enough, she could make it last just a little bit longer. *Smack.* Just a little bit . . .

His fingers left her and she whined. He slapped her backside once more.

"I'm going to spank your pussy until you come and then I'm going to fuck you until I come."

She gasped when she felt his hand again and came on the fourth swat to her oversensitized flesh. He stepped away just for a second. There was a rustle of clothes and then he was back, pressed hot and hard against her.

"This is for me, but you can come again if you're able," he said. "Hold on."

His hands held her waist as he entered her with a forceful thrust that slammed her into the table. Immediately, he pulled out and spanked her so hard she yelped.

"I told you to hold on," he said. "If I have to tell you again, you won't like what happens."

She wasn't going to find out what that would entail. She pressed forward as far as she could, grabbing hold of the end of the table.

"That's better."

When he thrust into her the second time, she was better prepared. True to his word, he pounded into her hard and deep. Each stroke of his cock stretched and pushed her toward another orgasm.

"Sir!" she shouted as he hit a particularly sensitive spot inside her.

"Like that?" His voice was breathless, but he drove into her over and over, each time hitting that very spot she needed.

"Yes!" she managed to get out right before she came with such intensity her vision went black for a few seconds.

Daniel followed soon after, holding still deep inside her, his fingers digging into her waist. He stayed pressed against her for several minutes, breathing heavy.

"Are you okay?" he asked, moving away and stroking her back.

She took a deep breath. "That was . . . intense."

She heard a rustle of clothes and then he spoke. "Stay here and don't move or get up. I'll be right back."

Even if she wanted to disobey, she couldn't. She didn't believe she could talk any of her body parts into moving. It was as if she'd turned into stone and didn't have the strength to do anything but wait for Daniel to return.

She sighed. Her backside stung pleasantly and there was a familiar ache between her legs. One that reminded her just how good it felt to be with him.

"Happy sigh?" he asked, coming behind her and rubbing an unscented cream over her sore bottom.

"Yes."

He worked his way slowly up her body, massaging and kissing every part of her. His hands were warm and it felt as if she sank into the table.

"I was so stupid to let you go," she whispered.

He kissed her shoulder and turned her around to face

him. "But how absolutely brilliant of you to come back," he said with a teasing smile. "Can you stand?"

"If you hold me."

"Always."

He helped her up from the table and gently pulled her close. She settled herself into his arms, tucking her head under his chin. How had she ever thought she could live without this?

"I love you, Daniel," she whispered against his chest.

"Julie." He lifted her head so their eyes met. "I love you so much."

His lips brushed hers. Her arms slipped around his neck. All was as it should be.

Later that night, they sat at Julie's kitchen table eating Chinese takeout. Speaking her mind had gotten easier, but there was something she wanted to discuss and she didn't know how to bring it up.

"Something bothering you?" Daniel asked, as if reading her mind.

"How do you do that?"

"Part of being a Dominant is being observant and I know you well enough to know when something's on your mind. Will you share what's troubling you?"

She looked down at her plate and piled up her remaining rice. They had only been back together a few weeks, so she wondered if maybe she should wait.

No, she told herself, she needed to know now.

She glanced up at Daniel, who waited with infinite patience. "Whenever you're ready," he said.

There was no way around it. She put her fork down and cleared her throat. "In the past when you . . . with your previous . . . did you . . . ah, hell."

He pushed back from the table, stood up, and held out his hand. "Let's go sit down and see if we can get to the bottom of what has you tongue-tied."

They made it into her living room, where he sat on the couch and pulled her into his lap. She took a deep breath, inhaling the smell of him and delighting in the feel of his arms around her.

"Let's try again," he said. "What was bothering you at dinner?"

She ran a finger down his arm, lightly brushing the hair on his forearm. "With your collared submissives, I know you said bedroom and playroom only, but are there, were there, rules? Things you expected?" She turned so she could look at him. He'd been right—it was easier to talk sitting on the couch, touching him. "I guess I'm looking for what the setup was like. The basics."

A look of momentary shock covered his face, but it was soon replaced with an easy grin. "Thank you for being honest. The truth is, the setup is what the people involved say it is. It won't be the same from couple to couple."

"But don't you have certain, I don't know, expectations?"

"Everything's negotiable."

"Okay, so what would be on the list you first brought to the table?" she asked. "If I were to wear your collar."

"What would be on my most wanted list?" At her nod, he continued. "For starters you would wear my collar every day. In fact, it would be locked around your neck and only I would have the key."

She nodded. That didn't sound so bad. In fact, she liked the sound of it.

"You would call me 'Master' any time we were playing or with the group."

"But all the submissives call you 'Master.'"

"No, they call me 'sir' or 'Master Covington.' 'Master' is reserved for my collared submissive's use alone."

"Oh." She liked the sound of that.

"You would shave your pussy and keep it bare for me at all times."

Ouch.

"All your orgasms would belong to me and you would only be allowed to have one following my permission."

"Forever?" she asked. "That seems a bit extreme."

"Have you felt sexually deprived in any way, shape, or form since you've been with me?"

Hell, no, she hadn't. In fact, she felt just the opposite—fulfilled, content, sated. She shook her head.

"Maybe I'm being a bit prideful," he said. "But I'd like to think I'm a generous Dom when it comes to permission."

She kissed his cheek. "You were very generous tonight."

"Thank you."

"Anything else?" she asked.

"I'd claim your ass."

"You don't mean by spanking, do you?"

"No, I'd claim it with my cock. I enjoy anal sex a lot and I believe I'd like fucking your ass very much."

Throughout their talk, she'd felt comfortable and warm. But the thought of anal sex scared her and she felt a light sweat break out over her skin.

"I've never . . . ," she started.

"I know you haven't," he said, tightening his arms around her. "And I know you're scared, but I would also expect you to know that we'd take it slow and easy. That I would make everything about the experience as pleasurable as possible and that I would only fuck you there when I knew you were ready."

"Well, when you put it that way."

He smiled at her.

"Your cock is huge, though. I may never be ready."

He laughed. "Flattery won't get you out of it. I'll fit."

"Says the one not getting it in the ass."

"Says the one who will treat you like the world's most precious and desired treasure." He shifted her so she reclined with her head on the armrest and her body resting along the length of the couch while he held himself above her. "Says the one who honors and respects your submission too much to ever give you cause to fear me. Says the one who will push you to your limits, but never past them.

And says the one who would rather cut off his own arm than cause you pain you don't want."

"As opposed to pain I do want?" she asked. He was hard between her legs; she doubted the conversation would last much longer.

"Did the spanking tonight in your shop hurt?"

"Yes."

"Would you want to do it again?"

Understanding flooded her mind. "Yes."

"Then there's a pain you do want." He started undoing the buttons of her shirt. "We can talk more about this later. Collaring is serious and should be discussed seriously and carefully. We have all the time in the world and I want to be sure you know exactly what you're getting into. Okay?"

She took a minute to think over her answer. So far he hadn't mentioned anything he'd expect that she didn't think she could do. She decided she'd trust him about the anal sex. There was no doubt in her mind he'd be as gentle as possible, while bringing her all the pleasure he could.

"Okay, sir."

He took both her hands in one of his, pulling her arms above her head, murmuring the entire time about how proud he was and how much she'd grown. She knew at that moment with certainty that it wasn't a matter of if she'd wear his collar, but when.

ELEVEN

*J*ulie sat in the middle of Daniel's spare bedroom, eyes closed in excitement, while Dena braided her hair and pinned it tightly to her head. She'd been planning this evening for weeks, ever since Daniel first brought it up.

"There we go," Dena said. Sasha held up a mirror for her inspection. Perhaps it was only her imagination, but her neck looked longer and conspicuously bare.

"Thank you." She gave Dena a hug, and glanced at the larger mirror over the dresser. She wore a simple cotton dress of white, with nothing underneath per Daniel's request. Vaguely, she remembered their first date and smiled at how much had changed between them since then.

Though she didn't live with him, she spent a good number of nights at his house each week. Since her return to him three months ago, their relationship had strengthened, both in his playroom and out of it.

"I love your nails," Dena said.

"Thanks," she said, admiring her new manicure. "Daniel treated me to a spa day yesterday and he insisted I get them done."

It was a small extravagance and wouldn't last a day at work, but for now, she had girlie nails. Silly how such a little thing made her feel pretty, but even more so, it made her feel loved and cared for. He'd remembered her comment about wanting girlie nails from the night at the benefit and gave that to her.

So much better than flowers.

"I'd better be going." Sasha picked up her purse and glanced around, looking to make sure she hadn't dropped anything.

Julie grabbed her in a hug. "It made my day that you came to help me. Thank you."

Sasha still fought her submissive side and while she never said as much, it was obvious she had misgivings about the step Julie was taking tonight. Yet she'd put that aside to stand beside her as she prepared.

When she pulled back, Sasha had tears in her eyes. "Daniel's a great man. I'm truly happy for you."

Julie knew what the admission cost her and choked back her own tears. "Thank you. See you Monday."

Someday, she knew, Sasha would find her own great man.

Sasha left after saying good-bye to Dena, and then Julie took a few seconds to take several deep breaths. Once calm, she took the barely opened white rose from Dena and headed outside where Daniel and Master Parks waited. While discussing the evening, one of the points she and Daniel had debated was whom to invite. Eventually, they agreed to invite only Dena and Master Parks.

Daniel stood on the deck overlooking the expanse of his backyard, the warm evening breeze ruffling his hair. He wore dark tailored pants and his white shirt was unbuttoned around his throat. An almost completely opened red rose sat in a vase on a nearby table.

Julie barely noticed Master Parks standing behind him. As she made her way to where Daniel stood, she found she couldn't keep her eyes off him. His eyes burned with a restrained intensity, though he gave her a warm smile when she made it to his side.

She drank in the sight of him, trying to take in every detail, knowing her time to do so for the next while would be short. He gently stroked her cheek with the back of his hand.

"Julie," he said in the voice that always made her knees weak. "Do you come here today of your own free will and desire?"

"Yes, sir."

"Kneel before me."

She gladly dropped to her knees on the pillow he had

waiting. In the last few months, she'd come to look forward to the times she surrendered to him. Those precious moments she yielded and allowed him to take over. Yet it felt even more intense in that moment.

Something rustled above her.

Daniel spoke low and rough. "I offer this as a representation of my dominance over you. I promise to love and respect you. To guide and to teach you. I will push you to help you become the best submissive you can be, but I will never betray or violate your trust. I will protect you with my life and hold you above all. Julie, will you accept my collar? Wear it always as a symbol of your submission to me?"

His words warmed her, wrapped around her in a promise she knew he'd never break. With all her heart, she answered with the words she'd prepared specifically for him and painstakingly memorized.

"Yes, sir, I will accept and wear your collar, acknowledging your dominance over me. I will serve you gladly and with my whole being, striving to be the best submissive possible. I will obey and honor your command, knowing you act only for my betterment. I offer my body for your use, your wish, your will, and my love and desire will be for you alone."

His hands were on her, slipping warm metal around her neck, and fastening it with the click of a key. It took all her strength not to reach up and touch it. There would be plenty of time for that later. She still wondered what it looked like.

"Thank you, kitten," he whispered for her ears alone.

"Thank you," she said, then added for the first time, "Master."

Saying the word made her shiver. She'd said it out loud alone in her house and in her head, but never to him. It seemed to magnify in power as she spoke it.

"Stand for me," he said, and his voice was heavy with emotion.

She stood as gracefully as possible and when he lifted her chin, she saw his eyes overflowing with emotion. Standing before him, seeing what she meant to him reflected in his gaze, she couldn't remember what she'd been afraid of.

Then he pulled her into his embrace and kissed her with a ferocity that left her needy and wanting. She moved closer to him and his arms tightened around her. Their witnesses were forgotten until Master Parks discreetly coughed.

Daniel pulled back and she felt his smile against her lips. "I think it's time our guests left."

"I couldn't agree more," she whispered.

They reluctantly separated just long enough to accept Dena's and Master Parks's congratulations. Dena hugged her close and whispered how happy she was for her. Julie wasn't sure, but she thought she heard a hint of longing in her voice. She wished she could assure Dena that everything would work out between her and Master Parks, but Dena had never shared their history. It didn't feel right to say anything other than she wished Dena every happiness.

Daniel turned to her when they were finally alone, his gaze heated. "It's time for me to fully claim my collared submissive so there's no doubt to whom she belongs. Hurry on to the playroom, I'll be there in less than five."

One of Daniel's requirements was that she be naked in his playroom. As she entered that night, she saw he had a hanger out for her dress. She slipped out of the white cotton and hung it up, excitement building with every second.

In the middle of the room stood something covered by a black cloth. Interesting, but she needed to mentally prepare, so she turned her attention inward, kneeling and calming her breathing the way Daniel had taught her. It wasn't long before she heard his footsteps coming down the stairs.

By the time he made it to where she waited, the room nearly buzzed with anticipation. And still he made her wait.

After what seemed like forever, he spoke. "You have no idea what it means to me, having you here, wearing nothing but my collar." He took a few steps away. "Just the very sight of you . . ."

The air around her moved, and all at once, she was covered by the black cloth she'd noticed earlier.

"Stand for me," he commanded.

She stood up and as she rose, he draped the cloth around her like a shawl. Because he was in front of her, she wasn't able to see exactly what the cloth had covered. But when he moved behind her, she noticed it was a mirror. Her eyes were immediately drawn to her neck and she gasped. The collar was more than anything she'd imagined.

He trailed a finger along its length. "You like it?"

"I love it, Master."

"The strand with the diamonds represents you." He stepped closer and she felt his warmth on her neck. "The beauty of your submission to me."

She couldn't take her eyes off it. How it looked on her. How it felt: warm and heavy against her skin.

"The plain strand is me and I'm surrounding you, protecting and holding you. But just as the collar would be incomplete without both strands, so are we incomplete without the other. My dominance is only possible because of your submission."

Ever so slowly, he pushed the cloth down, exposing her shoulders. He kissed one, caught her gaze in the mirror, and trailed his lips to the other side. "In this room, who does this body belong to?"

"You, Master."

"That's right, kitten, I'm your Master now. This body is mine to use as I wish." He moved even closer behind her and she felt him through the thin cloth. "Keep your eyes on the mirror."

She found herself unable to do anything else as he slipped the material down farther and her breasts came in view. His hands cupped her and she watched him pinch and tease her nipples. A moan left her lips as he rolled them between his thumb and fingers.

She didn't realize she'd closed her eyes until he bit her shoulder. "Watch."

Her eyes flew open in time to watch the black cloth fall to the ground. She didn't close her eyes again, but instead watched as he claimed every part of her body with his touch and kiss. While his hands explored her belly, his lips ran over her back, dipping low to kiss the curve of her bottom.

He worked his way down her body before starting back up. When he stood behind her again, he kicked her legs apart and slapped her ass. "Keep your eyes on mine, kitten. Watch me claim what's mine."

His fingers slipped between her legs and pushed inside. "Every part of you. Your sighs, your moans, your very breath."

Under his intense gaze, she almost wavered, but she refocused on him instead of her unease. She found if she kept her mind on him, it was easier to meet his gaze.

"That's it," he said, and she swore his eyes darkened.

To have him touching her so intimately while she watched was intensely erotic. He knew her body so well. Knew just how to touch and for how long to take her just to the brink without taking her over.

"Keep watching," he said, coming to her side and turning her so their profiles were reflected.

She gasped in surprise as he pulled her against him and lifted her right leg. Positioned as they were, he was poised just at her entrance. He teased her, all the while looking deeply into her eyes. Just when she thought he'd enter her, he pulled back.

"Beg."

It was almost too much, the combination of his ruthless gaze and his command of her body. From the corner of her eye she saw his collar and its meaning struck her anew as did his previous words. She was claimed and as she stood, balanced between need and want, she recalled what Dena once said about the right Dom.

"Please, Master."

His gaze never wavered. "Please, Master, what?"

"Please, Master, make me fly."

An animalistic growl was his only reply when he finally took her. And as he roughly drove them both to an unparalleled pleasure and later, when he carried her up the stairs to his room and made tender love to her, she knew she was finally free.

EPILOGUE

*D*ena walked to her car, Jeff at her side, having just left Daniel and Julie's collaring ceremony.

"They're good together," she said. "I think they'll be really happy."

Jeff didn't say anything. Ever since they'd played together months ago, he'd been even more withdrawn, more silent, more *absent* than before. Anger she could handle. It was the apathy that left her bewildered.

"I wish Cole could have been here. He'll hate he missed it," she tried again.

Still nothing.

"You going to say something or just pretend like I don't exist?"

They'd made it to her car. Jeff's scowl would have frozen most people in their tracks.

She put her hands on her hips. "You forget that look stopped working on me years ago."

"Dena, stop."

"Ah, he speaks."

"Sarcasm never was one of your more attractive traits."

She flinched. She'd forgotten how deeply his words could cut. "What happened to the man who held me so tenderly and kissed me with such passion?"

He shook his head. "Let's not rehash this. We're not good. Good in the playroom? Yes. But outside, we just hurt each other." Grief etched his expression. "And I love you too much to hurt you anymore."

Discover Tara Sue Me's original series,

the worldwide phenomenon

THE SUBMISSIVE TRILOGY

Here is an excerpt from *The Submissive.*

Available now from Headline Eternal.

ONE

"Ms. King," the receptionist said. "Mr. West will see you now."

I stood, wondered for the twenty-fifth time what I was doing, and went to open the door leading to the office I'd traveled across town to enter. On the other side was my darkest fantasy, and by stepping inside, I'd be making it a reality.

I was proud of the fact my hands didn't shake as the door opened and I walked into his office.

Step one: done.

Nathaniel West sat at a large mahogany desk, typing on a computer. He didn't look up or slow his strokes. I might as well not even have entered, but I dropped my eyes just in case.

I stood still while I waited. Face looking at the floor,

hands at my sides, feet spread to the exact width of my shoulders.

Outside, the sun had set, but the lamp on Nathaniel's desk gave a muted light.

Had it been ten minutes? Twenty?

He was still typing.

I counted my breaths. My heart finally slowed from the rocket speed it'd been racing at before I entered the office.

Another ten minutes passed.

Or maybe thirty.

He stopped typing.

"Abigail King," he said.

I started slightly, but kept my head down.

Step two: done.

I heard him pick up a stack of papers and tap them into a pile. Ridiculous. From what I knew of Nathaniel West, they would have already been in a neat pile. It was another test.

He pushed his chair back, wheels rolling over the hard-wood floor the only sound in the quiet room. He walked with measured, even steps until I felt him behind me.

A hand lifted my hair away from my neck, and warm breath tickled my ear. "You have no references."

No, I didn't. Just a crazy fantasy. Should I tell him? No. I should remain silent. My heart beat faster.

"I would have you know," he continued, "that I'm not interested in training a submissive. My submissives have always been fully trained."

Crazy. I was crazy to be here. But it was what I wanted. To be under a man's control.

No. Not any man. *This* man's control.

"Are you sure this is what you want, Abigail?" He wrapped my hair around his fist and gave a gentle tug. "You need to be sure."

My throat was dry, and I was fairly certain he heard my heart beating, but I stood where I was.

He chuckled and returned to his desk.

"Look at me, Abigail."

I'd seen his picture before. Everyone knew Nathaniel West, owner and CEO of West Industries.

The pictures didn't do the man justice. His skin was lightly tanned and set off the deep green of his eyes. His thick dark hair begged you to run your fingers through it. To grab on it and pull his lips to your own.

His fingers tapped rhythmically on his desk. Long, strong fingers. I felt my knees go weak just thinking about what those fingers could do.

Across from me, Nathaniel gave the faintest of smiles, and I made myself remember where I was. And why.

He spoke again. "I'm not interested in why you decided to submit your application. If I select you and you are agreeable to my terms, your past won't matter." He picked up the papers I recognized as my application and riffled through them. "I know what I need to."

I recalled filling out the application—the checklists, the blood tests he'd required, the confirmation of the birth control I was on. Likewise, before today's meeting, I'd been sent his information for review. I knew his blood type, his test results, his hard limits, and the things he enjoyed doing with, and to, play partners.

We stood in silence for several long minutes.

"You have no training," he said. "But you're very good."

Silence again as he stood and walked to the large window behind his desk. It was completely dark, and I saw his reflection in the glass. Our eyes met, and I looked down.

"I rather like you, Abigail King. Although I don't recall telling you to look away."

I hoped I hadn't messed up beyond redemption and looked back up.

"Yes, I think a weekend test is in order." He turned from the window and loosened his tie. "If you agree, you will come to my estate this Friday night at six exactly. I'll have a car pick you up. We'll have dinner and take it from there."

He placed his tie on the couch to his right and unbuttoned the top button of his shirt. "I have certain expectations of my submissives. You are to get at least eight hours of sleep every Sunday through Thursday night. You will eat a balanced diet—I will have a meal plan e-mailed to you. You will also run one mile, three times a week. Twice a week you will engage in strength and endurance training at my gym. A membership will be created for you starting tomorrow. Do you have any concerns about any of this?"

Another test. I didn't say anything.

He smiled. "You may speak freely."

Finally. I licked my lips. "I'm not the most . . . athletic, Mr. West. I'm not much of a runner."

"You must learn not to let your weakness rule you, Abigail." He walked to his desk and wrote something down. "Three times a week you will also attend yoga classes. They have these at the gym. Anything else?"

I shook my head.

"Very well. I will see you Friday night." He held out some papers to me. "These will have everything you need to know."

I took the papers. And waited.

He smiled again. "You are excused."

TWO

*T*he door to the apartment next to mine opened as I walked by. My best friend, Felicia Kelly, stepped out into the hallway. Felicia and I had been friends forever, having grown up together in the same small Indiana town. Throughout elementary and middle school we sat side by side, thanks to the alphabetical seating arrangements. After high school graduation, we attended the same college in New York, where we quickly learned that if we wanted to remain best friends, we should live as neighbors and not roommates.

Though I loved her like the sister I'd never had, she could at times be bossy and overbearing. Likewise, my need for regular quiet time drove her mad. And, apparently, so had my meeting with Nathaniel.

"Abby King!" Her hands were on her hips. "Did you have your phone off? You went to see that West guy, didn't you?"

I just smiled at her.

"Honestly, Abby," she said. "I don't know why I even bother."

"I know. Tell me, why do you bother?" I asked as she followed me inside. Settling down on the couch, I started reading the papers Nathaniel had given me. "By the way, I won't be here this weekend."

Felicia gave a loud sigh. "You went. I knew you would. Once you get an idea in your head, you just move right on ahead. You don't even think about the outcome."

I continued reading.

"You think you're so smart. Well, what do you think the library will say about this? What will your father think?"

My father still lived in Indiana, and though we weren't close, I was certain he'd have a definite opinion about my visit to Nathaniel's office. A very negative opinion. Regardless, there was no way anyone was going to discuss my sex life with him.

I set the papers down. "You're not saying a word to my dad, and my personal life isn't the library's business. Got it?"

Felicia sat down and examined her nails. "I don't got anything." She grabbed the papers. "What are these?"

"Give those back." I yanked the papers from her.

"Really," she said. "If you want to be dominated so badly, I know several men who would be more than willing to oblige."

"I'm not interested in your ex-boyfriends."

"So you're going to march into a strange man's house and let him do who-knows-what to you?"

"It's not like that."

She walked over to my laptop and turned it on. "So what is it like, exactly?" She leaned back in her chair while the screen booted up. "Being a rich man's mistress?"

"I'm not his mistress. I'm his submissive. Make yourself at home, by the way. Please, feel free to use my laptop."

She typed frantically on the keyboard. "Right. Submissive. That's *so* much better."

"It is. Everyone knows that the submissive holds all the power in the relationship." Felicia hadn't done the research I had.

"Does Nathaniel West know that?" She had pulled up Google and was searching Nathaniel's name. Fine. Let her find him.

All at once, his handsome face filled the screen. He was looking at us with those piercing green eyes. One arm was wrapped around a beautiful blonde at his side.

Mine, the stupid side of my brain said.

This Friday night through Sunday afternoon, the more responsible side countered.

"Who's she?" Felicia asked.

"My predecessor, I suppose," I mumbled, returning to reality. I was an idiot. To think he'd want me after he'd had *that.*

"You've got some pretty high stilettos to fill, girl-friend."

I only nodded. Felicia noticed, of course.

"Damn it, Abby. You don't even wear stilettos."

I sighed. "I know."

Felicia shook her head and clicked the next link. I looked away, not needing to see another shot of the blond goddess.

"Hello, baby," she said. "Now, I'd let *him* dominate me anytime."

I looked up to see a picture of another handsome man. *Jackson Clark, New York quarterback*, the caption said.

"You didn't tell me he was related to a professional football player."

I didn't know. But it'd do no good to tell Felicia any of this—she was no longer paying me any attention.

"I wonder if Jackson is married," she mumbled, clicking on links to bring up more information on his family. "Doesn't look like it. Hmm, maybe we can pull up more details on the blond chick."

"Don't you have anything better to do?"

"Nope," she said. "Nothing to do but sit here and make your life miserable."

"Show yourself out," I said, walking into my bedroom. She could spend all night digging up whatever she wanted on Nathaniel—I had reading to do.

I took the papers Nathaniel had given me and curled up on my bed, tucking my legs up under me. The first page had his address and contact information. His estate was a two-hour drive from the city, and I wondered if he had another property closer to town. He had also given me the security code to get through his gate and his cell phone number should I need anything.

Or in case you come to your senses, that annoying smart part of my brain chimed in.

The second page had the details of my gym membership and the exercise program I would have to follow. I swallowed the unease that thoughts of running brought up. More details followed on the strength and endurance classes he wanted me to take. At the bottom, in very neat cursive, were the name and number of the yoga instructor.

Page three informed me I'd have no need to bring any bags with me on Friday. Nathaniel would provide all the toiletries and clothing I needed. Interesting, that. But what else did I expect? It also contained the same instructions he'd given me earlier—eight hours of sleep, balanced meals—nothing new there.

Page four listed Nathaniel's favorite meals. Good thing I could cook. I'd look closer at those later.

Page five.

Let's just say page five left me hot, bothered, and waiting for Friday.

Here is an excerpt from *The Dominant*.

Available now from Headline Eternal.

ONE

The phone on my desk gave a low double beep.

I glanced at my watch. Four thirty. My administrative assistant had explicit instructions not to interrupt me unless one of two people called. It was too early for Yang Cai to call from China, so that left only one other person.

I hit the speaker-phone button. "Yes, Sara?"

"Mr. Godwin on line one, sir."

Excellent.

"Did I receive a package from him today?" I asked.

Papers rustled in the background. "Yes, sir. Should I bring it in now?"

"I'll get it later." I disconnected and switched to the headset. "Godwin, I expected you to call earlier. Six days earlier." I'd been waiting for the package just as long.

"I'm sorry, Mr. West. You had a late application I wanted to include with this batch."

Very well. It wasn't like the women knew I had a dead-line. That was something I would discuss with Godwin later.

"How many this time?" I asked.

"Four." He sounded relieved I'd moved on from his lateness. "Three experienced and one without any experience or references."

I leaned back in my chair and stretched my legs. We really shouldn't be having this conversation. Godwin knew my preferences by now. "You know my feelings on inexperienced submissives."

"I know, sir," he said, and I pictured him wiping the sweat from his brow. "But this one is different—she asked for you."

I stretched one leg and then the other. I needed a nice, long jog, but it would have to wait until later that evening. "They all ask for me." I wasn't being vain, just honest.

"Yes, sir, but this one wants to service only you. She's not interested in anyone else."

I sat up in the chair. "Really?"

"Her application specifically states she will sub for you and no one else."

I had rules about prior experience and references be-cause, to be frank, I didn't have time to train a submissive. I preferred someone with experience, someone who would learn my ways quickly. Someone I could teach quickly. I always included a lengthy checklist in the application to ensure applicants knew exactly what they were getting themselves into.

"I assume she filled out the checklist properly? Didn't indicate she would do anything and everything?" That had happened once. Godwin knew better now.

"Yes, sir."

"I suppose I could take a look at it."

"Last one in the pile, sir."

The one he'd held the package up for, then. "Thank you, Godwin." I hung up the phone and stepped outside my office. Sara handed me the package.

"Why don't you go home, Sara?" I tucked the envelope under my arm. "It should be quiet the rest of the evening."

She thanked me as I walked back into my office.

I got a bottle of water, set it on my desk, and opened the package.

I flipped my way through the first three applications. Nothing special. Nothing out of the ordinary. I could set up a test weekend with any of the three women and probably wouldn't be able to tell the difference between them.

I rubbed the back of my neck and sighed. Maybe I had been doing this too long. Maybe I should try again to settle down and be "normal." With someone who wasn't Melanie this time. The problem was, I needed my dom lifestyle. I just wanted something special to go along with it.

I took a long sip of water and looked at my watch. Five o'clock. It was highly doubtful I'd find my something special in the last application. Since the woman had no experience, it really wasn't even worth my time to review her paperwork. Without looking at it, I took the application and put it on top of my *To Shred* pile. The three remaining I placed side by side on top of my desk and read over the cover pages again.

Nothing. There was basically nothing differentiating the three women. I should just close my eyes and randomly pick one. *The one in the middle would work.*

But even as I looked over her information, my gaze drifted to the shred pile. The discarded application represented a woman who wanted to be *my* submissive. She'd taken the time to fill out my detailed paperwork and Godwin had held up sending everything because of Miss I-have-no-experience-and-want-only-Nathaniel-West. The least I could do was respect that woman enough to read her information.

I picked up the discarded application and read the name.

Abigail King.

The papers slipped from my hand and fluttered to the ground.

I was a complete success in the eyes of the world.

I owned and ran my own international securities corporation. I employed hundreds of people. I lived in a mansion that had graced the pages of *Architectural Digest*. I had a terrific family. Ninety-nine percent of the time, I was content with my life. But there was that one percent . . .

That one percent that told me I was an utter and complete failure.

That I was surrounded by hundreds of people, but known by very few.

That my lifestyle was not acceptable.

That I would never find someone I could love and who would love me in return.

I never regretted my decision to live the lifestyle of a dominant. I normally felt very fulfilled, and if there were times I did not, they were very few and far between.

I felt incomplete only when I made my way to the public library and caught a glimpse of Abby. Of course, until her application crossed my desk, I had no way of knowing if she even knew I existed. Until then, Abby had symbolized for me the missing one percent. Our worlds were so far apart, they could not and would not collide.

But if Abby was a submissive and wanted to be *my* submissive . . .

I allowed my mind to wander down pathways I'd closed off for years. Opened the gates of my imagination and let the images overtake me.

Abby naked and bound to my bed.

Abby on her knees before me.

Abby begging for my whip.

Oh, yes.

I picked her application up off the ground and started reading.

Name, address, phone number, and occupation, I

skimmed over. I turned the page to her medical history—
normal liver function tests and blood cell counts, HIV and
hepatitis negative, negative urine drug screen. The only
medication she took was the birth control pills I required.

I went to the next page, her completed checklist. Godwin had not lied when he said Abby had no experience.
She had marked off only seven items on the list: vaginal
sex, masturbation, blindfolds, spanking, swallowing semen,
hand jobs, and sexual deprivation. In the comment field
beside sexual deprivation, she had written, "Ha-ha. Not
sure our definitions are the same." I smiled. She had a sense
of humor.

Several items were marked "No, hard limit." I respected that—I had my own hard limits. Looking over the
list, I discovered that several of them lined up with hers.
Several of them did not. There was nothing wrong with
that—limits changed; checklists changed. If we were together for the long term—

What was I thinking? Was I actually thinking about
calling Abby in for a test?

Yes, damn it, I was.

But I knew, *I knew,* that if the application were from
anyone other than Abby, I wouldn't even give it a second
glance. I would shred it and forget it existed. I didn't train
submissives.

But it was from Abby, and I didn't want to shred it. I
wanted to pore over her application until I had it memorized. I wanted to make a list of what she had marked as

Excerpt from *The Dominant*

"willing to try" and show her the pleasure of doing those things. I wanted to study her body until its contours were permanently etched in my mind. Until my hands knew and recognized her every response. I wanted to watch her give in to her true submissive nature.

I wanted to be her dom.

Could I do that? Could I put aside my thoughts of Abby, the fantasy I would never have, and instead have Abby, the submissive?

Yes. Yes, I could.

Because I was Nathaniel West and Nathaniel West didn't fail.

And if Abby King no longer existed. Or if she was replaced by Abigail King . . .

I picked up the phone and dialed Godwin.

"Yes, sir, Mr. West," he said. "Have you decided?"

"Send Abigail King my personal checklist. If she's still interested after reviewing it, have her call Sara for an appointment next week."

Here is an excerpt from *The Training*.

Available now from Headline Eternal.

The drive back to Nathaniel's house took longer than it should have. Or maybe it just felt like it took longer. Maybe it was nerves.

I tipped my head in thought.

Maybe not nerves exactly. Maybe anticipation.

Anticipation that after weeks of talking, weeks of waiting, and weeks of planning, we were finally here.

Finally back.

I lifted my hand and touched the collar—Nathaniel's collar. My fingertips danced over the familiar lines and traced along the diamonds. I moved my head from side to side, reacquainting myself with the collar's feel.

There were no words to describe how I felt wearing Nathaniel's collar again. The closest I could come was to compare it to a puzzle. A puzzle with the last piece finally in place. Yes, for the last few weeks, Nathaniel and I had been living as lovers, but we both felt incomplete. His recollaring of me—his reclaiming of me—had been what was missing. It sounded odd even to me, but I finally felt like I was his again.

The hired car eventually reached Nathaniel's house and pulled into his long drive. Lights flickered from the windows. He had set the timer, anticipating my arrival in the dark. Such a small gesture, but a touching one. One that showed, like much he did, how he kept me firmly at the forefront of his mind.

I jingled my keys as I walked up the drive to his front door. My keys. To his house. He'd given me a set of keys a week ago. I didn't live with him, but I spent a fair amount of time at his house. He said it only made sense for me to be able to let myself in or to lock up when I left.

Apollo, Nathaniel's golden retriever, rushed me when I opened the door. I rubbed his head and let him outside for a few minutes. I didn't keep him out for too long—I wasn't sure if Nathaniel would arrive home early, but if he did, I wanted to be in place. I wanted this weekend to be perfect.

"Stay," I told Apollo after stopping in the kitchen to refill his water bowl. Apollo obeyed all of Nathaniel's orders, but thankfully, he listened to me this time. Normally, he would follow me up the stairs, and tonight that would be odd.

Excerpt from *The Training*

I quickly left the kitchen and made my way upstairs to my old room. The room that would be mine on weekends.

I undressed, placing my clothes in a neat pile on the edge of the twin bed. On this, Nathaniel and I had been in agreement. I would share his bed Sunday through Thursday nights, anytime I stayed over, but on Friday and Saturday nights, I would sleep in the room he reserved for his submissives.

Now that we had a more traditional relationship during the week, we both wanted to make sure we remained in the proper mind-set on weekends. That mind-set would be easier to maintain for both of us if we slept separately. For both of us, yes, but perhaps more so for Nathaniel. He rarely shared a bed with his submissives, and having a romantic relationship with one was completely new to him.

I stepped naked into the playroom. Nathaniel had led me around the room last weekend—explaining, discussing, and showing me things I'd never seen and several items I'd never heard of.

At its core, it was an unassuming room—hardwood floors, deep, dark brown paint, handsome cherry armoires, even a long table carved of rich wood. However, the chains and shackles, the padded leather bench and table, and the wooden whipping bench gave away the room's purpose.

A lone pillow waited for me below the hanging chains. I dropped to my knees on it, situating myself into the position Nathaniel explained I was to be in whenever I waited for him in the playroom—butt resting on my heels, back straight, right hand on top of my left in my lap, fingers not intertwined, and head down.

I got into position and waited.

Time inched forward.

I finally heard him enter through the front door.

"Apollo," he called, and while I knew he spoke Apollo's name so he could take him outside again, another reason was to alert me who it was that had entered the house. To give me time to prepare myself. Perhaps for him to listen for foot-steps from overhead. Footsteps that would tell him I wasn't prepared for his arrival. I felt proud he would hear nothing.

I closed my eyes. It wouldn't be long now. I imagined what Nathaniel was doing—taking Apollo outside, feeding him maybe. Would he undress downstairs? In his bedroom? Or would he enter the playroom wearing his suit and tie?

Doesn't matter, I told myself. *Whatever Nathaniel has planned will be perfect.*

I strained my ears—he was walking up the stairs now. Alone. No dog followed.

Somehow, the atmosphere of the room changed when he walked in. The air became charged, and the space be-tween us nearly hummed. In that moment, I understood—I was his, yes. I had been correct with that assumption. But even more so, even more important, perhaps, he was mine.

My heart raced.

"Very nice, Abigail," he said, and walked to stand in

front of me. His feet were bare. I noted he had changed out of his suit and into a pair of black jeans.

I closed my eyes again. Cleared my mind. Focused inwardly. Forced myself to remain still under his scrutiny.

He walked to the table, and I heard a drawer open. For a minute, I tried to remember everything in the drawers, but I stopped myself and once again forced my mind to quiet itself.

He came back to stand at my side. Something firm and leather trailed down my spine.

Riding crop.

"Perfect posture," he said as the crop ran up my spine. "I expect you to be in this position whenever I tell you to enter this room."

I felt relieved he was satisfied with my posture. I wanted so much to please him tonight. To show him I was ready for this. That we were ready. He had been so worried.

Of course, not a bit of worry or doubt could be discerned now. Not in his voice. Not in his stance. His demeanor in the playroom was utter and complete control and confidence.

He dragged the riding crop down my stomach and then back up. Teasing.

Damn. I loved the riding crop.

I kept my head down even though I wanted to see his face. To meet his eyes. But I knew the best gift I could give him was my absolute trust and obedience, so I kept my head down with my eyes focused on the floor.

"Stand up."

I rose slowly to my feet, knowing I stood directly under the chains. Normally, he kept them up for storage, but they were lowered tonight.

"Friday night through Sunday afternoon, your body is mine," he said. "As we agreed, the kitchen table and library are still yours. There, and only there, are you to speak your mind. Respectfully, of course."

Both of his hands traced across my shoulders, down my arms. One hand slipped between my breasts and dropped to where I was wet and aching.

"This," he said, rubbing my outer lips, "is your responsibility. I want you waxed bare as often as possible. If I decide you have neglected this responsibility, you will be punished."

And again, we had agreed to this.

"In addition, it is your responsibility to ensure your waxer does an acceptable job. I will allow no excuses. Is that understood?"

I didn't say anything.

"You may answer," he said. I heard the smile in his voice.

"Yes, Master."

He slipped a finger between my folds and I felt his breath in my ear. "I like you bare." His finger swirled around my clit. "Slick and smooth. Nothing between your pussy and whatever I decide to do to it."

Fuck.

Excerpt from *The Training*

Then he moved behind me and cupped my ass. "Have you been using your plug?"

I waited.

"You may answer."

"Yes, Master."

His finger made its way back to the front of me, and I bit the inside of my cheek to keep from moaning.

"I won't ask you that again," he said. "From now on, it is your responsibility to prepare your body to accept my cock in any manner I decide to give it to you." He ran a finger around the rim of my ear. "If I want to fuck your ear, I expect your ear to be ready." He hooked his finger in my ear and pulled. I kept my head down. "Do you understand? Answer me."

"Yes, Master."

He lifted my arms above my head, buckling first one wrist and then the other to the chains at my side. "Do you remember this?" he asked, his warm breath tickling my hair. "From our first weekend?"

Again, I said nothing.

"Very nice, Abigail," he said. "Just so there's no misunderstanding, for the rest of the evening, or until I tell you differently, you may not speak or vocalize in any way. There are two exceptions—the first being the use of your safe words. You are to use them at any point you feel the need. No repercussions or consequences will ever follow the use of your safe words. Second, when I ask if you are okay, I expect an immediate and honest answer."

He didn't wait for a response, of course. I wasn't to give one. Without warning, his hands slipped back down to where I ached for him. Since my head was lowered, I watched one of his fingers slide inside me, and I bit the inside of my cheek again to keep from moaning.

Shit, his hands felt good.

"How wet you are already." He pushed deeper and twisted his wrist. *Fuck.* "Usually, I would taste you myself, but tonight, I feel like sharing."

He removed himself, and the emptiness was immediate. Before I could think much about it, I felt his slippery finger at my mouth. "Open, Abigail, and taste how ready you are for me." He trailed his finger around my open lips before easing it inside my mouth.

I'd tasted myself before, out of curiosity, but never so much at one time and never off of Nathaniel's finger. It felt so depraved, so feral.

Damn, it turned me on.

"Taste how sweet you are," he said as I licked myself off his finger.

I treated his finger as if it were his cock—running my tongue along it, sucking gently at first. I wanted him. Wanted him inside me. I sucked harder, imagining his cock in my mouth.

You will not release until I give you permission, and I will be very stingy with my permission. His words from the office floated through my mind, and I choked back a moan before it left my mouth. It would be a long night.

Excerpt from *The Training*

"I changed my mind," he said when I finished cleaning his finger. "I want a taste after all." He crushed his lips to mine and forced my mouth open. His lips were brutal—powerful and demanding in their quest to taste me.

Damn, I'd have a stroke if he kept that up.